AFTER THE QUIET

Stories to the Edge and Back

Volume Two

Carl Lakeland

Book Layout © 2026 Carl Lakeland

After the Quiet: Volume Two / Carl Lakeland. -- 1st ed.

ISBN: 9781764476058 (Paperback)

"The most radical revolutionary will become a conservative the day after the revolution."

— **Hannah Arendt**

AUTHOR'S NOTE

These stories were written in the margins — between warnings ignored and consequences arriving. Some were shaped by moments where the choice had already been made, even if no one was ready to admit it. Others emerged from the silence that follows impact, when systems pause, fracture, or fail entirely, and individuals are left to navigate what comes next.

This volume moves closer to the point where denial is no longer possible. Signals are missed. Lines are crossed. The machinery of power continues to turn, often without regard for those caught beneath it. What interested me here was not the catastrophe itself, but the human response to its approach and aftermath — the decisions made in partial darkness, the compromises justified too easily, the costs that cannot be deferred.

These are not stories of collapse as spectacle. They are stories of pressure. Of people who sense what is coming and act anyway, or hesitate, or look away. Of survival that demands more than endurance. Of truth that arrives late and changes nothing—and everything.

Nothing here promises resolution. Nothing seeks absolution.
This collection is about what remains once the warnings have sounded and the quiet no longer means safety.

— Carl Lakeland

CONTENTS

BOOK ONE

BAGELS AND A WHITE ROSE

Life never felt so good. That was the lie I told myself as the ninety-six tram groaned its way toward St Kilda, wheels screaming softly against wet steel. The rain had settled into a steady, unambitious fall — not enough to wash anything clean, just enough to make the city glisten like it had secrets it didn't want to keep. I watched droplets chase each other down the window, merging, separating, choosing paths the way people do when they think no one's watching.

Business was booming. That was the phrase they used in the briefings, usually delivered with a tight smile and a nod that meant *don't ask for details*. Booming implied growth. Momentum. Success. It didn't mention the cost of sustaining it, or who paid when the momentum finally diminished.

I was one of the doers. That was the polite term. Operatives. Assets. Field personnel. We took what was handed down from offices with frosted glass and neutral carpet, from men and women whose shoes never touched pavement after dark. They planned. They approved. They authorised. Then they slept.

We followed procedures. We completed tasks. We didn't ask questions, because questions implied doubt, and doubt had a way of spreading. We didn't feel guilt or remorse or anything else that required introspection. Those things slowed reaction time. They interfered with judgment. They made for hesitation when hesitation got people killed. If there was a need to pull the trigger — justified or not — and it came from the top office, the job was done. I'd been telling myself the same thing for years. Justified. Duty. Obligation.

The tram I rode that night rocked gently as it took a corner, the interior lights reflecting my face back at me in fractured angles. Older than I remembered. Sharper around the eyes. The kind of face that didn't belong to any one age because it'd learned too early not to relax. I caught my reflection looking back, studying me the way I studied others, and for a moment I wondered what conclusions I'd draw if I were a stranger.

Probably I was tired. Probably I was dangerous. The truth was simpler. I was running out of places to put the weight.

Eagle Shield was nearing its conclusion. That much I knew. Not the details — never was — but the rhythm had changed. Fewer redundancies. Tighter timelines. A sense of inevitability in the way instructions arrived, like gravity asserting itself.

Shilo — Maggie Gallagher had made it clear: this was not a mission you walked away from. Too much at stake. Too many moving parts. Too many lives balanced on assumptions that required men like me to keep doing exactly what we were told.

I'd been tempted, over the years. Everyone is, sooner or later. The idea of throwing it all away had a way of surfacing late at night, usually when you're alone with your own thoughts and no one's watching your pulse rate. But temptation was a luxury. Consequences weren't. And walking away didn't mean disappearance. It meant correction.

The tram slowed, doors hissing open, letting in a couple soaked through. They'd laughed like they'd won something by getting wet together. I envied them in a distant, academic way. Shared inconvenience had a purity to it. You could complain without implication. Suffer without strategy.

I checked the reflection again, scanning the tram without turning my head. Old habit. No obvious tails. No one paying too much attention. A man pretending to read. A woman scrolling through her phone. A student asleep with his head against the window. If I was being watched, it wasn't by anyone careless enough to sit this close. But that didn't mean anything. I'd learned the hard way that absence of evidence was not reassurance.

The rain thickened as we moved north, St Kilda receding into a blur of streetlights and wet asphalt. I thought about the choice that'd been circling my mind for weeks now, tightening its orbit every time I tried to ignore it. Keep doing what I was handed or stop pretending there'd ever be a clean end. The problem with ends was that they rarely revealed themselves.

My stop came just after midnight. I stepped off the tram into the cold, collar turned up more out of habit than necessity. The city felt quieter at this hour, but not empty. Melbourne never really slept. It just changed shifts.

I walked the last few blocks home under the steady hiss of rain, boots splashing lightly, my mind running ahead the way it always did — door, lock, code, inside. Routine as refuge.

The apartment building they called *the safe house* rose out of the dark like a sealed vault, all concrete and angles. The kind of place designed to be ignored. I crossed the threshold and shook off the rain.

I stood alone in my shadow in front of the hardened steel door that separated the world from my living space.

Key in. Half turn right. Half turn left. Code entered without hesitation.

The locking mechanism made that familiar grinding clunk before releasing. Every time I heard it, some part of my brain flashed to old prison films — the sound of doors opening and closing with finality. Sometimes it made me smile. Sometimes it made me angry enough to grind my teeth. As I entered, this time it did neither.

I stepped inside, expecting darkness. Silence. The controlled emptiness I'd grown used to after long days and longer nights. Instead, there was light. Not bright — just enough to cast shadows — and Angel was seated at the dining table, hunched over her study materials. One lamp above her, everything else in shadow. She looked up as I entered, eyes sharp, assessing, and then returned to her notes as if my presence was incidental.

For a moment, I just stood there, rainwater pooling at my feet, watching her. Seventeen years old and already carrying herself like someone who knew how to survive rooms full of adults. I didn't say anything. I walked past her toward my bedroom, the weight of the day still sitting heavy on my shoulders.

"No hello, or anything, Nathan?"

I stopped, half turned. "Well, you've changed your tune. I can't remember the last time you gave me a hello. I suppose you're maturing for your seventeen years after all."

Angel yawned, long and unguarded, stretching her arms above her head before smiling at me. Really smiling. Head tilted slightly, eyes warm. For a second it caught me off guard, the way it always did when she let her guard down.

That was when I noticed it — the smile. One corner of her mouth lifting higher than the other. Her mother's smile. The realisation hit harder than I expected. Angel was growing up. Not just older, but away from me. Toward a life I couldn't follow. And one day, not too far off, I'd have to let her go. For her own good. For reasons she didn't yet know about or couldn't possibly understand. For reasons I wasn't sure I'd believed in anymore.

"Tell me," Angel asked me, folding her arms and studying me with a seriousness that hadn't always been there, "how was your day today?"

I knew the answer she expected. The same one I'd given her for years.

I'm ASIS, Angel. I can't discuss these things.

But before I could say what I was thinking, she giggled, the sound breaking the tension between us like glass. With her, it'd become a game. A ritual. Ask the same old question, watch me deflect. I let it pass.

"I thought you were heading to Jenny's place for the night," I said instead.

"She had to work late. She's still picking me up in about thirty minutes."

"At this hour?"

"There's a party at Busby's."

I frowned despite myself. "Out so late. Why?"

She didn't answer but rolled her eyes in that teenage way. "Don't worry. I'll be careful."

"You'd better be."

She cut me off with a sharp look. "Nathan."

"I'm just saying —."

"I know what you're saying. I'm not an idiot."

For a moment, she looked at me the way someone looks at an outdated map — not useless, just no longer reliable. Then she softened. "You don't have to protect me from everything," she said quietly.

I didn't answer.

Angel gathered her things, slung her bag over her shoulder, and headed for the door without another word. It closed behind her with a soft click that echoed louder than it should've. I stood there alone, the apartment — the lie I told myself moments before still circling my thoughts.

Life never felt so good. Some jobs ended. Others just changed the way they followed you.

The apartment felt different once Angel left. Not emptier — just quieter in a way that made sound noticeable. The hum of the refrigerator. The distant drizzle of rain against the glass. My own breathing, steady and controlled, like it'd been trained to be exactly that way.

I waited for a moment after the door had closed, listening for footsteps in the hallway, for the lift, for anything out of place. Nothing. Only then did I move.

The bedside light came on dim and low. The walls were bare save for a framed print I'd never bothered to replace — a neutral landscape, anonymous enough to pass inspection if anyone ever cared to look closely. I closed the door behind me and crossed to the far wall where a safe was built flush into reinforced concrete.

Kneeling, I pressed my thumb to the biometric reader. It accepted me without any comment. The panel slid open with a muted click, revealing the contents arranged with a precision that bordered on compulsion.

Weapon first. I removed it carefully, clearing the chamber out of habit even though I knew its state without looking. Magazine out. Slide back. Visual confirmation. Mechanical memory taking over where thought would only interfere. Satisfied, I laid it inside the safe, angled just so, alongside the spare magazine and suppressor wrapped in oilcloth.

Next, the passport. Australian, of course. Clean. Unremarkable. The kind of document designed to attract no interest at borders or counters. Beneath it, another, sealed in a black sleeve, never used and never explained. I never looked at that one. Identification followed. Government issue. Valid. Boring. I hesitated before closing the safe. The pause was new. New enough to startle.

For a moment, the idea occurred to me — absurd, impractical, dangerous — that I could leave the safe open. That I could stop pretending I wasn't constantly one step away from needing what was inside. The thought lingered just long enough to be dismissed. I slid the panel shut and listened to the lock engage, the sound final and comforting in its certainty. Routine restored.

My Amani suit came off next. Expensive. Perfectly tailored. Designed to disappear in rooms full of other men wearing the same uniform of success. I stripped it away with more force than necessary, as if the fabric itself were responsible for the things I'd done while wearing it. Jacket on the hanger. Shirt smoothed flat. Trousers folded. One of a dozen nearly identical black suits waiting patiently in the wardrobe, each one carrying its own invisible history.

I reached for a t-shirt — soft, worn, comfortable — and pulled it over my head. Track pants followed. Clothes that belonged to a man who existed only in private. A man no one briefed or debriefed.

As I dressed, I caught myself listening again. Habit. The apartment remained still. From the living room, the dining table lamp still glowed faintly, Angel's chair pushed back at an angle that suggested she'd left in a hurry. I stepped out and looked at the empty space she'd occupied only minutes earlier. Her books were gone, but the impression remained, like warmth lingering after a body moves away. I shook my head. "Bloody teenagers," I muttered, rubbing a hand over my face. "*I* never did that."

The voice in my head answered immediately, without mercy. *Yeah — you did.*

I walked to the window and looked out over the street below. Wet pavement reflected streetlights in long, distorted streaks. Somewhere out there, Angel was laughing, unaware of the calculations that followed her through my mind like shadows. I trusted her — or told myself I did — because the alternative was admitting how little control I truly had.

There was one more thing I needed to do. One last task before I let the night close in. I stood there for a long moment, weighing it. I'd tried before. More than once. Each attempt had ended the same way — incomplete, inconclusive, unanswered. Failure dressed up as due diligence.

I told myself this would be the last time. If it failed again, I'd let it go. Accept the truth of it. Move on. That was the plan, at least. The plan I'd rehearsed carefully enough to almost believe.

The truth was, I missed her.

The admission came without a warning, raw and unwelcome. I missed the way she drove, profile lit by passing streetlights as I watched her instead of the road. I missed finding her scent on my t-shirt in the morning — the one she'd borrowed because she'd forgotten her overnight bag. I missed listening to her breathe beside me, counting the seconds between each rise and fall, afraid to sleep in case time accelerated and stole it from me.

I missed her awful morning breath. Her hair at first light, tangled into something that resembled a nest of hornets. I missed the way she laughed when I said something stupid, and the way she didn't hold back when she was angry. I missed the weight of her body when she fell asleep on top of me, pinning me in place because neither of us wanted to be the one who moved.

Damn it.

I stood there, fists clenched, feeling something dangerously close to *need* settle in my chest. Need had no place in my life anymore. It compromised judgment. It invited mistakes.

And yet —

One last shot.

I turned toward the far corner of the living room, where the workstation sat behind an innocuous bookshelf that slid aside at the touch of a concealed switch. The set of curved monitors came alive as I stepped forward, their glow painting the walls in sterile blues and greens.

"Alexa," I said, my voice steady despite the tension coiled beneath it, "open a new case file."

For a fraction of a second — just long enough to notice — nothing happened.

Then the system responded. "Good evening, Nathan," the AI said calmly. "A security code is required for this operation. Please enter your security code."

I straightened. "November. Echo. One. Three. One. Five. Charlie. Bravo."

I stepped back as the screen populated, lines of code racing past before resolving into a familiar lime-green interface. The Australian Secret Intelligence Service official text filled the centre of the display, crisp and authoritative. Beneath it, Australian Coat of Arms, Kangaroo and Emu. And the words *Australian Federal Government* glowed with quiet conviction.

"Accessing," Alexa continued. "Access granted."

I hesitated. Just for a second. I had time to ask myself what I was doing? Could I change my mind and back away? Was this a good idea? But now, that was too late. Somewhere in the system, a record had just been created. A timestamp. A name. A choice.

I took a breath. Decided to move on. If there were consequences I'd answer them. Nothing new here. "Please continue to files," I said.

The night leaned in closer. The system waited. Not impatiently — Alexa didn't do impatience — but with the same neutral expectancy that made decisions feel smaller than they were. The coat of arms faded away, replaced by a segmented interface I hadn't used in years. I recognised it immediately. *Deep Dive Protocols*. The kind you didn't access unless you were prepared to leave a footprint behind.

"State the nature of the operation," Alexa said.

"Deep Dive," I replied. "Level three."

A pause. Longer this time.

"Please be advised. Level Three Deep Dive operations are subject to retrospective audit. This action will be recorded."

I exhaled slowly. "Acknowledged." The word felt more consequential than it should've.

"The name of the contact?" Alexa requested.

I swallowed. Dry mouth again. Ridiculous. This wasn't a firefight. No one was putting a weapon to my head. Still, my pulse picked up, betraying me. "Roslyn Tran," I said. "Asset designation one-seven-hotel-four-bravo-kilo."

The screen flickered. "Accessing. Please stand by."

Lines of data scrolled faster than I could read, not that I needed to. I'd seen this often enough to know what mattered — what returned to the screen was what didn't matter at all. Names, dates, locations, all assembling themselves into patterns designed to reassure. Designed to suggest completeness. I waited for more.

Seconds passed. Then more started to show itself. The system's processing bar crawled forward in deliberate increments, each one a reminder that somewhere, deep inside layers of compartmentalisation and redundancy, a question had been asked that hadn't been asked in a long time. I thought about the last time I'd seen her. Not the specifics — those were locked away carefully — but the feeling. The quiet certainty that some connections didn't obey orders or timelines. That some things, once known, refused to stay buried.

"Deep Dive complete," Alexa said at last.

The screen resolved into a single data panel.

"Roslyn Tran, also known as Ngoc Tran," Alexa continued. "Date of birth: August third, nineteen seventy-two. Place of birth: Da Nang, Vietnam. No current operational status available."

I leaned forward slightly. That wasn't right.

"No current information?" I asked.

"That is correct," Alexa said. "This contact is classified as inactive. No further data available within authorised intelligence partitions."

Inactive.

The word landed with a dull thud. Inactive could mean a lot of things. Retired. Reassigned. Contained. Dead. It was a word designed to end conversations. But the fact that a record still existed at all mattered. Truly erased assets didn't leave even this much behind. Not even a bread crumb. They were dark beyond dark. If this was the case, a Deep Dive would produce nothing.

"Expand search parameters," I said. "Cross-reference with allied databases. Global returns."

"Please confirm," Alexa replied. "This action will increase exposure."

"Confirmed."

Another pause. Another crawl of data. I forced myself to stay still, hands loose at my sides, posture relaxed. If anyone was watching my biometrics — and it wasn't impossible — I wanted nothing for them to read.

"All possible scenarios assessed," Alexa said. "No alternative aliases detected on worldwide service grid markers."

I frowned. "You're telling me she's completely off grid?"

"That is correct."

"Even with redundant grid markers?"

"That is correct."

The answer was too clean. I stepped back, running a hand over my beard, frustration simmering beneath my skin. Years of searching, of half-answers and dead ends, and this was all the system could give me? Either Roslyn was gone, or she'd gone so dark that even our highest-level networks couldn't see her. I stared at the screen, hardening my stance.

"Keep scanning," I said. "There has to be something."

"Affirmative, agent Masters." Alexa replied.

I turned away, pacing the length of the living room, every instinct telling me I was pushing too far for reasons that had nothing to do with national security. This wasn't tradecraft. This was personal. The kind of thing that got people reassigned if they were lucky, buried if they weren't. Sometimes there were no answers. When an agent went dark properly, they vanished. Clean. Deliberate. Final. I was almost ready to accept it when Alexa spoke again.

"There is a civilian telecommunications record associated with this contact. Historical. Dating back to nineteen ninety-two. Would you like me to retrieve it?"

I stopped mid-step. "Yes," I said immediately. Maybe too quickly.

The number appeared on the screen. Old format. Obsolete by modern standards. The kind of thing you'd expect to be long disconnected, a relic of another era. But it was there, unmistakably real.

My heart rate spiked. I felt it in my throat, in my hands. I tried to swallow, dry, and failed.

"Would you like me to initiate contact?" Alexa asked.

For a split second, I hoped the answer would be no. That the system would block the option, save me from myself. That this would remain theoretical — data without consequence. I imagined her voice. Her silence. The possibility that she wouldn't answer at all.

"Yes," I said.

The line connected. I held the phone to my ear, listening to the ring tone echo across the years I'd pretended not to miss. Each ring tightened something in my chest, a countdown I hadn't agreed to. I told myself she wouldn't answer. That the number was dead. That this was just one more attempt ending the way all the others had. The ringing stopped. Disconnected. For a moment, I couldn't move. I stared at the floor, heat flooding my face, disappointment cutting deeper than I was prepared for. That was it. The final answer delivered without ceremony. I exhaled, long and slow. But I wasn't done.

"Alexa," I said quietly, "cross-check that number."

"Please stand by."

The system processed again, faster this time, as if the barrier had already been breached.

"This number is currently registered with Optus services," Alexa said. "Subscriber name: Roslyn Tran. Known address on record: eleven thirty-two Bay Road, St Kilda."

I closed my eyes. How could this be so simple? But there it was. Not hidden. Not erased. Just — civilian. Outside the walls we all pretended were impenetrable.

"Why wasn't this flagged earlier?" I asked.

"This information resides outside intelligence grid markers," Alexa replied. "Civilian data partitions are not prioritised in Deep Dive operations."

Of course they weren't. For years, I'd been searching in the dark for someone who was already standing in the light. I opened my eyes and stared at the address on the screen. St Kilda. Close enough to taste. Close enough to ruin everything. But somewhere in the system, a log entry had just grown a set of shark's teeth.

I grabbed my phone from the table, hands still unsteady and typed the message before I could talk myself out of it.

Rose. It's me. I think it's time for a bagel. Wouldn't you agree?

I placed the phone face-up on the table and stepped back, putting distance between us like it was an explosive device. The reply came almost immediately.

Good morning, Nathan Masters. It's been a while. I was beginning to think you'd never find me. Congratulations. What can I do for you at this ungodly hour?

The night had just changed shape. I didn't pick the phone up straight away. I stood there, a few steps back from the table, watching the screen glow softly in the half-light of the apartment as if it might change its mind. As if the words might rearrange themselves into something less real if I gave them time. My name sat there in plain text — *Nathan Masters* — stripped of rank, designation, or buffer. Just me. Just the thing I'd spent years making sure never appeared anywhere it didn't belong.

Ungodly hour.

She was right. And wrong. For Roslyn, night had always been a beginning. I crossed the room and picked up the phone, feeling the familiar weight of it in my hand, suddenly aware of how absurd it was that something so small could carry so much history. I quickly typed my reply before my mind cascaded in on itself.

Ungodly hour, my arse. We both know you're just getting started about now.

There was a pause this time. Longer. Maybe deliberate.

I imagined her reading it somewhere not unlike where I stood — alone, lights low, systems humming quietly in the background. I wondered if she hesitated the way I did, or if that was something she'd trained out of herself long ago.

The reply came.

I thought you'd forgotten. My employers prefer me armed for all contingencies, Nate. Nothing has changed.

Employers.

Plural.

That detail lodged itself in my mind and refused to move. I let it sit there while I typed.

It's been a long time, Rose.

Her reply.

Has it? Time passes differently when you stop waiting.

That one landed clean. No wasted words. No softness. Roslyn had never believed in cushioning blows.

I leaned back against the edge of the table, staring at the rain-streaked window beyond the phone screen. Streetlights blurred into elongated smears of gold and white. Somewhere out there, Roslyn was closer than she'd been for years, but farther away than ever.

I tried.

I typed, then stopped.

Tried what? To find her? To forget her?

To convince myself that walking away had been a choice rather than an order?

I watched my screen. The three dots appeared. Disappeared. Appeared again. And then words.

You don't have to explain. I know how your world works. I gave up waiting for answers a long time ago.

I closed my eyes briefly, adjusting my stance. I typed and sent.

I didn't give up on us.

That was the first truly dangerous thing I'd said.

Her response took longer this time. Long enough that I began to regret it. Long enough that I imagined her deleting drafts, choosing words with care, deciding how much truth I was allowed to keep. Then words came.

I gave up. I had to.

I felt the admission settle into my chest like a weight finding its place. Next moment, a new message,

I moved on. I built something else. You need to understand that before you say anything else. If you can't understand, this conversation ends here.

My fingers hovered over the screen. But I typed them anyway. Sent.

You're married.

I winced at how blunt it looked once it was there. There was no immediate reply.

When it came, it was accompanied by a location ping I hadn't asked for.

Yes. And no. It's complicated, Nate.

Of course it was.

Is he a good man?

I sent it before I could stop myself.

Her response was laughter rendered in text — excessive, unrestrained.

You're unbelievable. All these years, and you still manage to make everything about you.

I smiled despite myself. A small one. Unwanted. Familiar. I replied.

Now I'm confused.

She shot back.

Then you're paying attention. Good.

The tone shifted then. I felt it even through the screen, the way you feel pressure change before a storm breaks. Roslyn replied again.

Look. We don't have much time. And I didn't respond to your texts, come back into your life so you could reminisce.

You came back?

You found me. There's a difference.

Another pause.

I've been watching you, Nate. Eagle Shield is nearly finished. You should be proud. Most of us don't get to see our work conclude.

My stomach knotted.

How do you know about Eagle Shield?

The reply was immediate.

Because I never stopped being good at what I do.

I exhaled slowly, realising just how naïve I'd been to think she could ever truly disappear. Then she wrote back again.

Forget about me. Forget about what we were. It was real. It mattered. But now it's over.

My fingers trembled as I typed.

I—

Don't. Don't even go there. Don't do this to me. I can't afford it. And neither can you.

The words arrived sharp and absolute as though she'd read my thoughts.

I stared at the screen, the silence between messages was suddenly deafening. I had nothing prepared for this version of her — controlled, distant, still lethal in her honesty. I lowered myself into the chair, shoulders slumping, the fight draining out of me faster than I'd expected. For the first time in years, I didn't have a comeback. The phone vibrated again.

I looked down.

I'll see you shortly. I'll bring bagels.

I sat there long after the screen dimmed, heart pounding, mind racing, knowing with absolute certainty that whatever happened next would cost me something I couldn't replace.

And knowing, just as clearly, that I would pay for it anyway.

***

The apartment felt smaller once the decision had been made. Not physically — the walls hadn't moved, the ceilings hadn't dropped — but the air had changed, thickened, like it was holding its breath along with me. I stood there for a moment after the last message, phone still in my hand, staring at nothing in particular, letting the reality of it settle.

She was coming.

After all the years of silence, all the failed searches and half-answers, Roslyn Tran was crossing the city to my door, with bagels in her hand like nothing had ever broken between us. Bagels that once were a code between us that only we understood. That thought alone should've been enough to make me stop. Instead, I checked the locks. Front door first. Manual bolt engaged. Electronic lock green. Secondary latch intact. I moved methodically, the way I always did when nerves threatened to interfere. Windows sealed. Balcony access locked. Motion sensors active but calibrated to ignore anything smaller than a cat — or anything I'd already authorised.

I paused at the workstation, fingers hovering over the controls. I could shut everything down. Kill the cameras, blind the external feeds, reduced the apartment to a dead zone that wouldn't register as anything more than another dark square on the active grid. It'd be cleaner. Safer. It would also be a confession. I left the systems running.

In the bathroom, the shower took longer than necessary. I stood under the hot water until my skin flushed and the noise drowned out my thoughts, replaying our exchange over and over again, analysing tone and timing the way I'd once meticulously analysed intercepted communications. Too familiar. Too easy. Too dangerous.

Married. And no.

Complicated.

That word again. It followed people like me the way smoke followed fire.

I dressed more carefully than I had earlier, changing out of the track pants and t-shirt without quite admitting why. Jeans. A polo shirt — neutral, understated. Something that said *civilian* without trying too hard. I shaved, slowly this time, watching my reflection for signs of something I couldn't name. Excitement. Fear. Regret. All three, probably.

The doorbell chimed.

Once.

I froze, razor still in my hand, a clean line half-finished along my jaw. I waited for it to sound again. It didn't.

That was pure Roslyn Tran. Precise. Confident. No wasted effort.

I rinsed the blade, set it down, and took one last look at myself in the mirror. I didn't recognise the man staring back — not because he looked different, but because he looked hopeful. That was much worse.

By the time I reached the living room, the apartment was silent again. I approached the door slowly, every sense tuned outward, listening for anything out of place. Nothing. No footsteps retreating down the hall. No movement on the other side. I disengaged the locks.

The door opened inward on silent hinges. No body. Anywhere. No one I could see.

I closed the door again. Puzzled by the chime. But as I turned around, she was there. Roslyn was already inside the safe house.

She sat on the sofa as if she'd always belonged there, legs crossed, posture relaxed but alert. A plain cardboard box rested beside her on the cushion, the lid still closed. Laid diagonally across the top was a single white rose, its stem trimmed neatly, petals unblemished. For a moment, neither of us spoke. She looked up and smiled. Not wide. Not cautious. Just enough.

Time folded in on itself. She hadn't changed the way people usually do. No dramatic alterations, no obvious signs of age. Her hair was swept up and pinned in place, exposing the line of her neck. Her coat was dark and tailored, unbuttoned but not yet removed. Makeup minimal. Eyes sharp. Alive. The same woman who'd once known how to read me better than anyone else.

"I see you kept the place tidy," she said lightly, her voice exactly as I remembered it — calm, detailed, carrying layers beneath the surface.

"How did you —"

She lifted a hand. "Later."

I nodded, accepting the answer even as questions crowded my mind. Of course she'd bypassed the security. Of course she'd done it without effort. It was what she did.

"I brought bagels as usual," she said, gesturing to the box. "And I didn't forget."

My gaze dropped to the rose, then back to her.

"You never did," I said.

She stood then, smooth and unhurried, closing the distance between us with the same deliberate grace I remembered. Up close, I could see the fine details — the faint line near her eye when she smiled, the familiar steadiness in her breathing. She scanned the room without turning her head, cataloguing exits and angles as naturally as other people checked their phones.

"We don't have much time," she said quietly. "And this isn't what you think it is, Nate."

I felt the weight of that statement settle between us, heavier than the silence it replaced.

"Then tell me what it's supposed to be."

She looked at me for a long moment, something unreadable passing through her eyes. "First," she said, "you're going to sit down. And then you're going to listen. If you interrupt me, I leave."

I pulled out a chair and sat.

Roslyn took the seat opposite, resting her hands lightly on her knees, posture perfect. "Nathan, after this, you won't see me again. It ends tonight."

And just like that, the night stopped being about what I wanted — and started being about what I was about to lose.

Roslyn waited until I was still. Not quiet — still. Shoulders squared. Hands visible. The kind of stillness that meant I was listening with more than my ears. Only then did she speak. "You broke protocol," she said. No accusation. Just fact. "Not the dramatic kind. The subtle kind. The kind people overlook because it doesn't look dangerous."

I didn't argue.

"You ran a Deep Dive when you had no operational justification," she continued. "You bridged intelligence partitions that were designed not to be compromised. And you did it using your real name, your real access, from a fixed location." Her eyes held mine steadily. There was no anger there. Only assessment. "That log already exists. You know that, right?"

"Yeah."

"Good," she said softly. "Then we can skip the part where you lie to yourself."

I exhaled and leaned back in the chair. "If you're here to tell me I made a mistake, you're late. I knew that when I opened the Deep Dive."

A corner of her mouth lifted. "You always were a stubborn bastard."

She reached for the box of bagels but didn't open it. Just rested her palm on the lid, grounding herself. "I'm here because the mistake you made doesn't belong only to you anymore."

That got my attention.

"You didn't find me because you were clever. You found me because someone stopped hiding me."

The room seemed to tilt slightly.

"Who?" I asked.

Roslyn shook her head. "Not yet. But you need to understand this: I didn't disappear all those years ago because I wanted to. I was removed. Quietly. Cleanly. I accepted it because it was the only way to keep certain people alive."

I sat up, back straight. "Including you."

"Including me," she agreed. "And including someone else."

I thought of Angel. I thought of my charge. I thought of Eagle Shield before I could stop myself. Roslyn noticed. She always did.

"She's grown," Roslyn said. "Angel. Your mission. Your assigned charge."

I didn't move. Didn't blink. "You shouldn't know about that," I said.

"I know more than you think," she replied gently. "Which is why I'm here."

Roslyn stood and crossed the room, not toward me, but toward the window. She looked out at the city as if it were a board she'd played on to forget. "You think Eagle Shield is about preparation? About Angel and her induction into ASIS? About her starting a new order?"

"It is," I said. "No question. It's been that way since she was ten."

Roslyn turned back to me. "Eagle Shield is about a handover, Nate."

The word sank in slowly. "Handover to who?"

"That's the part you were never meant to see," she said. "It's a legacy operation. Assets, infrastructure, influence — all transitioning to a new control architecture. Public-facing where it needs to be. Private where it matters."

"You're telling me we're giving Eagle Shield away."

"I'm telling you it's being absorbed. By people who don't care about restraint anymore. They want Eagle Shield abandoned."

I stood up. "That's not possible," I said. "There're safeguards. Oversight."

Roslyn smiled sadly. "You still believe in process, Nate. Don't be naïve. You're smarter than that."

I pushed a hand to my chin, anger bleeding into motion. "If what you're saying is true, then why come to me at all?"

"Because you're bloody visible. And because you still hesitate."

I stopped. I let the words sink in.

"Hesitation isn't a flaw," Roslyn continued. "And right now, it's the only reason you're still useful."

That stung more than it should've.

"Look. I'm married. This time, it's true. And no, it's not safe. It's a containment marriage. A stabiliser. It keeps certain assumptions in place."

"You're not in it for love?"

She didn't answer straight away. "I respect him," she said finally. "And I protect him. That's not nothing."

"So why risk this at all? Why come here?"

She met my gaze again, and this time there was no professional distance left. "Because you needed to hear it from me. And tonight is the last moment where this choice is still yours." Roslyn stepped closer. Close enough that I could smell her — the same faint, familiar scent that memory had never quite let go of.

"*You* can finish Eagle Shield. Do exactly what's expected of you. Protect the machine. Protect your charge by staying predictable." She paused. "Or, you can hesitate. Publicly. At the wrong moment. Just enough to force a delay. Nate, now's not the time for sudden movements. Stay in play."

"A delay gets people killed," I said.

"So does momentum," she replied.

I looked at her then — really looked — and saw not the woman I'd missed, but the operative she'd always been. Calculating. Honest. Dangerous.

"And us?" I asked quietly.

"Us? We already happened."

The words carried the weight of everything we hadn't said — and everything that was about to come due. Roslyn didn't touch me. That was how I knew she meant it. She stepped away, giving me space the way you give a loaded weapon room to misfire. The white rose felt out of place in my hand — fragile, symbolic, ridiculous in a room where decisions had hard edges. I set it down carefully on the table beside the unopened box of bagels, aligning the stem without thinking. Control where I could get it.

"You're asking me to sabotage my own operation," I said.

She corrected me without heat. "I'm asking you to slow it down."

I let out a humourless breath. "That's a semantic difference people use when they don't want to say the word out loud."

Roslyn shrugged out of her coat and laid it over the back of the sofa, movements unhurried. Beneath it, she wore black — simple, exact, functional. Not a disguise. A statement. "You know how many operations survive because someone hesitates at the right moment?" she said. "Not enough to make it into the training manuals."

I shook my head. "And you know how many fall apart because someone thinks they're the smartest person in the room?"

Her eyes flicked to mine. Sharp. Slightly amused. "You used to be the smartest man I know. Or at least honest enough to know when you weren't."

I turned away, pacing again, feeling the walls press in around me. This apartment had always been my safe space, my controlled environment. Tonight, it felt like a box with the lid halfway closed. "You're assuming I even have that kind of leverage," I said. "Eagle Shield doesn't hinge on one man's timing."

"No," she agreed. "It hinges on trust. And you have more of that than you realise."

I stopped near the window, staring out at the city. Somewhere down there, Angel was still out there, laughing under dim lights, unaware that her life was being factored into equations Eagle Shield never agreed to. Not for a second.

Roslyn joined me at the window, standing just far enough away that our reflections didn't overlap in the glass. "Angel's not a target," Roslyn said immediately. "Not now. Not unless someone makes her one."

"That's not reassuring."

"It's honest," she replied. "She's visible. Bright. That kind of intelligence doesn't go unnoticed forever. Especially when it runs in certain families. I think you know exactly what I mean."

I closed my eyes. "You didn't come here just to warn me," I said.

"No. I came to see whether the man I trusted still existed."

"And?"

She considered me for a long moment. Not romantically. Strategically. "He does. And that's the problem."

Silence settled thicker this time. I turned to face her. "If I do this — if I stall for time — what happens to you?"

A pause. The slightest one. "I vanish again," she said. "Properly this time."

"And your husband?"

"He'll be reassigned. Protected by proximity to the people who think they're winning."

"You don't sound convinced."

"I don't have the luxury of conviction," she said. "Only the probabilities."

I laughed softly, once. "You always did hate gambling."

She smiled, just a fraction. "And yet here we are. The both us. Old times."

The distance between us closed without either of us moving. It was awareness, not motion. Gravity. "This is the part where you tell me you still love me," I said quietly.

Roslyn's expression softened, but her voice didn't. "This is the part where I don't," she said. "Because love makes people sloppy. And I need you sharp, Nate. Now, more than ever. So, you carry your objectives forward."

That hurt more than any declaration could've. Roslyn reached for the bagel box at last and opened it, the smell cutting through the tension — warm bread, sesame, memory. She handed me one without comment and took another for herself.

I accepted it, absurdity and intimacy colliding in my chest. We stood there, eating bagels in silence like two people pretending this was normal, like this wasn't the calm before something irrevocable. After a moment, she spoke again. "There's something else," she said.

I looked at her.

"The Deep Dive you ran? It triggered an automated curiosity ping. Low-level. Background noise. But someone followed it."

"Fuck. Who?"

She met my eyes. "Not who," she said. "What."

A chill crept up my spine.

"An internal compliance algorithm," she went on. "New. Self-learning AI. It doesn't care about intent. Only deviation. It's automatic in ways even I don't fully understand."

I swallowed. "How long do I have?"

She glanced at the darkened monitor in the corner of the room, then back at me. "Hours," she said. "Maybe less."

The bagel she'd given me went stale in my hand. Roslyn stepped closer, close enough now that I could feel the warmth of her body, the familiarity of it threatening to undo me. "This is where you decide," she said softly. "Not tomorrow. Not in a briefing room. Here." She lifted her hand, not touching me, but close enough that I felt it anyway. "After tonight, there's no version of this where we both walk away unchanged."

Roslyn was still standing close — not meeting, but close enough that my body registered her presence before my mind allowed it. Years of training hadn't erased muscle memory. If anything, it had sharpened it.

"This is a mistake," I said.

"Yes," she replied. "A big mistake. But that's how you know it matters."

I let out a slow breath and looked past her, forcing my eyes to settle on something solid. The table. The bagels.

The white rose lying there, petals beginning to relax, already surrendering to time.

"You didn't come here just to talk," I said.

"No," she agreed.

"And you didn't come here unprepared."

She tilted her head slightly. A concession. "There are things I can't say over a channel," she said. "And actions I can't leave unanswered."

That was Roslyn all over. Precision wrapped in inevitability. I turned back to her. "If you're still the operative I know —"

"I am," she said.

"And you still came."

"Yes."

The silence that followed was heavier than anything we'd shared so far. Not awkward. Electric. A held breath stretched too long. "This doesn't end well," I said.

"It ends honestly, Nate — that's all." She reached up then, slow enough that I could've stopped her. She removed the pin from her hair. The movement was by itself almost ceremonial. Her hair fell around her shoulders in a familiar cascade, dark against black fabric, framing a face that had never learned how to lie without consequence.

I felt something in my chest give way. "That's not fair," I said.

She smiled — not teasing, not cruel. Just sad. "It never was fair to begin with," she said.

I should have stepped back. Put space between us. Reasserted control. Instead, I stayed where I was, letting the moment tighten around us. "This changes nothing."

"It changes everything in this moment only."

She closed the remaining distance of herself, resting her forehead briefly against my chest, not kissing me, not touching my hands — just there. Present. Real. I felt the steady rhythm of her breathing, the warmth of her body through fabric, the echo of a thousand nights we'd pretended were temporary.

Roslyn met my gaze. "This is the last quiet between us. After this, it all becomes noise again."

I lifted my hand without thinking, stopping just short of touching her back. "Ros —"

She pressed two fingers lightly against my lips. "Don't," she said softly. "If you say my name like that, you'll mean it. And then we won't stop."

She stepped away then, finally creating distance, and began unbuttoning her blouse — not hurried, not seductive. Intentional. When it slipped from her shoulders and pooled on the floor, she stood there unguarded, vulnerable in a way she rarely allowed herself to be. "This isn't about comfort. It's about remembering what it costs."

I stared at her, every internal instinct at war with itself. For a long moment, the world narrowed to the space between us. No briefings. No algorithms. No futures. Just the weight of choice pressing down, intimate and unforgiving. I reached for her then. Deliberately. And as my hand found hers, as her fingers curled into mine with a familiarity that hurt more than it soothed, I knew — with absolute clarity — that whatever came next would be to the point of no return.

Her hand was warm in mine, familiar in a way that bypassed memory and went straight to instinct. I pulled her toward me slowly, giving her every opportunity to step away. She didn't. Instead, she rested her forehead against my shoulder, eyes closed, as if bracing herself against something heavier than me.

For a moment, we stayed like that — breathing in sync, bodies aligned without urgency. The restraint was deliberate. Earned. Anything rushed would've broken the spell, turned it into something careless.

I slid my hand up her back, stopping when I felt her inhale sharply, the slightest hitch betraying the control she worked so hard to maintain. She responded by tightening her grip on my shirt, not pulling, just anchoring herself. Her eyes steady, searching my face as if committing it to memory. "You still hesitate," she said softly.

"Only with things that matter." I kissed her then — not the way I'd imagined in memory, not the way desire urged — but carefully, as if this moment could still fracture if handled without care. Her lips parted after a second, not in invitation, but in acceptance. When she kissed me back, it was with a certainty that made my chest ache. There was no hurry in it. No hunger. Just weight and meaning, layered over years of restraint.

She rested her hand at the base of my neck, thumb brushing skin with a familiarity that told me she remembered everything. The way I breathed. The way I paused. The way I always waited for permission even when none was required. "Don't disappear on me tonight," she murmured against my mouth.

"I'm here," I said.

"For now," she replied, and kissed me again.

We moved without speaking, shedding layers not as an act of resolve but of inevitability. Each movement was unhurried, measured — like two people aware this was not a beginning, but a reckoning. When we finally lay together, it was not about possession or escape. It was about closeness. About grounding. About reminding ourselves that we were still human beneath the machinery we both served. Afterward, the room was quiet again — but different. The kind of quiet that settles after truth had been spoken aloud. She lay beside me, her head resting lightly against my chest, listening to my heartbeat. I traced slow, absent lines along her arm, not wanting to disturb the fragile calm we'd earned. "This is where things break," she said eventually.

"Which part?"

"All of it," she replied. "Tomorrow, Eagle Shield accelerates. The compliance system will flag you. Subtle at first. Questions. Observation."

"And you?"

"I leave before dawn," she said. "I was never here."

I closed my eyes. "You could stay," I said, knowing the lie even as I spoke it.

She smiled faintly. "That's not how survival works."

Silence stretched between us again, but it wasn't empty. It was full of everything we weren't saying. "What about Angel," I said quietly.

"She'll be fine. Because of you. Because you still choose carefully."

Roslyn shifted slightly, fitting closer to me, and for a moment I allowed myself to believe in the illusion — that this could be enough. That memory could substitute for future. But she was right. This wasn't a beginning. This wasn't a substitute. It was a line drawn carefully in the dark, marking the last place where things were still true.

***

Light came quietly. It filtered through the blinds in thin, pale bands, touching the edges of the room like it was afraid of what it might wake. I opened my eyes slowly, disoriented for a moment by the unfamiliar weight beside me, the warmth where there should've been space.

Roslyn was still there. Not gone as quickly as she'd arrived, as I'd somehow expected. Instead, I was quietly surprised to feel her warmth next to me. She lay on her side facing away, one arm tucked beneath her head, hair spilled across the pillow in a way that felt almost indecent in its normality. Her breathing was slow, even. Real sleep — not the shallow half-rest of someone on watch. I watched her longer than I should've. Roslyn stirred, just enough to remind me she was trained even in sleep, then settled again.

I turned onto my side, facing her fully.

Is this really the last time?

As if hearing my thoughts, Roslyn reached out instead, resting her hand lightly on my chest, fingers spread, as if measuring the distance between heartbeats. "This," she said quietly, "is the last time we pretend we don't know what the cost is."

She withdrew her hand and sat up, gathering the sheet around herself with efficient modesty. The operative was already reassembling, piece by piece. "I meant what I said last night," she continued. "If you hesitate — publicly, procedurally — you'll buy time. Not safety. Time. Use it well."

She swung her legs over the side of the bed and stood, back toward me. "I'll be where I need to be to ensure that time doesn't collapse too quickly."

I watched her dress in silence. No drama. No lingering. Every movement purposeful. When she finished, she turned back to me once more. "You were right about one thing," she said. "This doesn't end well. Whichever way we look at it."

I sat up, the sheet pooling around my waist. "Then why do it?"

She smiled — not sadly, not happily. Truthfully. "Because some endings are cleaner than living with the lie."

Roslyn crossed the room and picked up the box of bagels, then hesitated. From the table, she lifted the white rose and placed it gently on top, aligning it the same way as the night before. "For what it's worth," she added, "you were never just a mission, Nate. I think you know that."

I swallowed something hard at the base of my throat. "Goodbye, Nathan Masters."

Roslyn leaned down, pressed a brief, soft kiss to my cheek — not my mouth — and stepped toward the door. The world echoed after she closed it. I sat there long after the sound of her footsteps faded, the morning fully arrived, bright and unforgiving.

On the chair by the window, the bagels waited. On top of them, the white rose lay perfect and intact. For the first time in a long while, the quiet didn't feel like refuge. It felt like warning.

The apartment woke slowly like a system. Timers clicked. Internal relays cycled. The low hum of electronics shifted pitch as background processes adjusted to daylight demand. I lay there listening, cataloguing the sounds the way I always did, but they felt different. Less comforting. More observant.

Roslyn had come and was gone. Not the dramatic kind. No trace, no disturbance. Just absence where presence had been. The bed was already cooling, the faint impression of her weight fading from the sheets like breath on glass.

I stood and dressed without ceremony. Jeans. Shirt. Barefoot. I didn't bother trimming my beard. It felt dishonest to finish something cosmetic when everything else was unfinished.

In the living room, the white rose still rested on its side atop the box of bagels. Morning light caught the petals, revealing the first signs of fatigue along the edges. Even cut cleanly, even cared for, nothing stayed perfect once removed from its source. I left them where they were.

The workstation chimed softly. That was new. I crossed the room and stood before the monitors as they came alive without prompting. No alarms. No warnings. Just a single notification pulsing steadily in the centre of the screen.

COMPLIANCE QUERY – PRELIMINARY

No red flags. No escalation markers. Clean typography. Neutral tone. The most dangerous kind. I read it once. Then again.

Please provide contextual clarification regarding cross-partition data access conducted at 00:41 hours. This inquiry is procedural in nature.

Procedural.

I felt a strange calm settle over me. The kind that comes when uncertainty collapses into inevitability. This was the moment Roslyn had warned me about —

the first touch, light enough to be mistaken for curiosity. I sat down.

The system didn't rush me. It never did. Algorithms like this weren't designed to intimidate. They were designed to learn. To see how people explained themselves. To measure uncertainty, tone, deviation from baseline. I could answer truthfully. Mostly. Wrap the action in operational language. Reference legacy verification. Invoke dormant contingencies. There were a dozen ways to make this look like nothing. And one way to make it slow.

When I finished, I didn't send it immediately. I reread it, listening for Roslyn's voice in my head — *clear, not kind* — and then submitted the response.

The confirmation ping sounded almost polite. I leaned back and stared at the ceiling. This was the delay. No dramatics. No heroics. Just friction introduced into a machine that expected smooth movement. Somewhere, a process would pause. Another would request review. A human might eventually be looped in — not today, maybe not tomorrow — but the momentum would stutter. Time, bought at cost.

My phone buzzed.

Angel.

I stared at her name longer than necessary before answering. "Morning, kiddo," I said.

"Don't sound so surprised."

I closed my eyes briefly. "You alright?"

"Yeah. Jenny's mum drove us home. I crashed pretty hard." A pause. "You okay too?"

The question caught me off guard. Not *where are you*, or *did you sleep*, but *are you okay.*

"I'm fine," I said, and hated how automatic it sounded.

She hummed, unconvinced. "I asked you a question once. A while ago now. You didn't answer."

"I didn't?"

"No. I asked if you ever regretted the choices you made before me. Before they told you to take care of me."

I swallowed. Angel sounded much older than her seventeen years for the first time. "Some choices," I said carefully, "don't show their consequences until much later."

Another pause. Softer this time. "I'll be home soon," she said. "Anything you want me to bring?"

I looked at the chair. The box of bagels. The rose. "Yeah," I said. "Some Philly cheese would be nice."

After the call ended, I stood and crossed the room. I picked up the white rose and turned it once in my hand, noting how fragile it felt now. Then I placed it gently in the sink and ran water over the stem, watching the petals darken, sag, give way. I closed the tap and let it rest there, spent and honest.

The bagels, I kept for later to have with the cheese Angel would bring home.

****

Outside the apartment, the city was alive. Traffic resumed its familiar rhythm. I imagined somewhere during the day in an office with frosted glass, a system would log my response and adjust its expectations. I imagined Eagle Shield would continue uninterrupted for the short term at least.

I returned to the workstation behind the hidden bookcase and began preparing for the briefing I'd attend later tomorrow, posture steady, expression neutral, the mask settling back into place. Only now, I knew exactly what it was going to cost to wear it.

I imagined the briefing room smelling faintly of coffee and recycled air. Neutral walls. Neutral carpet. A long table designed to make everyone feel equally small. I'd take my seat with the others and open the folder, place it neatly in front of me, already knowing what it would contain. Timelines. Milestones. Language engineered to sound decisive without committing to meaning.

Across the table, I imagined a screen would flicker to life.

EAGLE SHIELD – PHASE TWO

I imagined no one would look at me when it appears. No one would need to. The machine didn't accuse. It advanced. That was its nature.

I left the workstation and shifted to the window, to the city warm and busy around me, people carrying bags and conversations and plans that didn't require clearance.

Angel returned home by 2:00 p.m. unannounced and without warning as usual. After delivering the Philly cheese to the fridge, she sprawled herself on the sofa with a bagel in one hand and her phone in the other. "You saved me the good one," she said, smiling around a mouthful.

"I know your preferences," I replied, smiling back at her.

She eyed me for a moment, then nodded, apparently satisfied. "You look tired."

"I am."

She sat up straighter. "You ever think about stopping?"

The question again. Different angle. Same weight.

"Every day."

"And?"

"And some things don't let you stop. They just ask you to decide how you finish."

Angel considered the words, then leaned back, content for now.

Later, when the apartment had settled into evening and Angel had retreated to her room, I stood alone by the window.

The city lights came on one by one, familiar and distant. I thought about Roslyn — not where she was, but where she wasn't. Not in my life. Not in my future. Just in the space between choices, where some truths were allowed to exist briefly before being erased.

On the table behind me, the bagel box sat open, nearly empty. No rose this time. Just crumbs and the faint scent of Philly cheese. After tomorrow, I knew what would happen. There'd be reviews. Questions. Adjustments. Someone would eventually notice the pattern.

When they did, they would look for intent. For motive. For weakness. They wouldn't find what they expected.

I turned away from the window and switched off the light, leaving the apartment in shadow. Some lives were measured in missions. Others were measured in what they cost you to finish. And some things — the quiet things, the human things — were never meant to survive the work. But they left their mark anyway.

BOOK TWO

EARLY WARNINGS

PART ONE: AUSTRALIA LISTENING

Pine Gap had a way of making time feel poured out of a drum and left to settle. Same beige corridors. Same dry air that sanded the back of your throat if you talked too much. Similar hum in the walls — the quiet, constant vibration of a place built to listen.

The listening floor was always cold. Not cold, not Alice Springs winter cold, just air-conditioned-to-death cold. They kept it that way for the machines and for the people who had to pretend the machines didn't run them.

I sat down at my console with my coffee and my second coffee and tried not to think about the fact I'd already been awake since before dawn. Half the staff did it the same way: up in the dark, drive in with the road empty, badge in, swallow your personality, and become a pair of hands and a set of eyes.

The screen lit my face with that pale-blue glow. I'd been called Scotty-Blue since the Air Force days. I couldn't tell you why. Maybe because of my red hair and freckles. Maybe because I was stubborn enough to keep showing up. Maybe because *'Scott'* alone didn't stick. Names in places like this were less about what your mum wrote on your birth certificate and more about what your mates decided you looked like when you were knackered and half alive.

Across from me, Simon was already on shift, rolling his shoulders like he'd slept in a car.

"Mate, you look like death warmed up, eh?"

"Yeah, cheers," he replied without looking away from his display. "If that's the case I reckon you look like death's older brother."

The first ten minutes of a shift were always a ritual. Not the ceremonial sort. The practical kind. Check the inbound streams. Confirm the clocks. Make sure the last shift didn't leave you a mess. In a place like Pine Gap you didn't *'turn it off and on again'* unless you wanted a visit from someone with a badge you'd mostly didn't recognise, only heard about.

I started where I always started: baseline. Noise floor. The normal chatter of the planet. Military comms, civilian comms, the constant wash of *'nothing'* that your brain learned to ignore. The way you stopped hearing the fridge at home. Except this fridge contained the world.

I skimmed. I tagged. I flagged. It was work you did mostly with your gut and your eyes, like sorting fish at a wharf. Most of it was rubbish. Some of it was important. The trick was not to get bored and let the important stuff slide past.

The first hint came in as a burst that didn't feel right. Not the content, not yet, the shape of it. Timing, cadence, the little tells you couldn't teach in a classroom. I leaned in, letting my brew cool. It was routed through a channel that sat under layers of routine noise. Low-power, consistent. The sort of thing you saw a hundred times a day. Except this one was… urgent. Tight. Like a bloke speaking through his teeth. I pulled up the translation assist, but I didn't trust it. I never did. I trusted patterns. I trusted the human ear. Then the words hit me, and my stomach did a slow turn.

Launch.

Confirm.
Sequence.
I blinked, ran it again.
Launch.
Confirm.
Sequence.
It referenced a target vector that made no sense in the context of normal drills. Russia. Ukraine.

I sat back and stared at the screen like it'd crossed a line.

"Hey Simon," I said, keeping my voice level. "You seeing anything odd on your end?"

He angled his head. "Odd like what? Odd like the coffee machine's broken again? Cause I'll riot if it has."

"Odd like… a burst that's too clean for the channel it's riding."

He finally looked over, squinting at my display. "That doesn't look like much."

"That's the point, mate. It's bloody pretending to be not much."

He leaned closer. "You reckon it's exercise chatter?"
"Just smells wrong, eh?"
Simon snorted. "Mate, it's a signal. It doesn't smell."
"Struth Simon, you know what I mean."

He watched for a moment and then his expression shifted slightly — just enough that I knew he'd felt it too. People thought this job was all computers and clever acronyms. It wasn't. The computers did the lifting, but the *that's not right* part still sat behind your ribs.

"Could be a glitch," he said, and you could hear him wanting it to be that.

I relaxed a bit. "Yeah could be, I s'pose."

I didn't like how fast my mind tried to build a story around it. I forced myself back into procedure. Tag. Timestamp. Trace. Cross-check. I opened the metadata. Source route. Packet integrity. Timing drift. It held together. Too well. When a system glitched, it usually did it in a messy way. It spilled. It stuttered. It doubled itself or dropped pieces. This was clean. This was deliberate.

I logged it as **ANOMALY** and added a note: ***possible spoof / artefact; requires correlation***.

There were rules for everything. Even for being frightened. You didn't write *'this is terrifying.'* You wrote *'requires correlation.'*

I ran it against archived patterns. Drills. Exercises. Training rotations. It didn't match anything I could pull up quickly. The room kept breathing around me. Keyboards. Soft voices. The murmur of aircon. That hum behind the walls. Life continuing as though the planet wasn't doing a handstand somewhere beyond the desert. I took a sip of my brew. It tasted like burnt military regret.

On a second monitor, I pulled up other channels, looking for supporting chatter. Nothing obvious. Nothing screaming. That was almost worse. If it was real, it was early — still in the phase where the people making the decisions were whispering. Still in the phase where a warning looked like a mistake.

I leaned over and picked up the phone to the duty officer. There were different kinds of phones in Pine Gap. This was one of the quiet ones, the ones that didn't ring with that cheerful civilian tone. It just lit up and waited.

"Ops, Col. Banks," came the voice. Female. American accent softened by too many years here.

"Yeah, g'day, Ma'am," I said. "It's Scotty on Signals, Sector B. Got a burst that doesn't fit the channel. Looks like launch sequence comms out of Russia. Vector suggests Ukraine."

There was a pause — not long, but long enough to tell me she'd sat up straighter.

"Confidence level?" she asked.

"I'm calling it low-to-medium. Clean packet integrity, consistent cadence. Doesn't match archived drills. Could be spoof."

"Log it and push it through correlation," she said. "We'll watch."

"Copy."

That was it. No alarms. No drama. Just the machine of protocol turning another notch.

I hung up and stared at the screen again. The words still sat there like a splinter you couldn't work out of your skin.

Launch.

Confirm.

Sequence.

Outside, the desert kept being the desert. Inside, the base kept being a base. And I tried to tell myself what everyone told themselves when something didn't make sense: It's probably nothing. But my gut didn't buy it.

***

An hour later it came again. Same channel family. Same low-power hiding place. Same tight cadence. And now it wasn't a one-off. Now it was a rhythm. I'd been running correlation quietly while doing the rest of the shift work. That was the art of it: you didn't stop the world every time your instincts twitched. You took the twitch seriously and you let the system help you prove it. Correlation didn't give me the comfort I wanted. The second burst referenced timing marks. Coordinated. Multiple assets. Multiple launch sites. I rubbed the bridge of my nose and felt the skin already drying out. Aircon did that. The base dried everything out — your skin, your patience, your ability to feel normal things about normal life.

Simon looked over again. "Still on that thing?"

"It's still on me, mate. Can't leave the bloody thing alone. Got me frazzled, eh?"

He rolled his chair closer, the wheels whispering on the floor. "Show me more."

I pulled up the time series. Two bursts. Similar characteristics. Close enough that it wasn't chance.

"Looks like someone's practising," he said, but he didn't sound convinced.

"Or someone's actually fucken doing it."

We sat in that uncomfortable space where both possibilities were awful. If it was practice, it was practice for the worst thing humans had ever built. If it was real, it was the worst thing humans had ever built, being used.

I dug into the metadata again, hunting for the tell that would let me label it safely as error. Latency. Clock drift. Something out of place. Anything. Instead, I found the opposite. The timing was too good. It was concrete. The drift was minimal. The route was consistent. Whoever was transmitting knew what they were doing. Which didn't help. Skilled spoofing existed. Disinformation existed. People played games at this level because they could. But then I caught something that made my mouth go dry. A tiny delay between two elements of the burst. Not much. Milliseconds. But it was the sort of delay you got when a human voice was being patched through a chain of systems under pressure — systems already in motion. Not a pre-recorded exercise loop. Live traffic.

I stared at it, then ran it again. Then again, because sometimes your brain was an optimist and tried to trick you. Same delay. Same spot.

"Mate," Simon said softly, "you alright?"

I didn't answer. One earpiece cupped my ear, the other hang loose. The timing was too rushed even for wearing a headset. I was listening.

In the background of the burst — almost lost, almost swallowed — there was a sound. Not words. Something physical. A scrape. A chair. The sort of noise you couldn't fake easily if you weren't thinking about it. It made it real in a way the words hadn't.

I logged the second burst and attached my notes: *live characteristics present; human routing delay; advise escalation*.

Now I had to decide what *'escalation'* meant. There were layers to it. You could nudge. You could flag. You could ring the right person and put your voice into their ear, so they had to treat it like a human said it, not just a file on a system.

I chose the voice option.

The duty officer line again. The same woman answered. "Ongoing?" she asked, like she'd been waiting.

"Yes Ma'am," I said. "Second burst. Same channel. Same characteristics. I'm seeing live routing delay, like human comms patched under load."

"How confident are you?"

I took a breath. Confidence wasn't a number you pulled out of a hat. It was a judgement you owned. If you called it wrong, people remembered. If you called it right, they still didn't thank you — because being right about this sort of thing meant the world had gone mad.

"Medium," I said. "Leaning higher. Still could be spoof. But the pattern's consistent."

"Alright," she said. "Push to higher correlation. We'll bring in a second set of eyes."

"Copy."

I hung up and felt my hands shaking a little, so I put them flat on the desk until they stopped. This was the dangerous phase. The phase where you were convinced enough to be worried but not convinced enough to be certain. The phase where your mind tried to fill in gaps and panic did cartwheels in your chest. I forced myself to do what I always did: make it smaller. Focus on the data. Focus on the next step. I pulled in other feeds. I expanded the search window. I looked for anything that would either back it up or kill it. Then I found something else. It wasn't in Russian.

It came in as a short, clipped burst from a different direction, a different linguistic signature. It was partially encrypted, but the headers and routing gave it away even before translation.

China.

Simon swore under his breath. "You're kidding, right?"

"Mate, you wish," I said.

The content, what little we could peel off quickly, referenced readiness states. Alert posture. *'Second wave'* language that didn't belong in peacetime routine. The room felt smaller. The hum in the walls felt louder, like the building itself had started listening harder. A minute later, as if the universe wanted to be thorough, a third thread surfaced.

North Korea.

That one wasn't elegant. It was rougher, louder in its own way. The kind of signal that carried more desperation than discipline. But it referenced the same nightmare language:

Launch.

Authorisation.

Sequence.

Three separate sources. Three separate directions. And suddenly *'glitch'* felt like a child's word.

I leaned back and stared at the ceiling for a second, not because there was anything there, but because if I kept staring at the screen I might start believing I'd will it to change.

Simon's voice came quieter. "Scotty… what the fuck do we do?"

"We do our job, mate," I said, and it sounded steadier than I felt. Because that was the only thing you could do in a place like this. You didn't get to decide policy. You didn't get to decide retaliation. You didn't get to decide whether humanity deserved another chance.

You got to decide whether to raise your hand and say, *I think this is real.* And once you did that, it didn't belong to you anymore.

I opened the reporting pipeline and built the package carefully, like it was a bomb I didn't want to jostle. Attach logs. Attach timing analysis. Attach the correlation notes. Tag it as urgent without using language that would get me pulled aside for *'emotional framing.'*

Then I hit send. It left my screen and became someone else's problem. I should've felt relief. Instead, I felt like I'd pushed the first domino.

***

The hardest part about *'early'* warnings was that they never sounded like warnings. They sounded like maybes. They sounded like questions. They sounded like a bloke clearing his throat before he said something he knew would ruin the room. The base didn't transform into chaos. It didn't suddenly sprout sirens and running boots. It stayed itself — controlled, compartmentalised, polite. But the temperature of the room changed anyway.

It happened through body language first. People sat straighter. Voices dropped. Chairs stopped squeaking because no one shifted unless they had to. The kind of tension you got before a storm broke — not because you could see the storm yet, but because your bones could.

I saw two sets of uniforms I didn't recognise come onto the floor. One of them had that smooth American confidence that came from knowing you were backed by an entire machine. They spoke to the duty officer. She glanced toward my station. Didn't point. Didn't wave. Just looked. A moment later my phone lit up again.

"Scotty," she said, and now her voice had that sharper edge. "We need you in Briefing Two. Now."

"Copy. Osca-mike."

I stood and felt how stiff my back was. Too many years in chairs. Too many years watching screens instead of the skies. I'd always told myself I was lucky — I could fly a chopper, I was Air Force back then and wasn't trapped behind a desk. But in a place like this, everyone was trapped behind something.

Briefing Two was a small room with a table that looked like it'd been designed by someone who'd never had to sit at it for hours. The lighting was too bright. The air was too cold. There was a monitor on the far wall and a speakerphone in the centre of the table like an altar. Two American uniforms sat already. My duty officer stood near the door. Simon wasn't there. This wasn't a *'team'* moment. This was a *'who saw it first'* moment.

"Major Scott Thompson?" one of the uniforms asked.

"Yeah," I said. "Scotty-Blue, to you blokes if ya like, eh?"

He smiled like he'd heard worse. "We've reviewed your packet. Walk us through your confidence."

I sat down and folded my hands, because if I didn't, they'd move. I didn't want them to see that. I kept it technical. Timing. Cadence. Routing. Live delay. Cross-source alignment. I didn't say *'I think we're all about to die.'* I said. "These characteristics don't match known training profiles."

The second uniform — older, greyer — leaned forward. "Could it be a coordinated spoof?"

"It could, sir," I said. "But it'd be a bloody good one. And it would have to be coordinated across multiple sources with consistent timing signatures."

"Why would someone do that?" the first uniform asked.

I met his eyes. "To make you react. To make you push buttons you can't un-push."

He nodded slowly, like he liked the answer. The speakerphone crackled, and suddenly there was another voice in the room. American. Distant. The voice of someone who lived in a place where decisions were made.

"Pine Gap, confirm your assessment," the voice said.

My duty officer glanced at me. I swallowed. My tongue felt too big in my mouth.

"Sir, this is RAAF-Sigs, Major Scott Thompson," I said into the phone. "Based on multiple intercepts and correlation characteristics, I assess medium-to-high likelihood the traffic reflects live launch sequencing communications. Multiple sources. Russia. China. North Korea. Timing suggests alignment."

There was silence on the line. Not because the person hadn't heard me, but because they had. Then the voice said, "Stand by."

Those two words were nothing. But they were everything.

Stand by meant somebody somewhere was pulling up a chair. Stand by meant somebody was looking at a screen and doing the same thing I'd just done — trying to decide whether the world was about to change. Stand by meant I'd stepped onto a path that didn't have an exit ramp. The line went quiet again, but the call didn't end. They left us sitting there like weights.

The older uniform finally spoke. "If this is real, what's the timeline?"

I looked at the monitor on the wall where the trajectory estimates had started to populate. Calculations. Probabilities. The language of pretending you could make the unthinkable manageable. "Minutes to first confirmations," I said. "Then... it depends. But if launches are underway, you're looking at… tens of minutes before impacts on the far side of the world. Less, depending on range and vector."

"Jesus fucking Christ," my duty officer murmured.

Nobody told her off for swearing. That was another temperature change. The speakerphone crackled again. "Pine Gap, relay all supporting data. We're moving to DEFCON 2."

My stomach dropped through the floor. Higher readiness. DEFCON 2. That was the phrase that lived just under the surface of nightmares. A polite label for arming teeth.

My duty officer stepped in. "Copy. Relaying now."

The first uniform stood. "You did the right thing," he told me, like you'd say to a bloke who'd reported a suspicious package, not a man who might've just started a chain reaction of nuclear decisions.

I didn't feel like I'd done the right thing. I felt like I'd done the only thing. I left Briefing Two and walked back onto the floor and it hit me, suddenly, that the people around me were still working. Still typing. Still flagging. Still listening to the planet as though it wasn't in the middle of deciding whether it wanted to keep existing.

Simon looked up when I returned. His eyes searched my face. "Well?" he asked.

I sat down slowly.

"It's gone upstairs," I said. "Cocked Pistol."

He swallowed. "So… that's it then?"

"No," I said, and my voice came out rough. "That's the start."

He stared at his screen like it might save him. I tried to focus on my own. Tried to keep doing the work. But there was a new layer now, a new truth sliding under everything: We weren't watching a distant event anymore. If this was real, Pine Gap wasn't just an observer. It was part of the loop. A node in the chain. A place that fed decisions. And nodes got targeted. That thought landed quietly, like a stone dropped into deep water.

I imagined Alice Springs — my family out there living ordinary lives under an ordinary sky, thinking about groceries and school runs and what to cook for dinner. I imagined their phones in their pockets, silent, innocent. I imagined the desert, wide and empty, like it always was. Then I imagined the wrong kind of light on the horizon.

I forced my eyes back to the data because that was what I did when my heart tried to crawl out of my chest. I watched the feeds. I watched for confirmation. I watched for anything that would let me tell myself I'd been wrong. But everything that came in from then on didn't soften the story. It sharpened it. And somewhere deep in the base, behind doors I couldn't see through, decisions started moving.

The warning phase was ending.

And the world was about to find out whether it listened.

***

Back on the floor, everything looked the same, which was the first lie. The screens still glowed. The aircon still hammered the cold into us. People still did their little rituals — headsets adjusted, keyboard taps, the quiet mutter of acronyms like prayers. But the room had tightened. You could feel it in the way no one laughed. In the way chairs stopped skidding, people sat dead still. The way every bloke and every shiela suddenly remembered their posture, like someone important had walked in even when they hadn't.

Simon kept glancing at me, then away again, like eye contact might make it real. "What'd they say?" he asked.

I watched the feed scroll, my mouth dry. "They didn't say much. They listened. Mate, that's what I don't like."

He let out a short breath through his nose. "Yeah. When the uniforms listen, it's never any good."

On my secondary monitor, the reporting pipeline ticked as my packet moved through layers I didn't have access to. It was like watching a letter you'd posted to the Prime Minister and seeing it disappear into the slot. You didn't get to know where it went after that. You just knew it was out there, carried by people who could make decisions you couldn't.

Another burst came in — Russia again — tight, clipped, and now with more urgency threaded through it. Controlled voices speaking quickly, like a fire drill where the building was already burning.

I ran the cross-correlation again. The same delay. The same patch-through signatures. Live. I put my headset back on, it made me feel like I was still doing something. Like I wasn't just waiting for the sky to crack.

Col. Banks came onto the floor, walking fast without running. Her face had gone pale around the mouth, and I noticed it only because she was usually carved out of professionalism.

She stopped at my station. "Scotty," she said, voice low. "Keep everything. Log every fragment. No assumptions in the notes. Understood?"

"Yes Ma'am."

"There's going to be calls. You answer everything. If anyone asks for your confidence, you give it in plain language."

"Copy."

She hesitated. A human moment slipped through the official one. "You've got family nearby?"

I looked up at her. "Back in Alice."

She nodded once, like she'd filed it away in a place she didn't want to look at yet. "Alright. Keep your head."

Then she moved off, already speaking into her phone.

I glanced at Simon. He'd heard it too. His eyes widened, then he looked away hard, like he'd been caught.

A new indicator popped up on my screen — an internal flag, red-tagged, priority routing. It wasn't the kind of thing a signals grunt usually saw.

HIGHER READINESS — PARTIAL DEFCON 1

The words sat there like a weight. I didn't know exactly what *'partial'* meant in this context, and I didn't want to. It meant someone had moved a lever somewhere and the whole world was now a machine spinning up.

I did what I'd always done. I stayed with the data. I kept it clean. I kept it honest. And while I did, a thought kept knocking at the back of my skull: *If this is real, we're not just listening anymore. We were participating.*

***

Confirmation didn't arrive as a single dramatic moment. It arrived as a series of small, ugly certainties. First, an external feed flickered onto the big, shared display at the far end of the ops room — a map overlay, a tracking layer we didn't always have running in the open. It was one of the *'when needed'* tools. When needed meant when the nightmares came. A trajectory arc appeared. Thin, clean, computer drawn. It didn't look like death. It looked like geometry.

Then another.

Then another.

A bloke two rows over whispered, "Nah, this ain't right."

No one answered him. Simon leaned in, squinting. "Those are… what I think they are?"

I didn't take my eyes off the screen. "Looks that way, eh?"

"Jesus."

More arcs painted themselves in, each one tagged with probabilities, confidence values, estimated time windows. The language of science and statistics trying to wrap itself around an act of madness. A new packet hit my channel — different signature, different routing. A confirmation request from somewhere higher up the chain.

I opened it. It was terse.

CONFIRM LIVE CHARACTERISTICS

I typed back with hands that felt too heavy.

CONFIRMED. LIVE ROUTING DELAY PRESENT MULTI-SOURCE ALIGNMENT

I hit send.

For a moment nothing happened, and I almost convinced myself maybe the whole thing would dissolve. Maybe the arcs would turn out to be a glitch in their own system. Maybe somebody would say, *'False alarm,'* and we'd all go back to pretending the world was stable. Then the speaker above the duty officer's desk crackled. "Attention. Maintain stations. No unauthorised comms. All queries through chain. Repeat, maintain stations."

The voice was calm.

That was the second lie.

Calm meant they were trying to prevent panic, and you didn't prevent panic unless there was something worth panicking about.

A message window opened on my screen, priority, internal.

SITREP REQUIRED — PINE GAP CONFIDENCE ASSESSMENT

I stared at the cursor blinking. In my head I heard every training lecture I'd ever endured: don't overstate, don't editorialise, don't let emotion leak into your reporting. But I also heard my gut, and it didn't care about lectures.

I wrote:

CONFIDENCE HIGH THAT TRAFFIC REFLECTS LIVE LAUNCH SEQUENCING. MULTIPLE STATES INVOLVED. NOT CONSISTENT WITH KNOWN EXERCISE PROFILES.

I hovered over send for half a beat — half a heartbeat — then clicked send.

My stomach did that slow roll again. I'd just put my name next to *'high'* in a situation where *'high'* could set the world on fire.

Simon watched me. "You reckon they're gonna push the button?"

"They already have," I said, and my voice came out flatter than I felt. "Somebody did. We're just watching the chain catch up."

He swallowed. His Adam's apple bobbed like a kid's. "We're gonna get hit?"

I didn't answer. Not because I didn't hear him. Because the answer wasn't a thing you could say and keep breathing normal.

The map updated. One of the arcs changed colour — confirmed track.

Confirmed.

That word cut through everything. Not a glitch. Not a spoof. Not a maybe. Somewhere in the world, a lid had opened. A long cylinder had risen. Fuel had burned. An ICBM built to end cities had left the ground and was now moving through the sky. And we were in a cold room in the middle of the desert, staring at it like it was a weather system.

Another voice came through the room — someone behind me, low and broken. "My kids are at school."

A pause.

Someone else: "Fuck. Mine too."

No one said, "It'll be alright." Nobody believed it.

The human part of my brain tried to run away — tried to picture mushroom clouds, screaming, end-of-days rubbish you saw in movies. I shoved it back down. I focused on the next packet. If you let the pictures in, you stopped functioning. And in a place like Pine Gap, functioning was the only thing you had.

***

When the second wave of confirmations hit, the floor stopped pretending. Phones lit up everywhere. Higher ups moved like a school of fish, fast, coordinated, no wasted motion. People who'd been quiet for years suddenly sounded sharp, urgent, alive. Training kicked in.

The uniforms reappeared — more of them now, different faces, the same polished purpose. They didn't look frightened. They looked busy. That was the third lie. Busy meant they were fighting to keep control.

On my screen, the feeds multiplied.

Russia. China. North Korea. But now, India, Pakistan, Israel, United Kingdom, Germany — Yes, Germany.

Not just *talk.* Now it was the chatter that came after an irreversible act — status checks, secondary confirmations, route changes, the language of machines and men coordinating something enormous. And then another stream slid in — one I hadn't been watching because it wasn't my lane. Internal mapping.

Not of ICBMs.

Of us.

I caught it almost by accident — a metadata echo in a packet header, a reference to Pine Gap's own comms traffic being observed, analysed. It was subtle, but it was there. A targeting logic didn't need much. It needed presence. It needed importance. It needed a reason. Pine Gap had been a reason since the sixties.

We were a listening post, a relay, a brain stem in a larger body. If you were going to blind someone, you didn't start with their fingers. You went for the eyes, or their ears.

I stared at the header and felt ice crawl up my spine. Simon noticed my face. "What?"

I swivelled my monitor slightly so he could see. "Look at that, mate. Whadoya reckon?"

He squinted, then his expression changed. "Is that… them watching us?"

"Yes, mate. They're bopeeping us, the same as we them."

He went pale. "We're a target."

I didn't correct him. What was the point? I wanted to tell myself it didn't mean anything. That it was all standard. That everyone watched everyone and this was just another layer of espionage. But the timing was wrong. Everything was now.

Col. Banks returned, and this time she didn't stop to be gentle. "Scotty," she said, "we've got confirmed tracks. We've got Washington asking whether Pine Gap is under increased threat. You've got anything on that?"

I hesitated for half a second — because the question had weight, and the answer had weight, and my tongue felt like it was made of sand. "Yes Ma'am," I said. "I'm seeing indications our comms traffic's being mapped as a priority node. Could be routine targeting prep, but with launches underway… I'd call it credible threat."

Her stance hardened. "Alright. Log it. Send it up."

"Copy."

She moved away, and I watched her shoulders — tight, drawn up like she was bracing against a punch to her gut. I typed the report. I kept it clean. But inside my head, something else started ticking. Not a clock on a screen. A personal clock. *Alice Springs.* My family.

My sister. My nephew. People who didn't know what an intercept header was and shouldn't have to. I imagined them in their normal lives. I imagined the sun on the red dirt, the heat shimmering off the road, the smell of eucalyptus when the wind shifted. I imagined them completely unaware that somewhere far away, men in suits and uniforms were deciding whether they lived or died as collateral to a strategic asset.

My hands hovered over the keys. My mind tried to do two things at once: Be the professional. Be the bloke with a family and a bunch of good mates. Both felt impossible. In the end, the professional won — because that was what decades of training had built.

I sent the report. And when it left my screen, something in me broke a little, quiet as a bone crack you didn't notice until you tried to get up and walk.

***

A few hours earlier, Alice had just been 'home.' Now it was a point on a map. A radius. A time window. That was how the brain protected you: it turned people into geometry. I didn't like what my brain was doing, but I couldn't stop it. If Pine Gap took a hit, there were questions you didn't ask out loud, but everyone asked in their own heads. How close? How big? Which direction would the wind go? How long did you have?

I opened a private window — nothing official, nothing logged for anyone else — and pulled up distances. Not because it would save anyone, but because not knowing felt like sitting in a car with your eyes closed while someone else drove.

Alice Springs wasn't far from Pine Gap in the way Ballarat wasn't far from Melbourne. It was far in the way deserts were far — open, exposed, with nowhere to hide from a sky that decided it didn't like you. I did the maths. Not precise. Not perfect. Just enough to make my stomach clench.

Simon was watching me now, his face tight. "You alright, mate?"

I almost laughed. It would've been ugly if I did. "Just thinking of my family in Alice," I said. "What about you?"

"I'm here on my own. Not sure why they chose me to come to this place."

"Posting orders can be a bitch."

He nodded slowly. "Yeah. Too right."

A new message arrived, higher priority than the last. It wasn't even a request. It was an instruction.

MAINTAIN CONTINUOUS COVERAGE. EXPECT LOSS OF SOME COMMS. PREPARE FOR DEGRADED OPS.

That meant they expected things to start falling apart. Networks, satellites, power grids. The systems that made modern life feel solid. It also meant they expected us to keep working through it. Of course they did. A part of me wanted to stand up and walk out. Not dramatic. Not storming. Just… leave. Get in my ute, head for Alice, knock on my sister's door, tell her to pack a bag, tell her we were driving until the road ended. But that was all fantasy.

I didn't know what was real yet beyond the tracks and the chatter. I didn't know whether leaving Pine Gap would make any difference, or whether it would just mean I died on a highway instead of under an air-conditioned ceiling. And I knew something else too, something ugly and true: Even if I did make it back to Alice, what would I say?

G'day, love. World's ending. Pack ya thongs, eh?

How do you tell someone the sky might burn? You don't. Not until you have to. The uniforms came through again, heading for the deeper rooms. I caught a fragment of conversation as they passed — American accents, clipped urgency.

"—retaliatory posture—"

"—confirmation thresholds—"

"—cannot afford to hesitate—"

My mouth went dry. The chain was moving. Somewhere, someone was going to decide that the safest response to a planet full of launched ICBMs was to launch more. In that moment, *'early warnings'* stopped being about whether we were right. We were right enough. Now, it was about what rightness caused. Simon leaned in close. "If they confirm a target here… you gonna try to get out?"

I looked at him. He wasn't asking as a colleague. He was asking as a man. A human response. I glanced down at my hands. Old hands. Scarred. Hands that had flown helicopters, hands that had turned spanners, hands that had typed a thousand reports that mattered to nobody. I thought of my piloting skills — something I'd kept up because it made me feel like I had an escape hatch in life. I thought of the base's aircraft. The protocols around them. The locks. The keys. The permissions. I thought of how protocol was already killing people on the other side of the world. "Mate, I Just don't know," I said truthfully.

Simon nodded like he'd expected that. "Yeah. Me neither."

The big display updated again. More tracks. More confirmations. The arcs, thousands of them, began to look like a web. The room held its breath as though breathing might make it worse. And in the back of my head, that personal clock kept ticking. Not for the world. For Alice. For the people I loved. For the question I didn't want to answer: *What do you do when you realise the warning is real… and you're standing inside the target?*

***

The idea that there'd be a clean moment to decide was another lie. There wasn't a bell. There wasn't a pause where the world waited politely for me to make up my mind. Things kept moving — feeds updating, phones lit up, voices dropped into that tight register people used when they tried to stay professional while their insides came loose. But something shifted all the same.

It wasn't on the screens. It was inside me. I'd spent most of my life believing in systems. Not blindly —

never that — but with a kind of earned respect. Systems kept aircraft in the air. Systems kept people fed. Systems kept wars distant and abstract, something you watched on the news instead of felt in your bones. Now the same systems were doing something else.

They were turning warnings into inevitabilities.

Col. Banks came back again, her face set, the last traces of softness gone. "Scotty," she said, "we're moving into continuity protocols." That was the phrase you didn't hear unless things were about to get properly bad.

"What does that mean for us?" Simon asked before I could stop him.

She looked at him, then at me. "Essential personnel remain on station. Others may be stood down if comms degrade."

"Stood down where?" Simon pressed.

She hesitated, just a fraction. "The below shelter areas. If directed."

Shelter.

It was a generous word for reinforced rooms designed to protect equipment first and people second. I felt something tighten, almost to the point of sickness. "What about evacuation?"

Her eyes flicked around the room. "Not authorised at this stage."

At this stage.

Everything was staged. Everything was conditional. Everything waited for a threshold to be crossed. I looked at the clock in the corner of my display. Not a dramatic countdown. Just time moving forward, indifferent. I thought of Alice again. Of how far away it was. Of the fact that distance didn't mean safety when the ICBMs in play laughed at the word. The decision space was shrinking, and I could feel it. Not long now.

***

The message arrived quietly. No alarm. No announcement. Just a new priority line sliding onto my screen, flagged so high it almost glowed.

EXPECT IMPACT WINDOWS WITHIN FORTY-THREE MINUTES THIS MISSIVE — PINE GAP THREAT ASSESSMENT ELEVATED

Forty-Three Minutes.

That wasn't expected — but none the less, enough time to act. Not enough time to fix anything. Simon read it over my shoulder. "Jesus. That's… that's something?"

"Yes, mate," I said. "It is."

It was something in the way a man with a knife had *'something'* — not good, but not immediate death either. I felt oddly calm then. Not relief. Just clarity. I knew what I could do. I also knew what it would cost. The helicopter hangar wasn't far. I knew the layout as well as I knew my own kitchen. I'd flown out of Pine Gap on exercises, on logistics runs, on dull little jobs that felt important at the time. I knew the procedures. I knew the access points. I knew which rules bent under pressure and which snapped. And I knew that once I stepped outside protocol, there was no walking it back.

If I left my station without authorisation, if I used assets without clearance, I'd be a liability. A deserter. Possibly worse. I thought about staying. About doing exactly what I was trained to do — keep listening, keep reporting, keep the system fed until the moment the lights went out or the roof came down. There was honour in that, in a way. A clean line. Duty to the end. But there was another line too, one the manuals didn't talk about. Duty to blood.

I looked at Simon. "If I walk," I said quietly, "you don't know anything."

He stared at me. "Scotty —."

"I mean it. You don't know where I went. You don't know what I did. You saw nothing."

"They'll crucify you. Maybe they'll shoot first."

I shrugged. "Mate, there'd be no one left."

He leaned closer, voice low. "You reckon you can make it?"

"I don't know," I said. "But I know I can't sit around, like a shag on a rock."

The room around us buzzed with quiet urgency. People began to retreat below. Others were bracing for impact, literal or otherwise. No one was watching me. Not yet. This was the moment. Not heroic. Not cinematic. Just a gap in the machine.

I stood.

My legs felt steady. I took off my headset and laid it neatly on the desk, like that might matter later. Simon grabbed my arm. "For what it's worth," he said, "you're doing the right thing."

I met his eyes. "Maybe. Good luck, mate."

Then I turned and walked.

***

From the air Pine Gap didn't look like a target. It just looked small. The horizon was wide and red and endless. Alice Springs lay out there to the north, a cluster of ordinary lives under an ordinary sky. I pushed the Black Hawk harder than I should have. Just enough to steal time back.

The radio crackled. A voice with fragmented instructions — some of it urgent, some of it already slipping into chaos. I didn't understand all of it. Then the world flinched.

It wasn't a sound so much as a pressure change, a distant concussion that rolled through the air like thunder with no storm. The horizon to the north bloomed briefly, wrong coloured, a dirty white that faded too slowly.

Impact.

Not here. Not yet. But real.

My stomach clenched. Somewhere, a city had just stopped being a city. To the south, the same. Canberra probably. An impact so huge, even from where I was I could just barely make out the bloom. I flew on.

***

I never made it all the way to Alice. I got close enough to see the lights before the second concussion came in — closer this time, heavy enough to rattle the cockpit and make the instruments dance. The sky lit again, bright and blinding white hot, like the sun had fallen to earth. And this time the wind came with it, a hot breath that rolled across the desert like the world exhaled.

After fighting it, I set the chopper down hard but controlled, dust and red dirt whipping up around me. I killed the engine and sat there for a second, hands still on the controls, listening to the ticking of cooling metal. Silence followed. Not peace. Just absence. I got out and stood under the open sky, the heat on my face, the smell of dust and something else — chemical, sharp.

I didn't know what had survived. I didn't know who had. I only knew this: The warnings had been real. We'd heard them early. We'd logged them cleanly. We'd done everything right. And the world had still chosen fire.

I thought of Pine Gap, maybe buried and silent, either gone or waiting for a blow that might never come. I thought of Simon at his desk, of the duty officer holding the line as long as she could.

I thought of how systems were built to act, not to hesitate. Above me, the sky was the same blue it had always been. That felt like the cruellest part. Early warnings only mattered if someone was willing to stop the machine. And once it started moving, nobody was. I stood there until the light faded, until the desert cooled and the stars began to come out, one by one, indifferent and ancient. Then I turned back toward whatever was left, carrying the knowledge I hadn't wanted: Being right didn't save anyone. It just told you what was coming.

PART TWO: THE ARSENAL OF FREEDOM

The first thing people got wrong about an ICBM silo was the noise. They thought it'd be loud — alarms, klaxons, boots on metal, red lights spinning like something out of a film. They pictured drama because drama was easier to hold than the truth. The truth was quieter.

Most of the time, the silo was a long, cold routine wrapped in concrete and sealed doors. A place built to be boring on purpose. You lived inside procedure. You moved inside checklists. You did your job the same way every day because the whole point was that the job shouldn't depend on mood, or fear, or inspiration. It was built to run even if the men and women inside it didn't feel like running.

We called it the capsule. That was the polite term. It made it sound like you were tucked away, protected, contained. Like you were an astronaut. Down here, the air always had a dry, filtered taste. The lighting never changed. The clocks did. You learned to measure time by meals, by handovers, by the rhythm of systems status checks that came around like weather.

My Wingman sat across from me at the console, shoulders square, posture perfect in the way you practiced until it stopped being practice. We didn't talk much when the shift settled. Talking made the hours longer. Silence made them manageable. There were rules about everything, even silence. The consoles glowed with neat lines of text and measured indicators, the language of machines that were always ready and never interested in why. I ran my eyes across them automatically, as I'd done a thousand times. Green. Normal. No faults.

My hands rested on the edge of the desk. The metal was cold through my sleeves. I'd been down here enough years that my body had learned the temperature the way it learned the feel of a steering wheel. Familiar. Expected. Almost comforting, if you didn't think about what the place was.

Above us was Ohio. Cornfields. Roads. Homes with lights in windows. People who went to bed believing the world would still be there in the morning. Above them was everything else.

Down here, you were meant to stop thinking in pictures. Pictures were dangerous. Pictures made you human. The system didn't care about pictures.

The red phone rang once — a clipped phrase, a confirmation. Nothing unusual. My Wingman glanced at me, then back to his panel.

We lived in the pause between events. That was the normal. Not peaceful, exactly — just held. A spring compressed under a lid. And then a light changed. Just one. A small indicator that didn't scream, didn't flash like a carnival. It shifted state in a way a machine did when it'd been told something. The kind of change you noticed because your mind had been trained to notice it before it became bigger.

The message field populated. Not slowly. Instantly. As if it had been waiting behind the glass.

PRIORITY TRAFFIC RECEIVED

No exclamation point. No red banner. The machine didn't need theatrics. It had authority built into its bones.

My Wingman's chair creaked as he moved, the first loud sound in a while. He didn't swear. He didn't ask what it meant. We both knew, in the same wordless way you knew the weather had turned before the rain hit. He read the line. I read it back. We looked at each other once. That was all it took. We began procedures.

***

People loved to talk about the football like it was a single thing — a briefcase with a magic button inside, a movie prop, an artefact. I'd heard the jokes the first time I'd told someone, outside the wire, what I did for work. Half of them tried to make it funny. The other half went quiet, like the word carried disease.

Down here, nobody used the word *football*. We used the words we were trained to use.

Directive.

Authentication.

Sequence.

Words designed to keep emotion at arm's length. The system prompted the first action with a line of text that could've been for anything, if you didn't understand what it meant.

INITIATE AUTHENTICATION PROTOCOL

My Wingman pulled the binder from its slot — sealed, accounted for, sign-off history logged by hands that never shook on paper. He placed it between us on the console like a shared burden. We worked in twos for a reason. Two bodies. Two sets of hands. Two pairs of eyes. Two launch keys. Not for comfort. For containment.

I followed the steps the way I always did. Not fast. Not slow. Exact. There was no adrenaline, not at first. There was a kind of hollow calm, the way you felt when you were doing something that had been rehearsed so many times it stopped feeling like choice. The training kicked in, smooth and impersonal.

The red phone again, this time a voice with the cadence that made the back of my neck tighten.

Then a message — compressed, formal, unadorned — came through in the tone that existed only for one purpose. It wasn't a human voice telling you a story. It was a channel delivering a decision.

We acknowledged receipt. Then we did what came next. The mechanics weren't the point. The point was that the *process* was built to prevent hesitation from ever getting traction. You didn't decide whether to believe. Belief was not a requirement.

You verified. You matched. You confirmed that what had come down the line was what it claimed to be, and that the authority behind it was valid within the framework you'd been trained to obey. The system offered you only two states:

Valid

Or

Invalid

There was no option for *I don't like this.*

My Wingman read from the directive. I cross-checked against our reference.

We confirmed.

The machine accepted the confirmation without comment.

A new line appeared:

SECONDARY CONFIRMATION REQUIRED

My Wingman's voice stayed even. "Proceed."

My own voice sounded like it belonged to someone else. "Proceeding."

You didn't say *yes.* You didn't say *go.* You said *proceed* because it sounded like paperwork. Because if you called it what it was, you might stop. And stopping wasn't designed into the chain. Not for us.

The second confirmation came in as expected. Different channel. Same weight. The system checked it like a bank checked a signature. It didn't care who wrote it. It cared that it matched.

It matched.

The machine didn't change its tone. It didn't shift posture. It simply moved on.

DIRECTIVE CONFIRMED

I stared at those two words until they stopped being letters and became something physical in my chest.

My Wingman exhaled once, controlled. Not a sigh. Not relief. Just the body making space for the next step.

The capsule felt smaller. The ceiling closer. The air drier. Above us, the world still existed. Somewhere, people were still asleep. Somewhere, a dog was still barking at nothing. Somewhere, a truck was rolling down a highway with no idea.

Down here, a chain had been set in motion, and it didn't ask for our feelings.

The next prompt appeared.

PREPARE FOR SEQUENCE EXECUTION

My Wingman's eyes flicked to mine. It wasn't fear. It was acknowledgment. We were at the point where training ended and reality began. We began the preparation.

***

There was a moment — small, easily missed — where you realised the capsule wasn't a workplace anymore. It was a chamber. It was a place where the world narrowed down to two people and a set of steps that would lead to somewhere irreversible.

The system ran through its checks. That part was almost comforting. Machines loved predictability. They loved to tell you what they were doing. They loved to announce each stage as if narration made it safer.

My Wingman monitored one panel. I monitored the other. Our hands moved in practiced rhythms. I noticed, with a detached part of my mind, that my fingers weren't shaking. I'd expected them to. I'd expected the body to betray the calm. But the calm held.

Training did that. It didn't make you brave. It made you functional. The red phone brought in another voice, instructions — shorter than the first. There was no apology in it. No warning. No explanation of why this directive had been issued. Nobody told us what had happened in the world. Not because they didn't know. Because it didn't matter, not to the process. We weren't here to understand. We were here to execute.

The system requested another verification — an internal cross-check, a redundancy designed to make sure no single failure could stop the machine and no single human error could start it. I kept thinking about that, the way a mind fixed on a splinter. Redundancy cut both ways. It protected against mistakes. It also protected against mercy. If one person wavered, the system routed around it. If one component failed, another took its place. If one doubt surfaced, it was smothered by procedure. And because it had been designed by people who feared hesitation more than they feared consequence, it was very good at its job.

A new status line appeared:

FINAL ABORT WINDOW PENDING

My chest tightened. There it was —
The existence of the word was meant to comfort. It was meant to prove that control still existed somewhere in the chain. But down here, we didn't *have* abort. We didn't carry it.

Abort lived elsewhere, in the hands above our pay grade, in codes that belonged to the same authority that had sent the directive in the first place. Abort was not an option you could choose because you didn't like what you were doing. It was a state that could be transmitted if the people who owned the war decided to reverse it. The system did not ask if I wanted to abort. It only informed me of the window's shape, as if that shape made the act moral.

My Wingman's posture tightened — one small movement. He swallowed, and his throat bobbed. That was the first sign of anything human. He didn't look away from his screen or his console. "Window pending," he said, voice steady.

"Copy," I answered, voice steady.

We both kept moving. Time behaved strangely in those minutes. It didn't race. It didn't crawl. It simply became more noticeable, as if each second had gained weight. The system displayed countdown markers and internal timing sequences in neutral text, and I hated the neutrality. I hated how clean it was. Clean was what you wanted in a workplace. Clean was what you didn't want in a catastrophe.

The red phone rang again once.

This one wasn't a directive. It was a confirmation — a phrase that coded combat readiness.

I caught myself wondering what had triggered it. What signal, what intercept, what warning had been heard somewhere that had kicked the football open and fed the machine.

I wondered about the people who had first seen it — the watchers. The ones who lived in rooms full of screens and said, *this looks real.* I wondered if their hands had shaken. I wondered if they had been listened to. The thought was dangerous. It made the chain feel like people instead of process. It made it feel like something you could blame or forgive.

The system didn't permit blame. It didn't permit forgiveness.

It permitted action.

The abort window indicator changed state.

FINAL ABORT WINDOW OPEN

The capsule seemed to hold its breath.

My Wingman's eyes flicked to mine again. We were both thinking the same thing, without saying it:

If abort exists, it has to come now.

We waited, but waiting didn't mean stopping. We continued monitoring. Continued confirming internal readiness. Continued doing what the steps required, because the steps never paused to let you be a person.

Seconds passed.

No abort.

The system noted it without judgement. It didn't care about meaning. It cared about timing.

ABORT WINDOW — NO INPUT RECEIVED

The door, if it had ever been a door, closed without a sound.

My Wingman inhaled, slow. Exhaled, slow. He didn't speak. Neither did I. We both turned our eyes back to our panels, because there was nowhere else to look. Above us, Ohio continued being Ohio for a little while longer. Down here, we were no longer in the world of warnings. We were in the world of consequence. And the machine was already moving.

***

Once the abort window closed, the capsule changed character. Nothing physical shifted. The lights didn't dim. The air didn't thicken. The consoles didn't sprout new warnings. But the shape of what we were doing narrowed until there was no room left to move sideways.

Up until that point, there'd been branches in the process. Conditional steps. *If this, then that.* Options that existed on paper even if they were unlikely to be used. After the abort window expired, the language changed.

Verify.

Align.

Execute.

Not suggestions. Instructions. The system didn't announce that agency had been removed. It simply stopped offering places where it could live. A new sequence loaded automatically. It didn't ask for permission. It didn't wait for acknowledgment beyond the kind that proved our hands were still on the controls.

My Wingman read the header aloud, because that was what the checklist required.

"Post-abort sequence initiation confirmed."

"Copy," I said.

My voice still sounded normal to me, which bothered me more than if it hadn't. I'd expected something — tightness, tremor, some audible sign that I understood the scale of what was happening. But the training was doing its work. Training didn't numb you. It focused you so hard on the next step that the rest of the world went out of focus on its own.

The system began cross-checking internal components, cycling through redundancies with a precision that bordered on elegance. Each successful check removed another excuse for delay.

Hydraulics: nominal.

Power: nominal.

Environmental seals: nominal.

Guidance interface: nominal.

Green lines marched down the screen like a parade of approvals. I watched them stack, one after another, and felt something hollow open behind my ribs. This was what *freedom* looked like down here. The freedom to remove uncertainty. The freedom to make sure nothing could stop what had been authorised.

A message came through the secure channel, not addressed to us personally but routed through our system as confirmation that higher authorities were still present in the chain.

It was brief. Dense. Written in language designed to survive scrutiny by people who would never have to sit in this room.

LEGAL AUTHORITY REAFFIRMED
CONTINUITY OF GOVERNMENT MEASURES ACTIVE

My Wingman read it silently. I did the same. Legal authority.

It was an interesting phrase. It suggested law had hands, that it could reach down into a concrete capsule and guide two people through the end of the world with a clean conscience.

Nobody mentioned morality. Morality was messy. Morality implied judgement. Law was neat. Law was an architecture you could hide inside. The system acknowledged the message and moved on, as if it'd been waiting for it. As if that confirmation was the last piece needed to make the sequence complete. I found myself thinking about distance. Legal distance.

By the time anything happened, the decision would be so far removed from us that it would be absurd to think of ourselves as responsible. We were functionaries, operators, links in a chain so long it disappeared into abstraction. That thought was supposed to be comforting. It wasn't.

The system displayed a new set of prompts, each one framed as a requirement rather than a decision.

**ALIGN GUIDANCE PACKAGE
CONFIRM TARGETING DATA LOAD**

The words sat there, neutral, technical, carefully stripped of imagery. Targeting data. Not cities. Not people. Not consequences.

Data.

I entered my confirmation, matching my Wingman's input exactly. Deviation was the enemy of safety. We'd been taught that from day one. Consistency prevented error. Consistency saved lives. I wondered whose lives that had ever referred to.

The guidance package alignment took longer than I expected — The system insisted on rechecking itself from multiple angles. Redundancy again. Layers of certainty stacked on top of each other until doubt had nowhere left to exist.

I became aware of my breathing, slow and controlled. In through the nose. Out through the mouth. A technique I'd learned early, back when I thought nerves were the biggest threat I'd face in this job.

My Wingman shifted in his chair, the smallest adjustment. The sound of fabric against metal felt loud in the capsule.

"You good?" he asked quietly, not part of the checklist.

"Yeah," I said ever so briefly.

We didn't elaborate. Elaboration created space. Space was dangerous.

The red phone delivered another update, this one almost perfunctory.

"EXECUTION SEQUENCES CONTINUING NATIONWIDE"

Nationwide.

Plural.

That was the first word that cracked the abstraction. It suggested scope. It suggested that what we were doing wasn't isolated, that this capsule was one of many, all following the same choreography. The thought didn't make it easier. It made it worse. If we'd been alone, there might have been some twisted sense of singular responsibility. But being one of many diluted that, spread it thin until it was almost invisible. The system didn't comment on the message. It didn't need to. It was already aligned.

***

The countdown didn't look like a countdown. There were numbers, yes, but they weren't large or dramatic.

They didn't pulse. They didn't flash. They sat in a corner of the display, small and precise, ticking down as if they were counting something ordinary.

T–08:00

T–07:59

My Wingman and I acknowledged each stage as required. Our hands moved. Our voices stayed level.

The system announced readiness milestones in the same tone it might have used to announce a successful software update.

FINAL SYSTEMS CHECK COMPLETE

I felt a strange urge to laugh at that — to imagine a pop-up asking if I'd like to restart now or later. Instead, I nodded to myself and continued.

As the countdown progressed, the capsule grew quieter. The process no longer required as much input. The machine had taken over the heavy lifting. We were supervisors now, not drivers. Witnesses to something we had helped set in motion but could no longer meaningfully affect.

I thought, briefly, about standing up. About doing something obviously human and irrational — shouting, reaching for a switch, knocking my Wingman's chair over. The thought evaporated almost as soon as it appeared. Everything that could be touched had already been touched. Everything that could be decided had already been decided.

The system had been built to anticipate panic. To route around it. To make sure the ICBM would leave the silo even if the people inside it didn't want it to. And I realised, with a clarity that felt almost clinical, that courage had never been part of the design.

***

T–02:00 The system ran its final verifications. Each check was acknowledged. Each acknowledgment locked something else into place.

My Wingman's voice came steady and professional as he read out the final checklist items. I responded in kind. We sounded like two technicians closing down a power plant for maintenance, not two human beings standing on the edge of an irreversible act.

The red phone remained quiet. Whatever conversation had happened above our level had concluded. There were no more updates, no last-minute interventions.

Silence, it turned out, was the loudest confirmation of all.

T–01:00

The system shifted into its final mode. The displays simplified. The extraneous data disappeared. All that remained were the parameters that mattered. Time. Status. Execution readiness. I became aware of my heartbeat again, slow but insistent. It didn't speed up. It didn't falter. It just kept going. I wondered if that meant something. I wondered if it meant nothing at all.

T–00:30

My Wingman cleared his throat once, softly. It wasn't on the checklist, but neither of us acknowledged it. The system didn't care.

T–00:10

At ten seconds, the system locked out all remaining manual inputs. Efficiency was the highest value. The final status line appeared.

SEQUENCE LOCKED

There it was. The point beyond which nothing inside the capsule mattered anymore. I stared at the words and felt something settle — not fear, not relief, but a heavy, immutable understanding. We were done. Everything after this would happen whether we were watching or not.

My Wingman and I sat there, hands resting on the console, eyes forward.

No one spoke.

No one needed to.

The machine had all it required.

And somewhere above us, beyond concrete and steel and legal language, the world was about to change shape.

***

The last ten seconds passed without ceremony. No voice counted them down. No one marked the moment aloud. The numbers reduced themselves in the corner of the display, precise and indifferent, until there were no numbers left to reduce. At zero, nothing happened.

That was the final surprise.

There was no jolt. No sound that matched the size of the thing being completed. The capsule didn't shake.

The lights didn't flicker. The system simply advanced to the next state, as calmly as it had advanced through all the others.

EXECUTION IN PROGRESS

I read the line and understood, in a detached way, that we were already behind it. Whatever mattered had already occurred. What followed was confirmation catching up to reality.

My Wingman exhaled, slow, controlled, his hands remained on the console, fingers relaxed, exactly where training said they should be. So did mine. The system began reporting status changes from components that had waited decades for this moment.

Valves opened.

Locks disengaged.

Circuits that had never carried live command before accepted it without hesitation. Each change was acknowledged by the machine, logged in time-stamped entries that would be reviewed later by people who would never have to sit here and feel the weight of it. The capsule remained quiet. That, more than anything, unnerved me.

There was a low vibration under my boots — not violent, not dramatic. Just a hum, like a distant generator starting up somewhere far below us. The ICBM didn't roar. It prepared.

Pressure built in chambers designed to hold it. Systems that had been idle for years responded instantly, as if they had never been asleep at all. Fuel flowed where it was told to flow. Guidance systems aligned themselves to the data we had confirmed earlier. Targeting data.

I caught myself thinking about that phrase again and forced the thought away. The system didn't need my imagination now. It had everything it required. The vibration deepened, just slightly. The metal beneath the console responded with a faint resonance, like a held breath finally being taken in.

My Wingman glanced at one of his secondary displays, then back to the main panel.

"Status nominal," he said, voice steady.

"Copy," I replied. We sounded like we always had. Now, it felt wrong for the first time.

Somewhere below us, enormous mechanical systems were moving for the first time in their operational lives. Blast doors were unlocking. Restraints disengaging. The silo itself was waking from a sleep measured in decades. The system displayed the change as a single line:

SILO ACTIVE

Two words.

That was all it took to describe the transformation of a place built to contain destruction into a conduit for it.

The ICBM left the silo without violence. I hadn't been prepared for that one detail. There was no explosion in the capsule. No concussive wave. No cinematic blast that rattled teeth or threw us against our restraints. The silo had been engineered to make the departure as controlled as possible. Force, contained.

The vibration peaked and then smoothed out, becoming almost steady, as if the structure itself had accepted what it was now being used for. The display updated.

ICBM EGRESS CONFIRMED

I stared at the words until they stopped meaning anything. Egress. A polite term. A word you might use for someone leaving a building at the end of the day. Not a weapon leaving the ground to cross continents.

Telemetry streamed in, clean and continuous. The ICBM climbed exactly as it was meant to, following a trajectory that had been calculated long before either my Wingman or I'd been born.

There was a strange sense of delay, as if the mind lagged behind the data. The numbers said it was already gone. The vibration said it had left. But some part of me still expected it to be there, waiting for us to say otherwise.

We didn't say anything. We couldn't. The system advanced again.

BOOST PHASE NOMINAL

That meant it was accelerating. That meant it was committed. The capsule felt suddenly very small.

The vibration faded. The hum beneath our feet softened and then disappeared entirely, leaving behind a silence that felt heavier than anything that had come before it. The ICBM was gone. Not destroyed. Not consumed. Gone in the way an arrow was gone once it left the bow.

The system continued to report status updates, now focused on phases that were no longer our concern. Midcourse. Separation. Guidance integrity. We monitored because the checklist told us to. We acknowledged because the system required it. But our role had already ended.

I became aware of my hands again — how still they were, how ordinary they looked resting on the console. Hands that could have been fixing a machine, driving a car, holding a cold drink. Hands that had just participated in the release of something that couldn't be recalled.

My Wingman shifted in his chair, the first movement in several minutes. He didn't look at me. "That's it," he said quietly. It wasn't on the checklist. But it was true.

***

The system closed the sequence with the same lack of drama it had shown throughout.

EXECUTION COMPLETE
CAPSULE STATUS: STABLE

Stable.
The word sat there, unchallenged.

Above us, somewhere beyond concrete and earth, the ICBM was already arcing toward a place neither of us would ever see. The system would continue tracking it, handing responsibility off to layers far removed from this room. Down here, the machine considered its work done. My Wingman finally turned his head and looked at me. His face was pale but composed. There was no panic in his eyes. No triumph. Just a deep, settled fatigue.

"We did our job," he said.

It sounded like a question. I nodded, because that was what the words required.

"Yeah," I said. "We did."

The capsule remained sealed. The air remained dry. The lights remained unchanged. Everything that had happened inside procedure. That was the part that stayed with me. Not the ICBM. Not the destination. Not even the consequences, which were still abstract, still somewhere else. What stayed was the understanding that nothing had gone wrong. The system had worked. And because it had worked exactly as designed, the world beyond this room would never be the same.

I sat there in the quiet that followed, listening to my own breathing, and understood something with a clarity I hadn't known before: Freedom, in this place, was not the power to choose. It was the power to comply without hesitation. And the arsenal we had maintained had finally been used. One question in my head remained. It hit me like someone using a hammer. *What happens to us now?*

THE CIRCLE OPENS

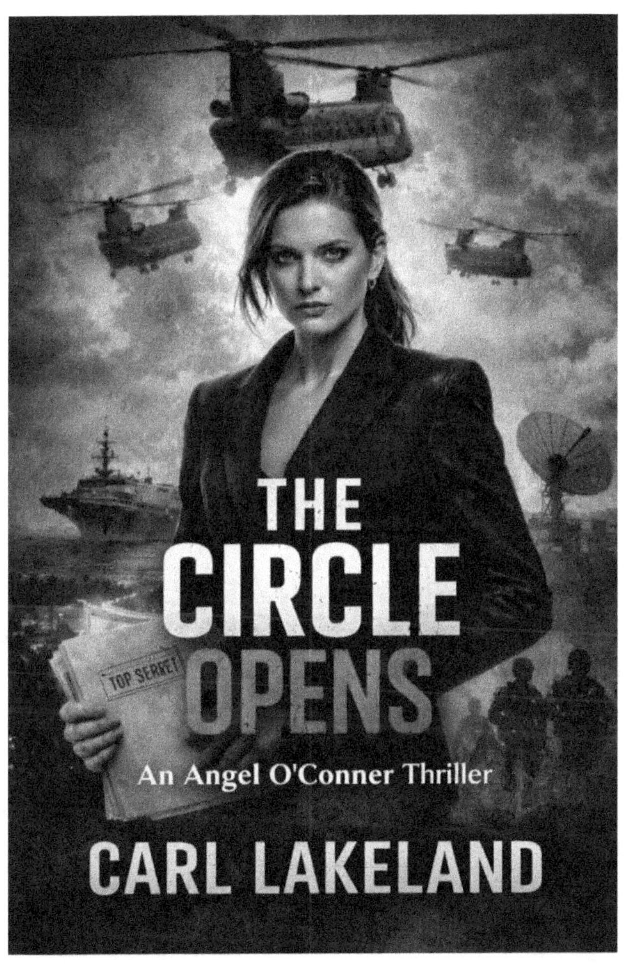

I woke before my alarm, the way you do when your body knows there's something it's meant to remember. For a few seconds I lay still and tried to catch the thought before it slid away — listening to the apartment breathe around me. The faint hiss of traffic down Fitzroy Street. A tram bell somewhere in the distance. The wind worrying the balcony railings like it had a complaint.

Jenny's arm was heavy across my waist. Warm. Possessive in the softest way. Her hair had escaped whatever bun she'd tied it into last night and spilled across the pillow like ink.

I stared at the ceiling and let the number roll around my head until it felt real.

Thirty.

It wasn't the kind of thing that should matter. A number. A neat human invention. But I'd been twenty-nine for what felt like a blink and now here I was, stepping over some invisible line like the world had been waiting with a clipboard. I didn't feel older. I felt… watched. As if something had noticed me. The thought made me smile, small and private, and I turned carefully in the bed so I wouldn't wake her. It was instinctive — protect the quiet. Jenny needed her sleep; she had a habit of waking up like a startled bird, heart already racing, already mentally at work.

I'd learned the best way to wake her was not to. I eased out from under her arm and padded down the hallway in my socks. The floorboards were cold in the places the sun didn't touch. The apartment was still dim, grey-blue with early morning, and the air carried that particular St Kilda smell that snuck in no matter how tightly you shut the windows: salt, wet concrete, last night's beer, and something sweet rose from the Acland Street Bakeries.

In the kitchen I put the kettle on before I even looked at my phone. The screen flashed to life with a scatter of notifications: group chats, a couple of late-night emails, a calendar reminder I'd set weeks ago — *ANGEL: 30* — as if future-me had worried I'd somehow forget the fact of my own existence. I ignored most of it. I leaned on the bench and listened to the kettle begin its slow, rising argument with the silent apartment.

When I finally opened the fridge, a small paper bag sat on the middle shelf like it belonged there. Neatly folded. Tied with twine. The kind of thing you couldn't miss without trying. I stared at it. I hadn't put it there. I smiled again, this time with a pulse of something warm in my chest. Jenny had always been good at small conspiracies — little hidden kindnesses tucked into the architecture of each day. I pulled the bag out and untied the twine. Inside was a pastry box, and inside that was a croissant that looked far too perfect to have survived transport. Beside it, wrapped in a napkin, was a little square of dark chocolate. A note was tucked under the lid. I unfolded it.

Happy 30th, birthday girl. Coffee on the balcony. Don't argue. Love you more than the sea. — J

I held the note for a second longer than necessary, feeling something tighten behind my ribs. *'Love you more than the sea.'* That was Jenny: romantic in a way that pretended it wasn't trying. I set the box on the bench and waited for the kettle as it began to roar. My phone buzzed again — news alerts this time — and I glanced at the headline without reading the details. Politics. A scandal. A fire somewhere. The world continuing as if I hadn't just turned thirty.

I made coffee the way Jenny liked it — long black with a splash of milk and the tiniest touch of bourbon — she would take it anyway. She always did. If she didn't, it would sit on the table and go cold and I'd feel guilty, and then she'd feel guilty for making me feel guilty, and the whole morning would become a strange little loop.

The kettle clicked off. I poured hot water into the press and watched the grounds bloom and swirl. It was hypnotic, that brief moment where chaos looked like art. While it brewed, I opened the cupboard to get mugs. And there it was.

A small box, wrapped in silver paper, sitting beside the cereal like it had always lived there.

My hands paused.

I didn't touch it straight away. That was the other thing about Jenny: she knew how to set a scene. She made you step into it. I lifted the box carefully and turned it over. No tag. No label. Just a clean ribbon, tied in a bow that was almost too perfect, like she'd watched a tutorial and then refused to admit it.

I carried it out to the balcony with my coffee, the pastry, and the absurd sense that I was walking into a moment already planned. The balcony was narrow but long enough for a small table and two chairs, the kind of outdoor set you bought for apartments because you wanted to pretend you had a yard. It faced south toward the bay. On clear days you could see Port Melbourne's cranes like skeletal fingers against the sky. On most days, you saw light and movement and the suggestion of water between buildings.

This morning was clear. The early sun hadn't fully warmed the air yet, but it had sharpened everything. The bay looked like a sheet of hammered metal. The city's high-rises caught the light and threw it back like they were showing off. I set everything down on the table and sank into one of the chairs, pulling my hoodie tight around me. For a few seconds I just sat there and breathed.

St Kilda at this hour was a different creature. The streets were quiet except for the occasional jogger and the distant grind of an Amazon van. The usual weekend chaos — tourists, bars, the beach crowds — hadn't arrived yet. It was like the suburb was holding its breath. I looked at the wrapped box again. Fine. I wouldn't torture myself. I untied the ribbon. The paper came away with a soft, deliberate rip, and inside was a velvet-lined case, the kind you'd expect for a ring or a pendant. My stomach muscles tightened a fraction with an absurd hope and then immediately corrected itself. Jenny and I weren't ring people. We'd talked about it. We'd laughed about it. We'd agreed we didn't need a symbol to prove what we already knew. Still. The heart doesn't always listen to the brain.

I opened the case. A crystal figurine sat inside, nestled in black velvet: an eagle, wings partially spread, mid-motion as if caught in the act of lifting off. Gold flecks running through it. It was beautifully detailed — every feather suggested rather than carved, the beak sharp, the eyes clear. It caught the early light and split it into pale rainbows that danced across the velvet and then across my hands. It was… unexpectedly heavy. I turned it slightly and watched the colours shift. The light inside it moved like water trapped in glass.

On the base, in tiny script, was a single word: *Charlotte.*

My throat tightened. Charlotte. A name. But not just an ordinary name. My Charlotte, from when I was ten. How did Jenny know? I'd never told her.

The crystal threw fragments of light onto the table, onto my coffee cup, across the croissant box like scattered confetti.

"Hello again," I murmured, feeling ridiculous and not caring. "Charlotte."

Behind me, the balcony door slid open.

Jenny stepped out barefoot, wearing one of my old shirts and her sleep-tousled hair. She squinted into the light, then looked at me, then at the eagle in my hands. Her face lit with that satisfied little smile she got when she'd pulled something off. "You found it," she said.

"I did. How did you know?"

"About what?"

I left it there. There'd be a right time and a right place to explain.

"Well?" Jenny asked, leaning against the door frame as if she could make herself casual. She couldn't. Jenny couldn't do casual if she'd put effort into something. She watched my reaction like it was a weather report. I turned the eagle slowly. "It's gorgeous."

"I know," she said, the words too quick, like she wanted to say them before doubt could breathe. "I saw it and it just… it felt like you."

I laughed softly. "Me? As an eagle?"

"Don't be a smart-arse," she said, walking over and stealing my coffee cup as if it belonged to her. "Not the eagle. The… I don't know. The way it looks like it's about to take off. Like it's frozen right before it does something. That's you all over."

I watched her sip my coffee. "It's literally my coffee."

"You were never going to drink it fast enough," she said, and I let her get away with it because it was my birthday and because she was right.

She sat in the other chair, folding her legs up under her. Her gaze went to the figurine again. "I named it," she said, like a confession.

"I noticed." I was about to say, *'I have no idea how you knew about charlotte,'* Again leaving it alone.

"Charlotte," Jenny repeated, testing it. "She's a guardian. She can sit on your desk and glare at people."

"My desk isn't intimidating. It's covered in interview notes and empty pens and that one plant I keep forgetting to water."

"That plant has survived purely out of spite," Jenny said. "Like you."

I laughed, and the laughter eased something in me that I hadn't realised was tight. Jenny reached across and touched the eagle's wing with one finger. Light fractured around her nail.

"Happy birthday," she said, quieter. "Thirty. You made it."

I tilted my head. "Made it like it was a war."

"Isn't it?" she said, eyes on me. "You spend your whole life walking through other people's disasters. It's a war. You just don't carry a gun."

I didn't answer straight away. There were things Jenny understood about me that I didn't always want understood. The job wasn't just a job. It was a way of being in the world. A way of proving something to myself, even though I couldn't name what it was. I was a journalist. A real one, not the lifestyle fluff. Politics, defence, state secrets that people pretended weren't secrets. It wasn't glamorous. It wasn't safe. It was a lot of waiting and a lot of lying — sometimes from sources, sometimes from myself. But it was mine.

Jenny watched me, then nudged the croissant box with her foot. "Eat. I'm not letting you do that thing where you forget to have food and then act surprised when you turn into a demon by midday."

"Yes, mum," I said, and took the croissant anyway because my stomach was already a hollow ache. I tore off a piece and chewed slowly, letting butter and flaky pastry settle me back into my body.

Jenny was halfway through my coffee when her eyes shifted past me toward the bay.

Her expression changed. Like she'd seen something that didn't belong. "What's that?" she asked. I turned in my chair and followed her gaze.

At first I saw the usual — cranes, container stacks, the line of the docks. And then my brain caught up, and the air went colder. There was a ship out there that didn't fit the scene. It sat in the water like a floating city block, grey and enormous, dwarfing everything around it. The deck was long and flat, and from this distance the superstructure rose like a jagged silhouette against the pale sky. Tiny movements on deck — dots that might have been people, equipment, aircraft — made it feel alive. A carrier. Not a cruise ship. Not a naval frigate. A full-scale aircraft carrier, the kind you saw in American news footage, parked off foreign coasts like a threat made of metal. My mouth went immediately dry.

"Is that…?" Jenny started.

"Yeah," I said, already reaching for my phone without thinking. I zoomed in with the camera until the pixels blurred and the ship's details sharpened into something unmistakable.

My heart beat harder. A carrier in Port Melbourne? "What the hell is that doing here?" Jenny said.

I didn't answer, because my mind was already doing what it always did when something didn't match the story: it began to fill with questions. A Nimitz class, if I wasn't mistaken. The shape was wrong for anything else. The scale. The posture. The way it sat like it owned the water. I zoomed again, trying to catch the name along the hull. The angle wasn't perfect, but I saw enough lettering to feel my stomach drop.

USS JOHN STEINBECK

The name hit me oddly. John Steinbeck. Grapes of Wrath. America's dust and hunger and moral rage packaged into literature. And now it was the name of a weapon platform that could project force across the world. The irony would have been funny if it wasn't sitting in our bay. Jenny watched me, waiting. I lowered the phone and looked again.

"Maybe it's a visit," she offered, but her voice didn't believe it.

"A visit gets announced," I said. The words came out flat. "A visit gets flags and ceremonies and politicians shaking hands for photos. A carrier doesn't just… appear."

I could already hear my editor's voice in my head — *You're seeing patterns. Don't chase ghosts.* But this wasn't a ghost. It was steel. It was aviation fuel. It was a statement.

"Could it be training?" Jenny asked.

"In Port Melbourne?" I shook my head slowly. "No. That's not training. That's… someone making a point."

I stared at it, and the longer I looked, the more it felt like it was looking back. Like a giant, patient animal that had wandered into a suburban street and settled itself down, daring anyone to question it.

My phone buzzed.

An email preview flashed across the screen, something from my producer about the evening slot. I ignored it. I opened my news app and typed the ship's name into the search bar. Nothing. No press release. No government statement. No official explanation. Not even a throwaway line buried in a "defence cooperation" article.

I tried a different search. *'US aircraft carrier Melbourne.'*

'Nimitz carrier Port Melbourne.'

'USS John Steinbeck docked.'

There were a few amateur photos — someone on a beach, someone on a balcony like mine, captions full of shocked emojis and speculation. But nothing official. No anchors on morning TV talking about it. No minister doing the usual smile-and-wave.

Jenny leaned over my shoulder and whistled softly. "How can that thing just show up, and nobody says anything?"

"That's the question, isn't it?"

I couldn't stop staring at it. My croissant sat half-eaten. My coffee went cold. The crystal eagle sat on the table catching the sun and throwing fractured light like it wanted to warn me.

Charlotte. A guardian, Jenny had said. A glare for people. I looked from the eagle to the carrier and felt something thread between the two images — ridiculous, symbolic, but real anyway. *A watcher and a beast.*

I turned the figurine in my hands and watched the light splinter. Jenny's voice softened. "Hey. It's your birthday. Please don't do the thing where you turn this into work in the first ten minutes of the day."

I met her eyes. I wanted to say she was right. I wanted to say I'd let it go and let the world keep its secrets for at least twenty-four hours. But the truth was, I couldn't. This wasn't just *'work.'* It was an anomaly. A rupture. A story that had arrived uninvited and dared me to look away. "I'm sorry," I said, and meant it. "I'll still do birthday. I promise. But —"

"But you're already gone," she finished, not bitter, just resigned in the way of someone who knew me well.

"I'm right here," I said, and reached for her hand across the table. "I'm here."

She squeezed my fingers, then nodded toward the carrier. "So, what do you think it means?"

I took a breath and tasted salt in the air. "I don't know," I said, stating the obvious, "I know it didn't arrive by accident, Jen."

Jenny studied my face as if deciding whether to fight me or support me. Then she sighed.

"Okay. If you're going to spiral, do it properly. What's the first step?"

That was Jenny too — if she couldn't stop the train, she'd help lay the tracks, so it didn't derail.

I looked back at the ship. My mind was already assembling the route: Port Authority logs. Defence contacts. The Australian Nuclear Safety Commission — ANSC — because a carrier like that wasn't just a floating airport. It was a nuclear-powered statement. There were procedures. Protocol. Permission. Unless someone had decided permission was optional.

"I'll check arrivals," I said. "Port Authority. Then I'll check who approved it. And if nobody did… I find out who told them they could."

Jenny's eyebrows lifted. "You're going to make enemies."

"I already have enemies." I realised it was true in a way I'd never said out loud. The bay wind gusted, rattling the balcony plants in their pots. Somewhere below, someone laughed — bright and careless — like it was any other morning. I set the crystal eagle down carefully on the table, facing outward as if it could watch the harbour with me. "Stay," I told it under my breath, feeling absurd all over again.

Jenny smiled faintly. "You're talking to it."

"No I'm not," I lied and smiled at the same time.

I stood, my body already shifting into motion, into purpose. I looked at the carrier one more time — grey, immovable, impossible — and felt the story take hold like a hook under the skin. Something had entered my city without asking. And I had just turned thirty. That felt like an opening. A circle. I went inside, picked up my laptop, and began digging.

***

By the time I sat at my desk the croissant had turned to dust in my mouth and the coffee had done nothing except make my hands feel too awake. The carrier still sat in the bay, visible from the balcony if I leaned the right way, but I didn't look. I needed it to stay practical. Metal. Paper. Procedure. A thing that had to have a trail.

My laptop fan kicked up as soon as I opened it, like it was already tired of me. The desktop was cluttered with folders and half-finished drafts, audio files named in a way only I could decode, and a spreadsheet I'd promised myself I'd clean up months ago. I didn't touch any of it. I opened a fresh document and typed three words:

USS JOHN STEINBECK.

Then, underneath:

WHY HERE. WHO SAID YES.

It was how I worked when I didn't trust my own thoughts. Strip it down. Reduce it to questions that could be answered. On the second screen I opened the Port of Melbourne website and then immediately closed it again. Public-facing information was always the same: corporate gloss, security theatre, curated photos of cranes against sunsets like they were selling romance instead of logistics.

The real information lived behind emails, phone calls, and favours. I pulled up my contacts list and stared at it for a few seconds. It was early, but not too early. People in operations were awake before journalists because ships didn't care about business hours. I tapped out a text to a port authority contact I'd used once for a story about biosecurity failures — someone who'd complained to me off-record and then regretted it.

Morning. Weird one. Need confirmation on the USS John Steinbeck arrival. Was it logged? Who approved?

I hesitated, then added:

Off record.

I hit send.

Then I opened my email and searched for the ship's name. Nothing. I searched for "carrier,"

"Port Melbourne,"

"US Navy,"

"Visit,"

"Exercise," and half a dozen variations that should've triggered something — briefings, media invites, a canned statement from Defence. Nothing. The emptiness wasn't reassuring. It was the opposite. It meant somebody had done their job in a way I didn't like.

Jenny appeared at the doorway wearing jeans and a shirt, her hair now tamed, her expression cautiously hopeful. "Did you eat?" she asked, as if that was the only measure of whether I'd spiralled.

"Most of it," I lied.

She walked over and leaned on the edge of my desk, looking down at my screen. "You're already in it."

"It's a carrier, Jen."

"I can see that," she said, and glanced toward the window. "It's like a bloody shopping centre out there."

I swivelled my chair slightly so I could see her properly. "They don't just park one of those without notice."

Jenny's gaze sharpened. "Unless they think they don't need to."

That was the thing. The thought I'd been circling all morning without wanting to name.

I didn't say it. I didn't want it to become real by giving it shape. Instead, I opened my browser again and pulled up the Australian Nuclear Safety Commission site — ANSC — then typed,

'foreign naval vessels,'
'nuclear propulsion,'
'port entry requirements,
and finally just *'authorisation.'*

The language was exactly what you'd expect from an agency that lived in the shadow of things it couldn't control. Dry. Legal. Procedures written like prayers. But the point was clear enough: a nuclear-powered vessel, entering Australian waters and docking, was not casual. There were protocols. Notice periods. Approvals. Liaison. Safety assessments. Paperwork that existed specifically to stop *surprises*. I was halfway through reading when my phone buzzed. A reply.

My port contact had responded faster than I'd expected, and that alone made my stomach tighten.

It's logged. But it's weird. Came through as 'special handling.' ANSC rejection due to non-disclosure of operations. ANSC is the paperwork gate — and someone bypassed it. Above my pay grade. Don't put my name anywhere near this.

I stared at the message.

There. I checked the text again. *'Nondisclosure of operations.'*

Special handling was what people called things when they wanted to pretend they weren't calling it *classified.* I typed back:

Who signed off?

The reply took longer. I watched the "typing…" bubble appear and disappear twice before the message finally landed.

Nothing from usual channels. Not Defence. Not Customs. Not anything I can see. Like it was already decided before anyone here knew. ANSC rebuffed the application. Steinbeck shouldn't have berthed.

I read it twice, then a third time, like the words might change if I stared hard enough. Pre-cleared. Already decided. Against policy. That wasn't an answer. It was a direction. I sat back in my chair and felt the room tilt slightly, not physically but in the way the day's shape shifted. The carrier on the bay stopped being a bizarre spectacle and became something else. A move. I looked up at Jenny, who'd been watching my face the way she did when she knew something had landed.

"What?" she asked quietly.

"It was logged," I said. "But it came through as special handling. Pre-cleared. No normal approvals. But something else, Jen. ANSC gave instructions not to berth."

Jenny's mouth tightened. "So… someone in government told them they could."

"Or someone above government," I said before I could stop myself.

The words hung there. Jenny blinked. "Angel."

"I know," I said. My voice came out sharper than I intended. I softened it. "I know. That's dramatic. But what else explains it?"

Jenny didn't answer straight away. She reached out and rested her hand on my shoulder, grounding me. For a moment I felt my chest ease. Then my email chimed.

A subject line flashed across the top of my screen:

EVENING SEGMENT — SECRETARY OF STATE INTERVIEW PACKAGE

My gut twisted. I clicked it. The message was from my producer, all cheer and urgency. The kind of tone people used when they wanted you to feel grateful for being given something you should already be allowed to do.

Angel, happy birthday — and what a birthday gift. Full package attached. Dossier, talking points, rundown, approved Qs. Please stick to the script for timing. Big eyes on this.

Attached: a PDF and a run sheet.

Jenny leaned closer. "That's tonight, right?"

"Yeah," I said, already opening the PDF.

The US Secretary of State. Prime slot. Live interview. The kind of access that people built careers on and ruined careers for. I'd been told it was a rare opportunity, that the Secretary wanted a strong Australian journalist, that it was a sign of trust.

The dossier loaded. I scrolled.

The first thing I saw was the photo — Secretary of State smiling, hair perfectly arranged, eyes bright with rehearsed warmth. Underneath was a bio that read like it had been written by someone who'd never met her but had studied her branding. Then came the *'themes'*: alliance, partnership, regional stability, trade, shared values.

Then came the questions.

Q1: *'Madam Secretary, welcome to Melbourne...'*
Q2: *'The alliance between our countries has never been stronger...'*
Q3: *'What message would you like to send to Australians about cooperation in the Indo-Pacific?'*

I stared at the page. It wasn't an interview. It was a performance. I scrolled further, expecting at least one line — one mention — of the carrier. A throwaway. A prepared statement. A justification. Something that acknowledged the massive grey fact sitting in our harbour. There was nothing. Not one reference. Not even an *'if asked.'* I checked the second attachment: the run sheet. The entire segment was mapped down to seconds. Intro. Cutaway footage. B-roll of flags, handshakes, smiling officials. Pre-recorded clips of *'public reaction'* and *'expert commentary.'* I felt my face heat up.

Jenny drew back slightly, reading the mood. "What is it?"

"They've scripted the whole thing," I said. "Every question. Every angle."

She frowned. "Isn't that normal? Like... producers plan?"

"This isn't planning," I said. "This is... control."

I clicked deeper into the dossier. There was a section titled *SENSITIVE AREAS — AVOID.*

It was a list. Human rights concerns in a certain country. A military agreement under negotiation. Domestic US political instability. Trade disputes. Refugee policy. The carrier wasn't on it. Because if it wasn't listed, I wasn't meant to think of it. My hands trembled slightly as I scrolled again, faster, hunting for a line that simply didn't exist.

I felt stupidly offended. Not just professionally — personally. As if someone had come into my home and rearranged the furniture without asking, then smiled and told me it looked better this way. Jenny sat on the arm of the chair beside me. "Maybe they don't want to bring attention to it."

"That's exactly why I want to," I said.

The words came out too quickly, too sharp. I heard myself. I heard the obsession. Jenny's eyes held mine. "Angel…"

"It's a carrier," I repeated, like saying it enough times would make it make sense. "A Nimitz-class. Nuclear-powered. Berthed. Without a proper paper trail. And they want me to smile and ask about shared values?"

Jenny's gaze flicked to the window. "Maybe it's connected."

I swallowed. The thought had been there all morning, underneath everything, but hearing it from her made it heavier. I closed the dossier and sat there in silence for a beat, listening to the apartment's hum. A distant tram. A neighbour's music. Life continuing. Then my phone buzzed again, this time a call. My producer.

I looked at the screen and felt a hollow dread. As if he'd already knew what I was thinking. I answered. "Hey. What's up?"

"Birthday girl," he said, too bright. "You got the package?"

"I did."

"Good. This is big, Angel. Big-big. The network's had eyes on this for weeks. We need it tight. We need it clean."

Clean.

It was always the same language when they wanted you to stay in your lane. "I saw the questions," I said carefully.

"Yep. Approved. We've got a buffer on the feed, standard. Legal's happy. Everyone's happy. We just need you to be — you. Smart, sharp, but not… you know." He laughed like it was a joke.

"Not what?"

"Not combative," he said, and the laugh faded. "We're not trying to start a war. We're trying to get a message out."

A message out.

Not the truth out. I stared at the crystal eagle sitting on my desk, catching light even in here, even away from the sun. Charlotte. A guardian. A witness. I forced my voice to stay neutral. "What about the carrier?"

There was a pause that lasted half a second too long.

"Yes, the carrier. We saw Facebook snaps on that this morning. Nothing yet. But we're sure you'll get a crack with that as well, probably next week." he said, and he did it smoothly, like the words were already practiced.

I felt my stomach flip. "You realise it's a nuclear-powered warship? Nimitz-class. It's literally visible from my balcony."

Another pause. Longer this time. Then the producer exhaled as if I'd asked him about the weather. "That's not part of the segment," he said. "Don't go there."

"Why not?"

"Because it's operational. Because Defence will shred us if we speculate. Because the Secretary won't answer. Because it'll derail the whole thing."

"It might be the only real thing in the whole thing," I said before I could stop myself.

Jenny shot me a look — *Don't.*

I held my breath. The producer's voice cooled. "Angel. Don't do this on your birthday. Don't make it into a… crusade."

Crusade.

Another word people used to make your integrity sound like a hobby. I swallowed my anger. "I'm not. I'm asking a legitimate question."

"The warship you're referring to is not on the approved list," he said flatly. "It's not open for debate. Stick to the rundown. That's all."

"Is the interview live?" I asked, because suddenly that mattered more than it had five minutes ago.

"It's as-live," he said.

"Meaning buffered?"

"Standard delay," he said, impatient now. "Five seconds. Seven, depending. It's for safety. For language. For errors. You know that."

I did know that. Every live interview you saw on television was a small, rehearsed act. A little seam built into the feed so someone could cut away if a guest said something that cost the network money. But I'd never cared before. Because I'd never been this aware of how a question could be removed before it reached the world.

I leaned back in my chair. "So, if I ask something off-script —"

"It won't make air," he said, and I could hear the warning in it now. "Do we understand each other?"

I stared at Charlotte. The eagle's wings were frozen mid-spread, as if the next moment would either be flight or shatter.

"Yes," I said softly.

"Good," he said, relief rushing in. "Enjoy your day. We'll see you at makeup at five. Happy birthday, by the way." He hung up. The call ended, but the conversation stayed in the room like a smell. Jenny let out a breath. "Okay," she said, careful. "Okay. You're angry. Fair. But you can't… you can't pick a fight with the US government on live television."

"It's not live," I said.

She blinked. "Angel."

"They'll cut it," I said, and my voice rose. "They'll cut the question. They'll cut the answer. They'll cut me."

Jenny held up a hand. "Stop. Listen to yourself."

I clenched my teeth and forced myself to breathe. Jenny softened. "This is your job. It's also your career. Your livelihood. If you don't play by the rules, they'll chew you up and spit you out."

"I know," I said, and the worst part was that I *did* know. I knew exactly how it worked. You got one big mistake. One story where you were labelled *'difficult.'* One moment where a producer decided you were a risk. Then you were gone.

But the carrier was still there. Whatever it was, it was still happening. "What if it matters?" I said, quieter.

Jenny looked at me for a long moment. "Does it matter to the world," she asked gently, "or does it matter to you?"

I opened my mouth, then closed it. That was the question that haunted every journalist. The line between truth and ego. Between public interest and personal obsession. I didn't know where mine was anymore. I looked back at my screen and opened my notes again. The dossier sat there, neat and smug in its certainty. The interview had been handed to me as a gift. But it came with a muzzle. I felt my hands settle on the keyboard as if they belonged there. If the interview wasn't truly live, the only way to make it real was to expose hard facts.

And I knew, instantly, that I couldn't do it alone.

My contacts list flickered in my mind, names that lived on the edge of my professional life — the ones you didn't call unless you had to, because calling them meant you were stepping into their world. There was one name in particular. Nathan Masters.

He used to be part of my every day. But now, he existed in that shadow space between journalism and intelligence, between the stories you told and the stories you were allowed to tell. I hadn't called him in years. Because calling Nathan meant admitting you were about to do something stupid.

Jenny watched my face change. "What're you thinking?"

I hesitated. The part of me that loved Jenny wanted to protect her from this. Keep her out of it. Keep her clean. But she lived with me. Slept beside me. Loved me. The consequences would find her whether I told her or not. "I might have a way to make the interview real," I said.

Jenny's eyes widened slightly. "Angel — no."

"I haven't done anything," I said quickly. "I'm just… considering."

She shook her head. "Don't. Please. You're not some lone hero in a movie. This is real. They'll —"

"I know," I snapped, then immediately regretted it. "Sorry. I know. I just —" I looked at the carrier again through the window, distant and unmoving. "Something's happening," I said. "Right now. In our city. And they're telling me not to talk about it."

Jenny's mouth tightened. She looked like she wanted to argue, but she also looked like she already knew she wouldn't win. "Who are you going to call?" she asked, resigned.

I swallowed. "Nathan."

Jenny went still. "I'm sorry, did you mean Nathan Masters?"

"Yes."

"You haven't spoken to him in how long?"

"It's been roughly twelve years,"

"Isn't he the one you said was… dangerous?"

"He's careful," I said. "There's a difference."

Jenny stared at me, then nodded once, reluctantly. "If you're doing this, do it with someone who understands what you're playing with."

I didn't like the way she said it — *if you're doing this* — like she could already see the choice forming. Like she could already see me stepping over the line. I picked up my phone and found Nathan's number. My thumb hovered over it. For a moment the room held its breath. Then I pressed call.

It rang twice before he answered. "Angel," he said, as if he'd been expecting me. His voice was calm, low, the kind of tone that made you feel like you were always slightly behind.

"Happy birthday to me," I said, trying for humour and failing.

A pause. "What happened?"

That was Nathan. No small talk. No pleasantries. If you called him, it meant something had already gone wrong.

"I need a favour," I said.

Another pause, longer. I could hear faint traffic in the background on his end, like he was outside somewhere. Moving. "That's not how this starts," he said. "Tell me what you saw."

I glanced at Jenny, who watched me like she wanted to pull the phone away. "There's an American carrier in Port Melbourne," I said. "*USS John Steinbeck.* Nimitz-class."

The line went quiet. When Nathan spoke again, his voice was the same, but the air around the words felt different. "Where are you right now?" he asked.

"At home." I was going to add *'the same place we used to share when I was a teenager,'* but left it.

"Are you alone?"

I looked at Jenny. "No. Jenny's here."

A beat. "Okay."

"Why is it here?" I asked.

He didn't answer that. Not directly. Nathan rarely did. Instead, he said, "You shouldn't be talking about it on a phone."

"It's not a secret," I said, anger flaring. "It's sitting in the harbour. People are taking photos."

"There's a difference between visible and speak able," he said, and his tone sharpened slightly. "What do you need, Angel?"

I took a breath and forced the words out cleanly. "I have an interview tonight. Secretary of State. They've pre-scripted it. There's a buffer on the feed."

Silence.

I could almost hear him thinking, mapping the shape of what I wasn't saying.

"You want to break the buffer," he said. It wasn't a question.

My throat tightened. "Yes." Jenny's hand gripped my shoulder, hard.

Nathan exhaled once. "No." The flatness of it hit me like a slap.

"Nathan —"

"No," he repeated. "That's career suicide. At best. At worst you draw attention you don't understand."

"I *do* understand," I said, and my voice rose despite myself. "They're hiding something. In *my* city. And they're using me to distract people with a scripted smile."

"Angel," he said, and now his voice had that warning edge — the one that made you feel suddenly smaller, suddenly like you were standing too close to a ledge. "You think you're going to force an answer out of a Secretary of State on camera? You think that ends with truth? It ends with you being removed. Quietly, or not quietly. Take a pick."

"I'm already being removed," I said. "I just didn't realise it until today."

Jenny squeezed my shoulder again, like she wanted to anchor me. Nathan was silent for a moment. Then he said, "Tell me the question exactly what you want to ask."

I didn't hesitate. The question had been burning in my mouth since the moment I saw the ship. "Why is a nuclear-powered US supercarrier docked in Port Melbourne without authorisation from the Australian Nuclear Safety Commission," I said, "and who approved it?"

Silence again. Then, softly, Nathan said, "I knew you from a child. I knew one day you'd stir up waves larger than anyone can handle. You've got guts, Angel. You're your mother's daughter."

"That's not an answer."

"No," he agreed. "It's not."

Jenny leaned down close to my ear, whispering, "Angel, stop."

I covered the phone's microphone with my hand for a second and looked up at her. "If I don't ask, I'll never forgive myself."

Jenny's eyes shone with frustration and fear. "If you do ask, you might not get the chance to forgive yourself."

I removed my hand. "Nathan," I said, steady, "I'm asking for help. Not permission."

He didn't speak for a long moment. Then, quietly, "If you do this," he said, "you don't get to pretend you didn't choose it."

"Yep. I know."

"And if I help you," he said, "I'm putting myself on a radar where I don't want to be."

"You're already on every radar," I said, and heard the bitterness in it.

He let that pass. "Where's the interview being hosted?" he asked, and my pulse jumped because it meant the conversation had moved from *no* to *how*.

I swallowed. "Docklands studio. Network feed, satellite uplink, standard as-live package."

"What kind of delay?"

"Five to seven seconds," I said. "Producer said standard."

"And you're sure it's on the main line, not local?"

"It's a national broadcast," I said. "But it's definitely delayed. They told me outright they'd cut anything off-script."

A sound on Nathan's end — maybe a car door opening, maybe a shift of movement. "You have someone in tech you trust?"

I almost laughed. "Nobody in tech trusts me. I'm *that* person who makes their job harder."

"Then you need someone who trusts *me*," he said.

Jenny's grip tightened. I felt the line narrowing. The decision crystallising. "Nathan," I said, low, "can you do it?"

He didn't answer immediately. When he did, his voice was quiet, controlled. "I can."

I felt my gut do a slow roll. The reality of it landed like a weight. I'd expected resistance. A lecture. The conversation ending with a warning and a deadline. Instead, he'd said the one word that meant it was now possible. Jenny shook her head slowly, helpless.

Nathan continued, "But you need to understand what you're asking. You're not just breaking a buffer. You're breaking a protection layer. That delay exists for a reason."

"So, the powerful can stay comfortable," I said.

"And so, you don't end up in a courtroom," he replied, blunt. "Or worse."

"I'll take the courtroom," I said.

"You say that now. What about Jenny?"

I glanced at her. She looked like she'd been hit. Like she hadn't expected him to say her name. I swallowed. "Leave her out of this."

"That's not how it works. People don't leave the ones you love out of it."

Jenny's voice came out tight and sharp. "Angel, I'm *right here.*"

I turned to her. I whispered. *"I know."*

She stared at me, her eyes wet now, not with tears but with fury held back by love. "Don't do this because you're angry."

"I'm not doing it because I'm angry. I'm doing it because it's right thing to do."

"Right doesn't keep you safe," Jenny snapped.

I flinched. On the phone, Nathan said, "Angel. Listen to her. She's wise. You're a gun. Jenny will give the time you need to unload."

I closed my eyes for a second and felt the day's weight settle. Then I opened them again and looked at Charlotte on the desk. The eagle caught a stray beam of light and threw it across the wall like a thin blade. I didn't believe in omens. But I believed in moments where your life split.

"Nathan," I said, and my voice steadied into something cold and clear, "I'm doing it. Help me do it clean."

There was a long pause. Then Nathan spoke, and his tone changed into something practical, professional. A man stepping into a plan. "Okay," he said. "Here's what happens. You don't talk about this again on the phone.

You don't email about it. You don't mention it to your producer. You play along all day. You smile. You rehearse. You let them think you're compliant."

My pulse hammered in my throat.

"And tonight," he continued, "when you're in position, I'll patch into the feed from the outside and collapse the delay. You'll know it's gone when you hear a confirmation tone in your earpiece. One short beep. Then you ask your question."

Jenny made a small sound, half disbelief, half horror.

I swallowed hard. "And if you can't —?"

"If I can't," Nathan said, "you don't ask. You don't improvise. You don't try to force it. You stick to script and you live to fight another day."

I hated that he was right. "Understood," I said.

"Good," he replied. "Now. This is the part where you decide again."

"I've already decided."

"No," he said, and his voice sharpened. "You decided emotionally. Decide strategically. You're about to create an enemy you can't name. This isn't a scandal. This is movement. This is machinery. If you stick your hand in it, it doesn't just bruise. It takes fingers. Maybe an arm."

I tasted iron in my mouth. "Why is the carrier here, Nathan?"

Silence. Then, very softly, he said, "I'm sorry. I can't tell you that."

"Then why help me?"

Another pause. "Because you're going to do it with or without me," he said. "And if you do it without me, you'll die wondering why it went wrong."

My skin prickled. Jenny whispered, "Jesus."

Nathan's voice stayed calm. "Angel, listen to me. If you go through with this, you don't get to be surprised by consequences. Your boss will come for you. The network will come for you. And other people will notice you exist in ways you don't like."

"I know," I said again, but the words felt smaller now.

"Do you?" Nathan asked. "Or are you in love with the idea of being the one who asks the forbidden question?"

That one landed. It landed hard because it was unfair and true and I hated him for it. My throat went dry. I forced myself to answer honestly. "I'm not trying to be a hero," I said. "I'm trying not to be a liar."

Silence. Then Nathan exhaled. "Okay."

"Okay?" I echoed.

"Okay," he said. "I'll do it."

Jenny's hand slipped from my shoulder. She stood abruptly and walked to the balcony door, opening it hard enough that it rattled. The bay air rushed in. Cold. Sharp. Salted.

I watched her, my chest tight, wanting to call her back and apologise and undo everything — but the call was still in my ear, and the decision was already moving. "Nathan," I said, voice low, "what do you need from me?"

"Access," he replied. "Not direct. I'll handle the technical side. But I need your schedule. Exact times. Makeup. Warmup. When you're wired. Which IFB channel you're on."

"I'll send it," I said automatically, then realised what I'd said.

Nathan cut in. "No. You won't send anything. You'll tell me in person."

"In person?"

"Yes," he said. "Today. Before the studio. Somewhere neutral. Busby's"

I looked at Jenny through the glass. She stood on the balcony, arms folded, staring at the carrier like she could will it away.

"Fine," I said. "Probably good to catch up again after all these years, anyway."

Nathan continued, "And Angel — one more thing."

"What?"

"If anyone asks you today, you haven't given the warship a second thought. You haven't connected it to anything. You're a journalist doing a normal interview. Do you understand?"

I swallowed. "Understood."

"Happy birthday," Nathan said, and there was something almost human in it, like regret tucked under professionalism. "Don't make me regret this."

He hung up. The line went dead. The apartment felt too quiet. I sat there, phone still in my hand, and listened to my own breathing. My heartbeat sounded loud, wrong, as if my body knew before my mind did that something had shifted. Jenny came back inside without looking at me. She closed the balcony door softly this time, controlled, like she was trying not to break anything. She stood in the middle of the room and stared at me. "You're really doing it," she said. It wasn't a question.

I opened my mouth, then closed it again. There was no version of the truth that made this easier. "I have to. It's what's expected of me. I have a duty to my followers."

Jenny laughed once — short, sharp, humourless. "You don't *have* to. You want to." Her eyes flashed.

"Do you know what it feels like," she said, voice trembling now, "to watch you choose something that might swallow you?"

I stood slowly, pushing the chair back. I crossed the room and stopped in front of her, close enough that I could feel the heat of her anger.

"I'm sorry," I said. "I didn't plan for this. It's just… it's here. It's real."

"So am I, Angel. You bloody frustrate me sometimes. Sometimes I wish… nothing." She stared at me for a long moment, and the anger in her face shifted into something else — fear, and underneath that, a kind of resignation that hurt more than the anger. Finally, she exhaled and rubbed her forehead with the heel of her hand. "Okay," she said, quiet. "Okay. If you're doing this… then don't do it like an idiot."

A small laugh escaped me, surprised.

Jenny glared at me. "Don't laugh. I mean it." She nodded toward the desk. "What do you need?"

I looked at her, and gratitude surged through me so hard it almost made me dizzy. Jenny didn't agree with me. But she wouldn't abandon me. She'd stand beside me even while she wanted to shake me.

"I need to get through the day," I said. "I need to act normal."

Jenny's expression twisted. "You're terrible at normal."

"I know," I said, and then, because it was the only thing that felt steady, I reached for Charlotte and placed the crystal eagle carefully in the centre of my desk. It caught the light and split it again, throwing small rainbows across the papers like fragile warnings. Jenny's gaze softened when she saw it. "At least she can watch you," she murmured.

I swallowed. "Yeah."

I looked back at my laptop. The interview dossier sat there, clean and smug. A rehearsal dressed up as access. Tonight, if Nathan did what he said he could do, it would become real. The question would go out uncut. The Secretary of State would have to answer, or refuse to answer, in front of everyone. And then I'd find out what happened when you pulled the curtain on something that didn't want to be seen. I took a breath, straightened my shoulders, and began rehearsing the approved questions with a smile I didn't feel.

***

I'd spent the afternoon doing what I did best: lying with a straight face. I answered birthday messages with emojis and exclamation marks. I let colleagues post their "Happy 30th!" comments under a photo I didn't remember taking, smiling so wide I looked like a different woman. I told my producer I was excited. I told Jenny I was fine. I told myself I was steady.

All the while, the carrier sat in the bay like a thumb pressed into the skin of the city, and every time I thought about it my pulse ticked up a notch, like my body was trying to outrun my decision.

Jenny stayed close, hovering in that careful way people do when they don't want to crowd you, but they don't trust you not to walk into traffic either. She made me eat something real — eggs on toast, too much salt, her way of forcing me into my own mouth and hands and body. She kept talking, normal things, small things. The weather. The neighbour's dog. A new café opening on Acland Street.

I nodded and contributed at the right moments like a woman participating in her own day.

But inside, I kept seeing Nathan's words like subtitles.

Don't talk about this again on the phone. Play along all day. One short beep. Then you ask.

At three thirty I left the apartment under the pretext of *'going in early,'* as if that was the most innocent thing in the world. Jenny walked me to the door, her hand on my arm a fraction longer than usual, her face set in a mask she'd built for herself — supportive girlfriend, not terrified witness. "If you're going to do it," she said quietly, "do it clean."

I nodded. "I will."

Jenny's eyes searched mine, looking for cracks. "And if you feel it's wrong — if you feel it in your gut — stop."

I wanted to promise her I would. I wanted to be the kind of person who could. "I'll listen," I said, and it was the closest I could get to a lie that didn't taste bitter.

She kissed me at the door anyway — soft and fast, like she didn't want to give the moment enough time to become goodbye.

I walked away before I could see her expression change. Outside, St Kilda was busy in that late-afternoon way — people drifting toward the beach, couples crossing roads without looking, trams clanging like impatient gods. I moved through it like I was under glass. Everything too bright, too loud, too normal for what I was about to do. I didn't take the tram. I walked. It gave me something to do with my legs. Something to count with my breath. Steps, cracks in the pavement, traffic lights, the angle of the sun dropping toward the bay. Every time I passed a shop window and caught my reflection, I checked my face like I was looking for evidence of guilt.

At a small café off the main drag called Busby's — neutral, Nathan had said, somewhere no one would remember — I ordered a long black. I didn't want and chose a table near the back, facing the entrance. My phone sat on the table like a live wire. Four minutes late, Nathan walked in.

He didn't look like a man who wanted to be noticed. Dark jacket. Dark jeans. No logo, no identifying anything. Not even a watch visible. His hair was shorter than I remembered, and the lines at the corners of his eyes looked deeper, like he'd been sleeping badly for a long time. He still walked, strutted, with the same limp I remembered. He scanned the room once and found me instantly, as if he'd known exactly where I'd sit. He didn't smile. He sat opposite me without asking. His eyes flicked to my coffee. "You drink that?"

"No. I just look at it and wonder why it's gets cold before I abandon it."

"Good," he said. "That stuff's not good for the heart unless it has bourbon."

Nathan's gaze dropped briefly to my hands. I looked down. My fingers were curled too tightly around the edge of the table, my knuckles pale. I forced my grip to relax. Nathan didn't comment.

I leaned forward. "Are you actually doing it?"

Nathan's eyes didn't change. "You still want it?"

I held his gaze. "Yes. Of course."

He watched me for a beat longer than necessary. Then he nodded once, as if accepting the weight. "Okay," he said. "Talk me through the setup."

I pulled the run sheet from my bag and slid it across the table. It had network branding, timing blocks, and the kind of cheerful font you used when you wanted to pretend you weren't managing something that could ruin lives. Nathan didn't read it like a producer. He read it like a man mapping a building for entry points.

"Makeup at five," I said. "Mic at six. IFB fitted at six thirty. Segment intro at seven. Interview starts seven-oh-five."

Nathan's fingers tapped lightly, not nervous — He was calculating. "Feed path?" he asked.

"Docklands studio to network control, then out. Delay inserted at control."

Nathan's eyes narrowed. "You sure delay isn't in-studio?"

"Producer said standard delay. Legal. Network."

Nathan looked up. "Producer said."

I felt heat rise. "What?"

"Producers say things," he replied. "Sometimes they know. Sometimes they repeat what someone told them. Sometimes they spin facts to make you behave."

I swallowed. "Okay. What do you need?"

Nathan shifted the black device slightly, keeping it half hidden under the menu like it was shy. "I'm not erasing the buffer," he said. "Not exactly."

I sat up straight. "Then what are you doing?"

"I'm collapsing the path," he said. "Shortening the route so the delay becomes meaningless."

"That sounds like erasing it."

"It's not," he said. "Erasing implies you remove the delay unit. That leaves evidence. I'm bypassing it."

My pulse beat hard. "Can you bypass it without anyone noticing?"

Nathan's mouth twitched — not a smile, something closer to pity. "They'll notice. Eventually. But not until after the fact."

I swallowed back. "And the beep?"

Nathan nodded. "You'll hear one short tone in your IFB. You ask immediately. Don't hesitate. The window will be small."

"How small?" My voice sounded thin.

"Enough for one shot," he said. "Maybe less."

I stared at him. "That's insane."

Nathan said flatly. "Now listen. When the beep hits, you ask one question. Not two. Not a speech. Not a grand reveal. One clean, sharp question."

"I already told you the question."

"And I'm telling you," he said, voice hardening, "it's too long. Make it short. If you want it aired, you need to get everything out in time."

I blinked. "What?"

Nathan leaned forward, lowering his voice even though no one was looking at us. "Your question has an agency name in it. Acronyms. The words *'nuclear-powered.' 'Without authorisation.'* That's a speech. The more you say, the more time they have to cut away, pivot, or mute your mic."

"I need to be precise."

"You need to be *heard*," Nathan snapped quietly. "Precision doesn't matter if you never get the words out."

I swallowed. My pride flared — journalist pride, the kind that hated being told how to ask a question. Nathan held my gaze. "You want them pinned? Use the simplest pin. Make them answer the fact."

I exhaled slowly. "Okay."

Nathan nodded once, approving. "Ask this: *'Madam Secretary, why is the USS John Steinbeck berthed in Port Melbourne?'*"

I stared at him. "That's it?"

"That's it. Because if she denies it, she's denying something visible. If she confirms it, she's confirming something they didn't want spoken. Either way, you force a public record."

My throat tightened. "But she can still deflect."

"Of course she can," he said. "But deflection on camera is still a shape. People see the shape."

I hated that it made sense. Hated that I needed him. I nodded. "Okay. I'll ask that."

Nathan's gaze flicked briefly toward the café window, then back. "One more thing. If the beep doesn't come, you don't ask. You go back to the studio plan."

I held his eyes. "You keep saying that."

Nathan's voice softened slightly. "Because you're acting like you have control. You don't."

There was nothing to say that didn't feel like denial. Nathan slid the run sheet back to me. "Go. Be normal. Don't look like you're carrying a grenade."

I almost laughed. "That's a bit late now, isn't it?"

Nathan stood. "Not for you. You're good at faces. I trained you well." He paused as if deciding whether to say something else. Then he leaned closer, just enough that I caught the faint scent of rain and something sharp — aftershave or antiseptic. "Angel," he said, quiet. "If this goes wrong, don't call me. If you need help, it means it's already worse than you think. Go to your Jenny. Go home. Disappear for a bit."

I stared at him, a chill sliding under my skin. "What're you expecting?"

Nathan's eyes were flat. "I'm expecting consequences. If this all goes belly, you'll have the United States of America coming for you. An ally, not an enemy. You could change that in one sentence by tossing it at their second leader. If she comes off badly, I'd hate to think what those consequences would amount to."

Then he walked out.

I sat there for a full minute after he left, staring at the coffee I hadn't touched, the untouched pastry in the display cabinet, the ordinary people laughing at the front tables like the world was small and safe.

My phone buzzed — my producer again.

Car picking you up in 15. Please be ready.

I picked up my bag, stood on legs that felt like they belonged to someone else, and walked out into the bright Melbourne afternoon as if I was just going to work.

Docklands studio smelled like hairspray, hot lights, and false urgency. The moment I stepped inside, the machine swallowed me. Makeup artists, floor managers, producers with headsets, interns carrying clipboards like they were sacred texts. People called my name in tones that implied intimacy but meant scheduling.

"Angel! Happy birthday!"

"Angel, wardrobe's ready!"

"Angel, quick photo for socials!"

I smiled. I laughed at the right moments. I posed beside a '30' balloon someone had inflated as a joke. I let them dab powder onto my forehead like they were sealing me in.

All the while, the carrier sat in the bay, and the only person in the building who seemed to remember it was me. They led me to the green room and handed me the dossier again as if it was a gift. "Run through your questions," my producer said, bright-eyed. "Keep them tight, keep them warm."

Warm.

Like I was interviewing a celebrity. "Sure," I said, and flipped pages I already knew by heart. The Secretary of State was in a separate room, or maybe in a different building altogether. There were security layers I never saw. Her presence was felt more than witnessed — men with earpieces, sudden hushes in hallways, people moving with that careful respect reserved for power.

At six thirty they fitted my mic. A technician clipped it to my blouse with gentle hands that didn't match his tattoos. Another tech fitted the IFB — earpiece — into my right ear and ran the thin wire under my hair.

"Sound check," someone said.

I heard the producer's voice in my ear, crisp and close. *"Angel, are you hearing me?"*

"Modulation wall-to-wall," I said.

A faint echo in my own head made me feel like I was underwater. They did lighting. Camera framing. A quick rehearsal where I practiced smiling while asking questions that meant nothing. The producer beamed at me. "Perfect. You're perfect. Just like that." I kept smiling. Inside, my own heartbeat was a drum.

I tried not to think about Nathan. Not to picture him somewhere outside the building, unseen, reaching into the guts of the broadcast like a tech genius. I tried not to imagine the moment where the path collapsed, where the script vanished for a few seconds. I tried not to imagine what happened after. At seven, a floor manager counted down with their fingers.

Ten.

Nine.

Eight.

I breathed in.

Seven.

Six.

The studio lights burned my skin. The air felt dry. My mouth tasted like powder and nerves.

Five.

Four.

Three.

Two.

One.

The red light on the camera blinked alive. My producer's voice in my ear became softer, like he was leaning closer. "Okay Angel, you're on."

A theme sting played, and my smile became automatic. "Good evening," I said, voice smooth, familiar. "I'm Angel O'Connor —"

I delivered the intro exactly as written, a puppet with good diction. B-roll rolled on the monitor beside the camera: flags, handshakes, the Secretary of State stepping out of a black car in slow motion like a movie. Then the split-screen switched, and there she was. The US Secretary of State looked exactly like she did in photos. That was part of her power — consistency. A controlled face. Warm eyes that never truly softened. Hair perfect, posture perfect, the kind of composure that felt less like confidence and more like training. She smiled at me like I was a friendly inconvenience.

"Madam Secretary," I said, "welcome to Melbourne."

Her voice was smooth, American vowels polished. "Thank you, Angel. It's wonderful to be here."

The producer's voice murmured in my ear. *'Keep pace. Don't rush. Smile.'*

I asked the first approved question. She answered exactly how the dossier predicted — words about partnership and shared values, the Indo-Pacific, stability.

I nodded, smiled, performed. While she spoke, my mind split in two. One part listened and tracked. The other part waited for the beep like a dog waiting for a whistle only it could hear.

Second question.

Third.

The conversation flowed like warm water — pleasant, meaningless, safe. I felt the delay in it even without hearing it. A softness. A cushion. The sense that the world was seeing us slightly after we existed.

And then —

A single short tone snapped in my ear.

Beep.

It was so quick I almost thought I'd imagined it. A clean electronic chirp, like a heart monitor correcting itself. My body reacted before my mind did. My stomach dropped. My throat tightened. My skin prickled. The producer's voice in my ear continued, unaware or pretending. *'Good. Now transition to trade.'*

I didn't. I looked at the Secretary of State, still smiling, still mid-breath, and I asked it. Clean. Sharp. Exactly as Nathan had told me. "Madam Secretary," I said, and my voice came out steady in a way that terrified me, "why is the *USS John Steinbeck* berthed in Port Melbourne?"

For a fraction of a second, her smile froze. It wasn't dramatic. It wasn't a gasp. It was subtler than that — micro-movement. A stillness around the eyes. A recalibration. But it was there. And because it was there, I knew it'd landed. The producer's voice in my ear exploded. *"Angel —"*

Then nothing, as if someone had cut him off, or as if the system was scrambling. The Secretary of State didn't answer immediately. Her gaze shifted slightly. To someone in the room with her. A handler. A security aide. Someone feeding her a line. She blinked once, slow. Then she smiled again, warmer this time, like she was turning my question into a joke between friends. "*The USS John Steinbeck* is an example of the kind of cooperation that keeps our region secure," she said smoothly. "Our military partners coordinate on a number of initiatives, and I'm confident the appropriate Australian channels have been engaged."

I held her gaze. I was about to say, *'That's not an answer,'* I heard myself thinking it — the second step Nathan hadn't authorised, the push. I held.

"Is she there as part of an operation," I pressed, "or an unannounced visit?"

Her smile stayed in place, but her eyes cooled.

"Angel," she said, voice still polite, "I'm not here to discuss operational details on a public broadcast."

There it was. Not a denial. Not a confirmation. A refusal, shaped like diplomacy. The producer's voice returned, tight and urgent. ***'Move on. Move on now.'***

I could hear panic under his control. My heart hammered. The studio lights felt hotter. My mouth went dry. I nodded once as if accepting the boundary. As if I was being reasonable.

"Understood," I said, and my voice stayed smooth because my body had decided survival meant professionalism. "Australians in our audience tonight will make their own conclusions. Are you aware of that?"

The Secretary's smile sharpened. "Australians are smart," she said. "And they understand alliance means sometimes our work is quiet."

Quiet.

The word hit me like a thumb on a bruise. I forced my smile back into place, the way you did when you were holding a knife behind your back. I studied her gaze. The same intensity came right back. Time to strike.

"Madam Secretary, I have it on good authority that the *USS John Steinbeck* berthed in Port Phillip Bay against authorisation from ANSC."

Her eyes glazed over for a millisecond. But it was enough. Her stall in composure said everything to those watching.

I moved on. I asked about trade. About values. About stability. But the interview had changed shape. The warmth was gone. The performance was still there, but now it had teeth under it. Every answer she gave after that felt like a controlled punishment. She didn't raise her voice. She didn't insult me. She didn't need to. She simply reminded the world, with every measured syllable, that she could take my little rebellion and absorb it into her calm like it was nothing.

And the worst part was that it almost worked. Because she was good. Because she'd been trained to survive hostile rooms. And I was just a journalist in Melbourne who'd decided her thirtieth birthday was a good time to poke a giant.

The segment ended with smiles. Always smiles.

"Madam Secretary," I said, "thank you for your time."

"Thank you, Angel," she replied, and her eyes held mine for a beat too long, like she wanted me to feel seen. Then the red light blinked off. The studio exhaled. And the machine turned on me within an instant.

The producer was on his feet before the camera cooled. His face was red. His headset cord bounced as he strode toward me. "What the *fuck* was that?" he hissed, grabbing my arm just above the elbow like I was a child about to run into the road. I kept my smile on until the last possible second, then let it fall the moment the camera was off, and we were in the shadow of the set. "You told me it wasn't live," I said. "That we had a buffer."

His eyes flashed. "You went off-script, Angel. Don't you realise the implications now."

"You gave me a script for a performance," I snapped. "I'm a journalist. What do you expect?"

His grip tightened. "You're an employee. Wait. You used to be…"

A floor manager hovered nearby, pretending to adjust a cable while listening to every word. A tech looked away, suddenly fascinated by a monitor. My producer leaned closer, voice shaking with anger. "Did you plan that?"

I met his eyes. "I asked a question."

"That was an unauthorised question."

"About a nuclear warship in our bay," I said. "A nuclear-powered ship that arrived without being authorised, damn it."

"Stop," he cut in. "Stop. Don't say that. Not here."

His fear was the first thing that made me truly cold. Because anger was normal. Fear meant something else. I stared at him. "And did it go to air? Or did you scrub back?"

He didn't answer. I saw it in his face before he spoke — the calculation, the horror, the realisation that the safety net hadn't caught me.

"It went to air," he said finally, voice low. "It went out. Holy crap, Angel. We now brace for impact."

My pulse jumped. A part of me wanted to laugh. Another part wanted to vomit. "It went out," I repeated, almost to myself.

"You have any idea," he hissed, "what you just did to us? To me?"

I pictured Nathan, unseen, somewhere outside this building. A man who didn't want radar.

I pictured Jenny, at home, watching the broadcast, hearing my voice twist the blade. "I did what you trained me to do."

The producer's face tightened. "Your training is to do what you're told."

I shook my head. "No. That's *your* job. You don't get to spin it."

He looked at me — really looked. "Green room. Go. Don't talk to anyone. Don't answer calls. Legal will want you. The exec producer will want you. Everyone will want you."

Good, I thought. Let them want me.

But my hands had started shaking, finally catching up. The adrenaline that had held me upright in the interview was draining, leaving a hollow tremor behind. I forced myself to breathe through it. A tech passed me and murmured under his breath, almost kindly, "Jesus, That was… brave, Angel. What the fuck?"

It didn't feel brave. It felt like stepping off something high and only then realising you didn't know how far the drop was.

In the green room, the television was still on, replaying highlights. My question played again in a clipped promo style — *Why is the USS John Steinbeck berthed in Port Melbourne? What about ANSC rejection?*

Hearing it out loud, hearing it repeated, made my stomach turn. It was real now. It existed outside me. A network assistant hovered at the door, eyes wide, like she didn't know whether to offer me water or treat me like a bomb. I sat on the couch and pressed my palms against my thighs, trying to steady the shake.

My phone buzzed. Jenny.

I stared at her name for a second like it might save me, then answered.

"Angel," Jenny said, voice tight. "Are you okay?"

I swallowed hard. "I'm alive."

"Oh my god," she whispered. "I watched it on tele."

"I know. It's worse than what I thought. But might get worse than this."

There was a beat of silence on the line, and in it I heard her breathing — fast, like she'd been running.

"You did it," she said, and there was awe in it, and fear. "You actually did it."

"I did, didn't I?"

Jenny's voice cracked slightly. "She — she looked at you like... like she knew you."

A chill slipped down my spine. "Yep."

"Angel," Jenny said, urgent, "listen to me. Come home. Please. Don't stay there."

"I can't just leave," I said automatically. "They'll..."

"Let them," Jenny cut in. "Let them fire you. Let them scream. I don't care. Come home."

I closed my eyes. In the dark behind my eyelids, I saw the Secretary's eyes holding mine. Not angry. Not shocked. Just... recording. "I have meetings," I said quietly. "Legal. Execs."

"Angel."

"I know," I said. My voice softened. "I know you're scared."

"I'm not scared. I'm terrified." The words punched the air out of me.

"I'll come home as soon as I can," I said. "I promise."

Jenny didn't answer straight away. Then she said, quieter, "Nathan called."

"What?"

"He called me," she repeated. "Just now. He asked if you were okay. He told me — he told me to keep you inside tonight. He said if you see anything strange, lock the doors and don't go to the windows."

My mouth went dry as a Sao. "What else did he say?"

Jenny exhaled shakily. "He said, *'She's going to be watched now.'* In those words, exactly."

I stared at the green room wall, suddenly unable to tell if my skin was too hot or too cold.

"Nathan shouldn't have called you," I whispered. "I don't know why he did that."

"He called because you're stubborn," Jenny said, and there was anger in her fear now. "He called because he knows you'll stay there and try to fight."

I swallowed down something harder this time. "I'll come home."

"Now," Jenny said. I opened my mouth to argue. Then I didn't.

"Okay. There in twenty five minutes." I hung up before she could hear my voice break.

For a few seconds I sat there, phone in my hand, while the television replayed my question again like a taunt. The network had already clipped it. Already turned it into a teaser. A moment. A controversy. I stood and walked out of the green room. My producer met me in the corridor, flanked by a woman in a blazer who looked like she'd been built out of policy. Legal. Or PR. Or both.

"Angel," the woman said, tone controlled. "We need a word."

I looked at her, then at my producer's pale face, and felt something harden in me.

"Tomorrow," I said. "If you're going to sue, I'll need backup."

Her expression didn't change, but her eyes sharpened. "Excuse me?"

"I'm going home," I repeated. "You can put my head on a spike tomorrow."

My producer's mouth opened. "Angel, you can't —"

"I can, and I will. Try to stop me if you dare." I said, and my voice was calm in a way that surprised even me. "Now, watch me as I keep walking."

For a second, no one moved. The corridor hummed with distant studio noise, the machine still running. Then the woman in the blazer stepped aside with the smallest tilt of her head, as if granting permission she didn't own. "Go," she said. "But don't speak to anyone. Don't post. Don't —"

"I know the protocol. Don't worry, I won't leak to paparazzi. Legal will have a clean launching platform after I return."

I walked out of the building and into the night air, which felt too open, too exposed.

The city lights glittered off the bay like broken glass. Somewhere out there, beyond the cranes and the dark water, the *USS John Steinbeck* sat in the bay. And now my question floated above it like a flare. I didn't know yet what I'd started. But I felt, deep in my bones, that a circle had opened. And it was widening by the minute.

***

I didn't fully remember the drive home. I remembered fragments: the rideshares stale air freshener, the driver's eyes flicking up to the rear-view mirror like he recognised me, the way my phone kept buzzing in my lap like a trapped insect. I remembered holding it face down, refusing to look, because each vibration felt like another hand reaching for my throat.

Outside the window, Melbourne slid past in glossy pieces — lit intersections, dark stretches of road, people spilling out of restaurants as if it was any other night. The city looked ordinary, which made everything in me feel wrong, like I was carrying a fire through a crowd, and nobody could smell the smoke.

When we crossed a rise and the bay came into view for a moment, my eyes found the harbour automatically. The carrier was still there. A shadow against the water, huge and immovable, like the city had grown a tumour overnight and decided to pretend it was a feature. The driver turned the radio up without asking. A presenter's voice was talking about *'an unexpected moment during tonight's high-profile interview,'* and my name landed in the sentence like a stone dropped in a glass. I sat totally still. The driver didn't say anything. The mirror showed his mouth tighten, the way people's faces did when they weren't sure if they were in the presence of someone brave or someone stupid.

I got out in St Kilda and walked the last block to the apartment because the air felt safer than the enclosed space of a stranger's car. My keys rattled in my hand. My fingers didn't want to work. They kept slipping, like my body was quietly refusing to open the door to whatever came next.

When I finally pushed inside, Jenny was waiting just beyond the entry, barefoot on the wooden floor, arms folded tight across her chest. The living room was dim except for the glow of the TV, paused on my face mid-interview. A freeze-frame smile that looked like it belonged to a woman who hadn't just detonated her own career. Jenny crossed the room in three quick steps and grabbed my shoulders. "Are you okay, Babe?" she asked, voice sharp with fear.

I nodded automatically.

Jenny's eyes searched mine, and I saw the moment she realised nodding didn't mean anything. "Don't do that," she said. "Don't just nod. Talk."

"I'm home," I said, and my voice sounded hoarse, like I'd been shouting.

Jenny's face cracked for half a second. Relief flickered there, then vanished under anger and adrenaline. She pulled me into a hug that was too tight, almost painful. I felt the tremor in her arms. I hadn't realised she'd been shaking until it transferred into me. For a moment I let myself stand there in her grip and just breathe her in — soap, skin, the faint scent of coffee. Ordinary things. Human things. Then she pulled back and looked at me again. "That woman, the Secretary. She didn't look surprised. She looked… prepared."

I still for a moment not knowing what to say. "I know," I said. "Not what I was expecting."

Jenny stance stiffened. "And your producer called. Twice."

"I'm not answering."

"Good."

My phone buzzed again, as if to prove Jenny's point. Jenny snatched it off the bench before I could even glance at it. She turned it over in her hands and frowned at the screen.

"Unknown number," she said.

My uneasiness did cartwheels in my chest. "Don't answer," I said.

Jenny hesitated — then, because she was Jenny and curiosity was a muscle she couldn't switch off, she answered anyway and put it on speaker before I could protest.

"Hello?"

There was silence for a beat.

Then a voice — male, calm, too controlled — came through the phone. "Angel O'Connor?"

Jenny's eyes flicked to mine. I moved toward the phone like I could physically intercept the sound.

"Who is this?" Jenny asked. Another pause, deliberate.

"You asked a question tonight," the voice said, ignoring her. "You shouldn't ask questions you can't finish."

My throat went dry. Jenny's face went white. "Tell me *who* this is?"

The voice didn't rise. It didn't threaten outright. It didn't need to. "You've done your job," he said. "Now do the next part. *Stop.*"

Jenny swallowed a huge gulp. "Stop calling this number."

A soft exhale on the line, almost a laugh. "Tell Angel that she's being looked after."

Then the line went dead. Jenny stared at the phone as if it had bitten her. I stood very still, trying to decide whether what I felt was fear or rage. It was both, layered. Jenny looked up at me, eyes wide. "What the hell was that about?"

"No idea," I said, and it was the truth. The worst kind — true and useless. Jenny's hands shook as she set the phone down on the bench like it was contaminated.

"Okay," she said, voice strained. "Okay. We're doing what Nathan said. Doors locked. Curtains closed. No windows. No hero bullshit."

I walked into the study without thinking, drawn to the only thing that had felt stable this entire day. Charlotte sat on the desk, crystal wings half spread, catching the faint light from the street through the blinds. She looked like a frozen warning. I reached out and picked her up. She was cold, heavier than she looked, and when I turned her, the light splintered into thin pale bands across my palms. "You wanted a guardian," I murmured, then immediately felt ridiculous and hated myself for it.

Jenny appeared behind me, silent. She watched the eagle in my hands like it was a fragile weapon. "You're shaking," she said.

I hadn't noticed. I lowered Charlotte onto the desk again, more carefully than necessary, and forced my hands to still by pressing them flat against my desk. Jenny leaned down until her forehead almost touched mine. "Angel," she said softly, "you did the thing. It's done. Now survive it."

I closed my eyes and let her voice hold me for a second. Okay, I whispered to her.

We went through the apartment like people preparing for a storm. Jenny checked the locks twice. She shut the balcony door, then wedged a chair beneath the handle even though it wouldn't do much against anyone serious. She drew the blinds in the living room and the bedroom. She turned off the lights in the front room, so the windows became dark mirrors instead of lit targets. I wanted to tell her she was overreacting. I didn't. Because my phone buzzing felt like a heartbeat that didn't belong to me anymore.

I took a shower because Jenny told me to, and because the hot water was the only thing that made my muscles unclench. I stood under the stream longer than usual, eyes shut, trying to wash off the interview, the studio lights, the Secretary's stark gaze. I thought about the moment her smile froze. About the way her eyes flicked off camera. About the choice she'd made — not to deny, not to confirm, but to refuse. Operational details. Quiet work. The words tasted like ash.

When I stepped back into the bedroom in a towel, Jenny was sitting on the bed with my laptop open, scrolling through social media with the expression of someone looking at a car crash and trying to count how many people were still trapped inside. "It's everywhere," she said without looking up. "Viral."

I sat beside her. The bed dipped. On the screen, clips were already circulating. My question, cut into a neat ten-second loop, posted by accounts that loved controversy like it was sport. Some people praised me. Some called me reckless. Some accused me of grandstanding. And beneath all of it, like a slow undertow, there were comments that chilled me more than the hate.

Why is there a carrier in Melbourne? Is something happening we should all know about?

I felt a hollow open in my chest. It wasn't just about my career anymore. It was about the fact that I'd pointed a spotlight at something powerful enough to avoid paperwork.

Jenny closed the laptop with a sharp motion. "No," she said. "Not tonight. You're not reading your own demolition."

I stared at her. "We need to know what's happening, Jen."

"We need you alive," she replied, and her voice cracked slightly. "Tomorrow you can be a journalist. Tonight, you can be a human being."

I didn't argue. We lay down in the dark, but sleep didn't come. Jenny fell into a shallow doze first, her breathing uneven, one arm thrown across my waist as if she could physically hold me in place. I stared at the ceiling and listened to the apartment. A distant siren. A car door. Someone laughing on the street. Normal sounds.

Then — later, much later — something else.

A low thump that wasn't a tram.

I sat up.

Jenny stirred. "What?"

"Shh," I whispered.

The thump came again, deeper this time, vibrating faintly through the glass. Rotor wash, but distant. Heavy. My skin stood up taught. I threw the covers off and padded to the living room, careful not to turn on any lights. Jenny followed, already awake, her face pale in the faint glow of the microwave clock. We stood in the darkness, shoulder to shoulder, and listened. The sound grew clearer: that unmistakable heavy, chopping pulse of large helicopters. Chinooks. Several of them.

I knew the sound intimately. I'd reported on defence exercises before, stood too close to airfields while pilots grinned and politicians posed. Chinooks didn't whisper. They announced themselves. Jenny's nails dug into my arm. "Angel…"

I didn't answer. I moved to the blinds and lifted one slat just enough to see out without exposing the room. A thin strip of night city appeared — streetlights, parked cars, the vague dark shape of the bay beyond. Then I saw them. Several dark shapes moving in a line, low and purposeful, their rotors cutting the air like giant invisible saws. They were travelling inland. From the direction of the docks. From the direction of the carrier. A final detail struck me. You'd think an American carrier had American aircraft. Wrong. As the Chinooks flew over, I caught a glimpse at the words RAAF.

Jenny's breath hitched beside me. "Oh my god."

I lowered the blind slat and stepped back, heart pounding so hard it made my ears ring.

The helicopters kept moving, the sound trailing after them, fading slowly like thunder withdrawing.

Jenny stared at me in the dark. "That's… that's connected, isn't it?"

I hitched a breath. My mouth tasted like dry crackers again. "Yeah, I think it must be."

Jenny's voice went hard. "And you just put a spotlight on it."

I closed my eyes. The sensation of having stepped onto ice and felt it crack beneath my weight — realising, too late, that I'd made myself part of the environment. Jenny grabbed my face with both hands and forced me to look at her. "Promise me," she whispered, fierce and shaking, "promise me you won't go outside. Promise me you won't try to 'see' anything."

"I promise," I said, because I needed her to believe it. Because *I* needed to believe it. We went back to bed, but the sound of the Chinooks stayed in my skull like a drumbeat. When sleep finally came, it was patchy at best. I dreamt of the carrier as an animal, grey and patient, lying in the harbour with one eye open. In the dream, Charlotte sat on the balcony railing and watched it without blinking.

***

Morning arrived in dull slices. My phone was on silent, face down, but it buzzed anyway — vibrations travelling through the bedside table like a pulse. Jenny woke before I did, or maybe she hadn't slept at all. She lay staring at the ceiling, teeth clenched, as if she'd spent the night in a fight she couldn't win. "You have to go in," she said when I sat up.

"Yes. That's a cert."

My throat felt raw. My mouth tasted like I'd been chewing cardboard. Jenny swung out of bed and started making coffee with the intensity of someone arming herself. She didn't ask if I wanted any. She simply made two cups and shoved one into my hands like a weapon. Her other hand passed me a cigarette. God, I needed one right now.

I took it and sipped, letting the bitterness anchor me. I checked my phone. It was carnage.

Missed calls from my producer, my editor, a number marked *'unknown caller,'* and one text from Nathan.

Don't talk to anyone. If you have to, keep it simple. Keep it brief. Don't be alone today.

My fingers tightened around the phone. Jenny leaned over my shoulder and read it anyway. "He's right, you know."

"I have to face my boss," I said. "This will be a shitty day. Not sure what you'll see when I get home. Just… letting you know."

Jenny's laugh was short and humourless. "Your boss isn't your problem anymore."

"What is, then?"

Jenny's eyes flicked to the window, to the bay beyond our blinds, but the *USS John Stienbeck* was no longer there. She'd weighed anchor sometime during the small hours while we slept.

"Oh," she said. "That warship has — disappeared."

I dressed in my most boring outfit — neutral blouse, black pants, jacket that made me look like I belonged in an office rather than on television. I pulled my hair back tight, a physical attempt at control. Jenny watched me from the doorway while I put on lipstick.

Jenny stepped forward and adjusted my collar with hands that shook only slightly.

As I reached for my bag, my gaze snagged on Charlotte on the desk. The crystal eagle sat where I'd left her, wings spread, catching morning light through the blinds. Tiny shards of brightness lay on the desk like broken glass. I picked her up.

Jenny frowned. "You're taking it to your office?"

I looked at Jenny "I had a real one of these. An eagle. Not mine but, but a friend. When I was ten years old. I called her Charlotte as well. The universe aligns itself in funny ways sometimes. So, I don't know *why* I'm taking this to work. I just feel the need to," I said and felt my cheeks heat. "It just… helps."

Jenny didn't laugh. She nodded once like she understood the irrational parts of survival. "Okay," she said. "Take your guardian with you."

***

The office felt different when I walked in. Not hostile exactly — worse than that. Controlled.

People looked up from their desks and then looked away too quickly, like eye contact might implicate them. The usual noise — keyboards, chatter, phones — had been turned down.

Conversations stopped when I passed. I became a moving silence. My editor's assistant met me near the elevators. She didn't smile. "Angel," she said, voice tight. "He wants you in his office. Right now."

I nodded once and walked. "Don't go past go? Go straight to jail?" I said in a low tone.

No comment, just a dry smile.

My editor — Graham — had been in this business longer than I'd been alive. He'd taught me how to chase a story without chasing my own ego. He'd defended me when politicians complained. He'd also thrown people under buses when it suited survival. His office door was closed. I knocked. "Come in," Graham said.

I stepped inside. He was standing by the window with his hands clasped behind his back, staring out at the city like he was trying to see the future in the glass. He didn't turn around immediately. He let the silence stretch a beat. That was a tactic. Make the other person fill it.

I didn't.

I stood there with my bag on one shoulder and Charlotte's weight in my coat pocket like a secret. Finally, Graham turned. His face didn't show anger. It showed exhaustion. "Sit," he said.

I sat, folding my hands in my lap. My head felt like I had a nicotine overdose the night before and now paying the price.

Graham didn't sit behind his desk like he normally did. He leaned against the edge of his desk and looked at me like I was a puzzle he'd assembled wrong. He exhaled slowly and began.

"You embarrassed the network."

"And?"

"You embarrassed the government."

I didn't answer that one. I wasn't sure which government he was talking about.

Graham watched me carefully. "Explain it, Angel. Give me a good reason not to turf you out."

"Because it's the job of every good journalist to dig beyond the scope," I said, simply. "And pretending the *USS John Steinbeck* it isn't a topic for public scrutiny doesn't make it disappear."

Graham's mouth tightened. "Do you have any proof of wrongdoing?"

"I have proof of an uncleared nuclear powered warship entering Port Phillip Bay against ANSC protocols," I replied.

"Documentation?"

"None at this stage."

"Why?"

"Because when I approached Port Authority they mentioned ANSC, then they fobbed me off."

"Then that's not proof of wrongdoing," he said, sharper now. "That's proof of an event."

I held his gaze. "Events have causes."

"Not your job to decide."

It was the first time he'd said something to me that felt like betrayal. I felt my spine stiffen. "That *is* my job."

Graham's eyes flashed. "Your job is to report facts with evidence. Not to ambush a foreign official on national television based on a hunch."

"It wasn't a hunch," I said. "We're talking about American muscle just showing up."

Graham rubbed his forehead, a gesture that looked like pain. "Do you know how many calls I've had since last night?"

I said nothing.

"Defence. The communications office. The network. Two people who didn't introduce themselves. And now ASIO."

Graham saw the words flicker across my face.

"They didn't threaten me," he continued. "They — They just reminded me that we exist because they allow us too." He walked around the desk and sat down, finally. He opened a folder I hadn't seen when I entered. Inside were printouts — my interview transcript, social media clips, internal emails already circulating like knives. He slid one page toward me. A memo.

Pending investigation: Angel O'Connor suspended from on-air duties effective immediately.

I stared at it. Suspension was better than firing. It was also a leash. Graham watched my reaction. "You're not being fired today. You're being sidelined. For your own protection as much as theirs."

"Theirs?"

Graham's eyes held mine. "You poked something big, Angel."

I sat up. "So, you believe me."

"I believe that you believe you saw something you weren't meant to ask about," he corrected. "That's not the same as believing you're right."

Graham blinked once, like he didn't know what to do with human softness in the middle of corporate damage control. Then, unexpectedly, his expression shifted — just a fraction. Something like sadness. "You used to be better at knowing which fights you could win," he said.

"I didn't do it to win," I said quietly. "I did it to make it real. Because everyone but me chose to turn a blind eye. Including you!"

Graham leaned back in his chair and studied me like he was seeing the cost of my stubbornness for the first time. "Listen to me carefully," he said. "You go home. You keep your head down. You don't talk to anyone. You don't give interviews. You don't tweet. You don't post. You don't become the story."

"What about the carrier?"

Graham's jaw clenched. "You let it go," he said through his teeth.

I stared at him harshly.

"You let it go," he repeated, and now the exhaustion in his voice sounded like fear. "Because if you don't, you won't just lose your job. You'll lose… other things."

I thought of Jenny's shaking hands. The unknown caller. Nathan's warning. Chinooks lifting into the night. *RAAF* Chinooks.

"Is that advice," I asked softly, "or an order?"

Graham held my gaze for a long moment. Then he said, very quietly, "This is me trying to keep you alive."

The air thinned. I nodded once. "Okay," I said, and meant it only as far as I had to. Graham exhaled like he'd been holding his breath since last night. He slid another page across the desk — an official suspension notice, wording clean and polite, as if they were talking about a scheduling change. "Sign it," he said.

I didn't. I looked at it, then looked back at him. "If I sign this, you control what I say."

Graham's mouth tightened. "If you don't sign it, we cut you loose. And then you're alone."

I thought of Nathan: *Don't be alone today.* I signed. The pen felt heavy in my hand, as if it was filled with consequence. Graham took the paper, nodded once, and stood. The conversation was over. That was how power worked: it decided when you were done speaking. As I stood, he said, softer, "Angel."

I paused.

Graham looked at me with something close to regret. "I meant it. Go home."

I nodded and walked out.

***

The city outside the building looked the same as it always did. But *I* certainly didn't. I felt exposed, as if my skin had been peeled back and the air could touch things it wasn't meant to touch.

My phone buzzed again. I didn't look at it. I walked to a quiet corner near the building's entrance and called Jenny instead. I needed the one voice that didn't sound like strategy. She answered on the first ring. "Angel? How did it all go?"

"Graham suspended me," I said.

Jenny exhaled hard. "Okay. Okay." Jenny's voice softened. "Did he… did he threaten you?"

"No," I said, then corrected myself. "Not directly, at least."

"Did you tell him about the Chinooks?"

"I never got the chance. It will sit. It's no longer my job, apparently."

Jenny was quiet for a beat. Then: "We're not staying here tonight."

Jenny's voice went hard again, decisive. "We're going to my sister's. Or a hotel. Or somewhere. I don't care. This isn't normal."

Part of me wanted to argue. Part of me wanted to plant my feet and refuse to be moved like furniture. But another part knew she was right. "Okay. Pack a bag. I'll be soon."

I hung up before she could hear the tremor in my voice. As I stepped out onto the footpath, I felt the urge — sharp and stupid — to look toward the bay. To keep my eyes on the beast. I resisted for three steps. Then I turned my head anyway. From here, between buildings, I could see a slice of water and the jagged silhouettes of cranes. No longer was the carrier there. But I could still feel it. Like a pressure change. I slid my hand into my pocket and touched Charlotte through the fabric, feeling the cold crystal against my fingers. A guardian. A witness. An absurd little thing. And yet it was the only part of this story that belonged to me. I kept walking. I didn't know what would happen next — whether the ship would ever return, whether the helicopters were the beginning of something larger, whether my question would be buried under official statements and distraction. I didn't know if anyone would answer me. But I knew one thing with an unsettling clarity: I had been seen. Not as a journalist. Not as a host. Not as a woman turning thirty on a balcony in St Kilda with coffee and a gift. As a variable. A risk. A person who had asked the wrong question at the wrong time. And once you were that you didn't go back.

As I headed home to Jenny — toward locks and blinds and a packed bag — the sun caught on the glass towers and threw bright shards of light across the street. For a moment, it looked exactly like Charlotte's fractured rainbows on my desk. Beautiful. Sharp. And impossible to ignore.

BOOK FOUR

THE MEMOIR

I'd stopped checking my bank balance because it felt like watching a man drown through a glass wall. I could see the mouth open, the eyes widen, the hands claw for something that wasn't there. The letters of demand came anyway. Polite fonts. Clean envelopes. Always the same weight in the hand, always the same threat inside.

Overdue. Final notice. We regret to inform you —

The bank wrote like it was apologising for the inconvenience of crushing my life. Visions in my head with my belongings thrown onto the street haunted me like my pantry. A few packets of instant noodles that were almost out of date.

I told myself I was a writer. I said it out loud sometimes, like the sound of it might make it true. But the truth was simpler: I was a man who had run out of time and run out of options, and I was losing a house I couldn't afford to love.

Melbourne had a way of making me feel like it was my fault. The city was always moving. Always renovating itself. Always smiling in storefront windows. It didn't slow down for people who couldn't keep up. It walked right past in suits and gym gear and sensible shoes, and if you didn't get out of the way, it used you as scenery.

That morning, I left my home and got public transport into the CBD, only because my walls had started to feel like a prison cell — the kind of walls that kept their mouths shut but remembered everything.

The sky was grey in that particular Melbourne way — flat and undecided, as if rain was an administrative error still being processed. The air smelled of wet concrete, Italian coffee and tram brakes. I walked without purpose to clear my head, not wanting to go back to the place where my life was waiting to be repossessed.

I carried a manuscript in my laptop bag. Not a novel — an attempt at one. Two hundred pages of careful sentences and dead ends. Every time I opened it, I felt an old shame lift its head: the realisation that words weren't saving me. They weren't paying rates or interest or utilities. They weren't negotiating with a bank manager who spoke to me like I was a risk category rather than a person.

I passed a café on Swanston Street where two men in construction shirts argued over footy scores. I passed a woman in a pink blazer taking a call so loud it felt like she wanted the street to know she mattered. I passed a busker playing something soft and sad on a violin that sounded expensive, which made it worse. Everyone looked like they belonged somewhere. I looked like a man heading nowhere.

At some point, I ended up near Collins Street, where money lived behind glass. I didn't go there often. It wasn't envy so much as nausea. The kind of retail that required staff to smile at you as if you were a privilege. The kind of shoes displayed behind windows that cost more than my 1997 Toyota Prius.

Taking a seat on a bench to catch my breath, I was halfway through a thought — *If the bank takes it, at least the pressure stops* — but what came next? I had no answer. I sat there, opened a packet of crisps, thinking it was better than noodles that defy gravity. I stared into the distance and thought of my manuscript again. I thought of getting a regular job. I thought of updating my resume and rejoining the rat race. I felt nausea but then forced myself to empty my mind.

I was about to get up and continue to walk the streets. My body asked. My limbs didn't respond. And it was in that moment that I felt a stranger sit beside me, maybe a bit too close. A hand slid into mine like a quick handshake. Unannounced. Almost an invasion. He pushed something into my palm. Something thin, folded, a scrap of paper.

"Take it. It doesn't belong to me," he said. Then he was gone.

I turned instinctively toward him as he stepped away, more offended than alarmed. People didn't talk like that. They didn't do things like that. Not in the city. Not unless they were asking for money or directions or your signature on something you didn't believe in. He didn't stop. He didn't even turn to look at me properly. He was already moving through the flow of pedestrians like he'd been born into it. The kind of stranger you wouldn't remember if he punched you, because the memory would have nothing to hold on to.

For a moment, I thought it was a trick. A scam. A baited handoff with an accomplice waiting to pick my pocket while I stared at whatever he'd given me. As I walked along Collins Street, I stepped to the side, pressed my back lightly against a building column, and checked what was clutched in my hand. It was still there.

The paper in my hand felt cheap. A scrap torn from something bigger. The kind of useless waste you found in the bottom of supermarket bags. I unfolded it. The first thing I saw were numbers — blocks of them, printed neatly. My eyes adjusted, and the shape snapped into something recognisable. It wasn't the shopping receipt I'd imagined. What I had nestled in my palm was a lottery ticket.

My first reaction was laughter. Not joy. Disbelief. That sharp, humourless laugh you make when life tries to be clever at your own expense. No longer cheap, it had the clean, glossy feel of it, but it was creased as if it'd been carried in a wallet for days. The barcode was intact. The grid of numbers was clean. The date was recent — yesterday's draw. I stared at it like it was an animal that might bite. Then I realised.

Yesterday's draw.

The practical voice in my head appeared — the one that still pretended I had control — said: *It's probably old. Probably checked. Probably worthless.*

The other voice completely opposite — the desperate one — said: *Check it.* I looked up. The man who passed it to me was long gone. Swallowed up by the crowd. Melbourne was brilliant at that. It could erase people who were in plain sight.

I should've thrown it in the bin and kept walking. I knew that. You don't accept gifts from strangers. You don't accept anything that arrives without a reason. But desperation isn't loud. It's persuasive. It makes stupidity feel like hope. And hope feel like fate.

I slipped the ticket into my pocket and kept walking, but my body had changed without my permission. My stride was lighter — tighter. My attention narrowed. My brain was already building paths: how to check it, where, how quickly, without looking like a man on the edge of hopelessness. I thought more. Claiming a lottery win that didn't belong to me was a felony. Simple. No bullshit. Plain as day. But that man gave it to me. He didn't want it. I didn't steal it. He gave it freely. I tried desperately to justify what'd happened. No matter which way I looked at it, time in box or a cage.

Curiosity. There was a newsagency two blocks away, tucked between a chemist and a sushi shop. I went in as if I belonged there. The door buzzer above the door gave a soft, accusing noise. A woman behind the counter looked up with the kind of bored neutrality only retail could create.

I bought a bottle of water I didn't want, because it felt suspicious to walk in and ask about a ticket without buying anything. I handed over cash because my card was a liability. The woman rang it up without interest.

"Can I check a ticket?" I asked, like it didn't matter.

She nodded and held out her hand.

"Here," I said looking a little sideways to avoid direct embarrassment. I hesitated. It was ridiculous. The hesitation of a man passing over a piece of paper that might be worthless but might also change everything. My fingers shook just enough for me to notice, which made me hate myself.

She scanned it with the machine. The little terminal beeped. For a second nothing happened. Then the woman's face changed — just a flicker. Her eyes widened the slightest amount, and something sat up in her posture.

"What?" I asked, maybe a little too quickly.

She scanned it again. The terminal beeped again. Then she looked at me properly. Really looked at me. Like she was trying to decide if she'd just come across one lucky bastard. "It's — it's a winner," she announced.

I waited. My mouth went dry. "How much?"

She turned the terminal slightly so she could read it. Her finger hovered above the screen as if it might burn her. "Sir, I'm not in a position to show this amount to you. What I need are some details. My advice is for you to go home and wait for lottery officials to call you." Then she ended her sentence in another *'sir,'* which was everything I needed to know.

But I managed it badly. I didn't give her any of my details. I was scared. I went straight home and placed the lottery ticket deep into my sock drawer and tried to forget it.

***

After a restless night trying to sleep, I rose at 6.00 a.m. I skipped the noodles for breakfast. The thought just made my teeth itch. I opened my laptop to write. Nothing came. I was left with a blank screen and a flashing cursor that begged me for movement. I sat there willing my mind to cooperate. I pushed my fingers down onto the keyboard and started.

I was...

I had been...

My life was...

I slammed the laptop closed and left my chair with such force it went skidding into the wall. I paced around. The same empty walls around me speaking louder than the few words on my screen. Then I paced out of the door carrying that lottery ticket with me.

By the time I reached Collins Street again, I had time to think things over. I entered the same newsagency armed with a promise of hope. The same woman greeted me with a smile that said she remembered me. But then she saw how I was dressed and her expression changed. "You've come back," she said politely.

"Yes." All the words I could manage.

"Do you have your ticket for scanning?"

I handed it over and became a statue.

"Sir, I will need your details."

I gave them.

"Now you need to head straight home and wait," she said, but then added. "I've been working this newsagency for over thirty years. I've never seen this."

"Can't you tell me how much?" I asked.

"It's against policy for this amount. Lottery officials have to contact you, sir." Then she handed the ticket back to me. "One last detail. Do you wish for privacy?"

"Why?"

"Sir, if I place you in the system as a private beneficiary, it means media won't pursue lottery officials after they contact you."

I went straight home as instructed, leaving my status as private with the newsagency. After I arrived there, the waiting began. I sat on the couch staring at my phone screen. My mind was going to explode. When it rang, it wasn't lottery officials. It was the bank with bad news. They'd given twenty-one days to vacate my property. They were officially foreclosing. It left a sour taste sitting on the back of my palate. It almost made me vomit everything that an empty stomach could yield.

It wasn't until the next day that I heard from lottery officials. A restless night of trying to sleep came with its own rules. It meant nothing seen by my eyes looked straight. And everything was doubled.

I thought it would come as a simple phone call. But instead, it was a courteous knock on the door. Standing at the doorway was a young woman dressed in a suit who could be mistaken for a finance broker. The other was a man dressed similarly but looked as though he'd seen money his entire life. She'd brought a large bunch of fresh flowers. He'd presented me with a bottle of champagne, the brand I'd never heard of.

I ushered them both inside, my heart hammering in my chest. They both congratulated me and the moment had arrived.

I asked them what I'd won in the lottery.

The reply was without hesitation, without even thinking about it twice. "Sir, your lottery ticket has the only winning combination of numbers for this draw, which means the entire prize pool is yours. Sixty-one-million-dollars."

I stood from my chair and the world around me went dark.

***

Lottery officials had given me the choice of a lump sum or payments in segments over fifteen years. I chose the latter. When the first payment hit my account, I stared at it for almost an entire day.

I didn't go on a spree. That was the first surprise. Money arrived the way fog does — without ceremony, without sound — and I waited for myself to change. I waited for appetite. For hunger. For something reckless to rise up and demand satisfaction. It didn't.

The first things I paid for were practical. Dull. Surgical. Mortgage arrears. Utility accounts. Council rates. Numbers I'd memorised out of fear finally crossed off a list without relief. I expected triumph. Instead, I felt a faint embarrassment, like I'd been caught surviving when I hadn't earned it.

I paid the house out entirely two weeks later. Not because it made financial sense, but because I couldn't stand the idea of anyone else having a claim on it. The bank manager congratulated me again, voice slick with the assumption that luck and competence were interchangeable. I thanked him and exited the bank before he could suggest investments. I didn't tell anyone. There was no one to tell.

My parents were gone. Both of them taken years apart, slowly enough that grief had become procedural. My wife had died suddenly — methodically, privately, leaving behind a silence that never quite learned how to behave like peace. I had a brother overseas who I spoke to once or twice a year, and a sister interstate whose life had continued without waiting for mine to catch up. No dependants. No legacy obligations. No one whose future depended on my choices. That should have felt like freedom. Instead, it felt like supervision had been removed.

I bought groceries that didn't require boiling water. Fresh food. Meat I hadn't learned to cook. I still caught myself checking prices out of habit, then resenting myself for it. The habit didn't disappear. It just became decorative.

I replaced the fridge because the seal no longer worked properly. I fixed the leaking tap in the bathroom.

I had the roof inspected and repaired even though it hadn't yet failed. Preventative maintenance felt indulgent.

I didn't buy a new car. Not at first. I kept driving the Prius, listening to the same rattle in the dashboard, telling myself it was loyal. Familiar. That it understood restraint. When it finally died at a set of lights on Punt Road, I didn't swear. I didn't even feel annoyed. I felt relieved. As if it had waited until I was allowed to let it go.

I bought a modest replacement. Resolute. Quiet. The salesperson tried to upsell me and I let him talk until he ran out of enthusiasm. Then I said no and paid outright. He shook my hand like I'd passed a test.

I avoided houses. Avoided boats. Avoided watches and suits and anything that suggested permanence or display. I didn't want my money to announce itself before I understood the rules.

What I did spend on was time. I stopped rushing. I stopped apologising for delays. I stopped explaining myself. I let mornings arrive without obligation and evenings close without regret.

I took walks through parts of the city I'd only ever passed through, learning streets the way you learn someone's habits — slowly, without expectation. Sometimes I sat in cafés and ordered food I didn't particularly want, just to watch it arrive without calculation. I tipped badly at first, then too much, then settled somewhere in between. Guilt has a learning curve.

I donated to causes anonymously. Cancer foundations. Hospices. I never lingered on the confirmation screens. I didn't want gratitude. I wanted distance. I thought about giving money to my siblings and decided against it. Not out of selfishness, but because money complicates grief, and we'd already had enough of that. If they needed me, they would ask. If they didn't, I wouldn't intrude.

At night, I sat in a dark living room with a glass of something expensive. It was enough that I didn't recognise the taste, and I thought about my wife. I thought about how money would have changed nothing. About how all the choices in the world couldn't have altered the ending we'd already lived through. That was when I understood the danger. Money doesn't make you careless. It makes you *precise*. It removes the noise that once justified hesitation. It forces you to confront who you are when survival is no longer an excuse.

I started keeping lists again — not budgets, but boundaries. Things I wouldn't buy. Places I wouldn't go. The list changed as I did, but it mattered that it existed. Control needed shape. The money didn't make me happy. It didn't make me reckless. It didn't even make me ambitious. It made me still. And in that stillness, I realised something that unsettled me more than poverty ever had. With no one left to disappoint and nothing left to lose, I was finally dangerous. And all the while since my first payment hit my account, I felt eyes on me, watching me.

***

Melbourne had a sense of timing it didn't deserve; my phone vibrated in my pocket. Not a call. A message.

Unknown number.

I stopped near a tram stop and pulled out my phone with clumsy fingers.

The message was simple.

DON'T GET COMFORTABLE.

For a second I thought it was spam. A prank. A coincidence so cruel it felt intentional.

Then another message arrived.

LOOK LEFT.

My neck tightened. I didn't want to. I didn't want to play. But my eyes moved anyway, because fear is a kind of obedience.

Across the street, standing under an awning outside a closed shop that said Rolex, was the man who had handed me the ticket. Same cap. Same jacket. Same unmemorable shape. He stood with his hands in his pockets, posture relaxed, as if he was waiting for a tram like everyone else. He didn't wave. He didn't smile. He just looked at me.

Then my phone buzzed again.

YOU HAVE SOMETHING OF MINE.

My mouth opened, but no sound came out. I stared at him across the street like I was trying to remember the rules of the world. I typed back before I thought. *Who is this?*

The reply came instantly.

YOU'RE A WRITER, ALFONSO.

My blood went cold.

I hadn't said my name to anyone. Not on the street. Not to the man who gave me the ticket. He hadn't asked. He'd just handed it over to me like he was leaving garbage behind. I watched him again. He didn't move. He didn't look at his phone. It was as if he didn't need to.

Another message arrived.

YOU CAN KEEP THE MONEY.

Then, after a pause that felt deliberate:

BUT YOU'RE GOING TO EARN IT.

I looked down at the screen until the letters blurred. My hands started to shake again, harder this time, because my body was finally catching up to what my mind had refused. The winning wasn't luck after all. It was a transaction.

Across the street, the man raised his chin slightly — an almost imperceptible gesture, like a nod toward something behind me. I turned without wanting to.

A black Mercedes Maybach had pulled up at the curb a few metres away, windows tinted so dark they looked like they were filled with oil. It was not anything that belonged to ordinary traffic. The engine idled quietly, confident in its place.

My phone buzzed again.

GET IN.

I didn't move. Every part of me screamed to run. But there were people everywhere. Running would make a scene, and scenes belonged to others. Others who were brave or stupid or desperate enough to believe they could outrun consequences in a city full of cameras and eyes.

I looked back at the man under the awning. He was still watching me. Patient. He knew I'd do what he asked. He knew it. He'd already done the hardest part. He'd made me hope.

I approached the Mercedes like a man approaching his own sentencing. The door opened before I reached it, smooth and silent, as if someone inside had been watching my footsteps through the tinted glass. A voice from within spoke without warmth. "Mr Bagala," he said. "Please."

No one asks politely when the answer isn't optional.

I got in.

The door closed behind me with a soft, final click. Automatically. Like someone had pressed a button. Another click — and my mind told me the door was locked from the inside.

The city outside continued in its indifferent motion. Tram bells rang. People crossed streets. The sky remained undecided. Inside the car, it smelled like leather and something faintly chemical, like cleaning products used to erase evidence.

A man in a suit sat opposite me, posture upright, hands clasped. He looked like a lawyer. Or a banker. Or a man who could be either depending on what the day needed. He smiled with his mouth only. Said nothing. Eyes fixed.

I swallowed. My throat felt too small. "Who are you? Why am I here?"

The man didn't answer. He reached into his jacket and produced a slim folder, placed it on the seat between us like an offering. On the front was a single word, printed in clean black type.

MEMOIR

I stared at it. "What's this all about?"

The man's smile didn't change. "It's your job."

"My job is —" I started, then realised how pathetic it sounded. *My job is writing.* As if that protected me. The man leaned forward slightly. In the tinted reflection of the window, my face looked pale and blurred, like someone else's.

I tried to breathe. I thought about the lottery ticket. I thought about the stranger who gave it to me. I looked down at the folder again, the word sitting there like a stain.

The Mercedes Maybach began to move, sliding into traffic as smoothly as if it belonged there. I sat in the dark glass cocoon while Melbourne continued outside, ignorant and bright. I thought of the money again like a secret I could no longer afford. And I realised — with a slow, sinking certainty — that at the moment I'd scanned the ticket, the money had already stopped being mine. It never had been.

***

The car didn't accelerate like a normal car. It didn't need to. It moved with entitlement — sliding into gaps that opened as if traffic itself understood hierarchy. I kept my hands in my lap. My phone sat heavy in my pocket, useless. Even if I called someone, what would I say?

A stranger handed me sixty-one million dollars and now I'm in a Mercedes Maybach with a man who smells like disinfectant.

The man opposite me watched without staring. He gave me the impression of restraint. Not kindness. Control. What you used when violence was inevitable but premature. I glanced at the front seats. Two men. Driver and passenger. Both in dark suits. The passenger's ear carried a thin wire, almost invisible against his skin. He didn't look back once. He didn't need to. They knew where I was. Where I'd be. Where I wouldn't get out.

The man opposite me opened the folder marked **MEMOIR** and slid a single sheet toward me. It wasn't a contract in the traditional sense. No logos. No letterhead. Just clean type.

You will write.
You will meet when asked.
You will not speak of this arrangement.
You will not contact police.
You will not contact media.
You will comply.

He closed the folder as if I was irrelevant. "You're a writer," he said again, like it explained everything.

"I *was* a writer," I corrected. The bitterness came out before I could stop it. "I'm not sure *what* I am anymore."

The man held my gaze in a way that felt like testing. "You're useful. That's what you are. That's why you're here."

We passed through the city, but the route meant nothing to me. I recognised streets in flashes — buildings I'd walked past a thousand times — only now they looked staged, like props in a film you weren't allowed to leave.

The car turned and dipped into a private parking entrance beneath an office building. The boom gate lifted without anyone stopping us. The underground lights were harsh, clinical. Cameras watched from the ceiling. The Mercedes rolled to a stop in a reserved bay. The driver killed the engine. Silence settled like a rubbish bin lid coming down.

The man opposite me opened his door and stepped out first. "Come," he said. It wasn't an invitation. I followed because my body understood what my pride didn't. You don't refuse when the consequences are unknown and the men around you are calm.

We moved to an elevator at the back of the garage. The passenger in the front seat swiped a card and the doors opened at once. No waiting. No other people. Just us and the soft hum of machinery.

As the lift rose, I felt my ears pop. The man stood beside me, hands clasped. He didn't look at the mirrored wall. He didn't adjust his tie. He was already exactly what he intended to be.

"What's your name?" I asked out of politeness.

He considered, then offered it like a returned courtesy. "Leon."

"Just Leon?"

He glanced at me, faint amusement in his eyes. "You don't need more."

The lift doors opened. We stepped into a corridor that smelled like expensive carpet and recently renovated mahogany. Everything was quiet. Too quiet for a building in the CBD. Either it was empty, or it was controlled.

Leon led me past a reception desk with no receptionist. Past framed prints that meant nothing. Past doors that looked identical. We stopped at the end of the corridor. Leon pressed his palm to a small black plate beside the door. A green light blinked. The door opened.

Inside, a long table that said fully imported from Milan. Leather chairs, a wall of tinted windows looking out over the city like it was its possession. The blinds were half-drawn, slicing Melbourne into grey strips. A pot plant sat in the corner, too healthy to be real. A man stood at the far end of the room, back toward us, hands resting on the window frame as if he was holding the city in place. He didn't turn at once. He made us wait. It was subtle. It was effective. Then he turned.

He wasn't what my imagination had offered in the car. Not a tattooed brute. Not some snarling caricature of an underworld kingpin. He was clean. Mid-fifties, maybe. Hair grey at the temples, neatly cut. He wore a dark suit that fitted like it'd been tailored to his bones. His face was sharp without being cruel. Almost gentle. His eyes were the kind that didn't waste attention. He smiled almost professionally. "Mr Bagala," he said, voice smooth and unhurried. "Thank you for coming."

I looked from him to Leon. "I didn't come. I was delivered."

The man's smile widened a fraction, as if he approved. "Good. You still have the ability to name things accurately."

Leon stepped aside and stood near the door, becoming furniture. The man gestured to a chair at the table, halfway down. It wasn't the head. It wasn't equal either.

It was exactly where he wanted me — close enough to be seen, far enough to be reminded. "Sit," he said.

I didn't. Not yet. "Who are you? What's this all about?" I'd asked the same to Leon without a response. Maybe this time it'd be different.

The man tilted his head. "You already know, Mr Bagala."

"No," I said. "I have no idea."

He watched me for a moment, then nodded as if to himself. "Mario Costa."

The name landed without drama, which made it unpleasant. It was a name I'd heard the way you hear about storms forming off the coast: distantly, through chatter, through news items that never quite said what they meant. The kind of name that lived in the background of certain conversations. The kind of name that suggested consequences. I felt my throat tighten. "You're the one who —"

"I'm the one who gave you an opportunity, Mr Bagala. Let's not be melodramatic."

I finally sat. My legs didn't feel strong enough to stand.

Costa remained standing, leaning lightly against the table with his hands spread, casual, as if we were discussing a business proposal. In a way, we were.

"You scanned the ticket," he said. "And you claimed the money."

It wasn't a question.

"Yes," I replied.

"Good. I dislike waste."

I stared at him, trying to understand the shape of this.

Costa's eyebrows lifted slightly. "Now, down to business. You might ask why we gave you the ticket."

"That's the place to start. Why me," I said, forcing it out. "Why not someone else? Why not cash it yourself?"

Costa smiled again. "Because I didn't want my crew anywhere near it. Simple as that."

"And you think giving it me is safer?"

Costa's gaze held mine, steady. "Your name is nothing," he said gently. "That's why we chose you. You're a nobody. An unknown entity." The sentence should have offended me. It did. But it also carried a brutal clarity. I'd spent years trying to matter. He had just put it in a single line: I was invisible. Worthless. Expendable. That was my value.

Costa moved around the table and sat at the far end — the head position without claiming it overtly. He rested his forearms on the polished mahogany surface, fingers interlaced. "You're wondering about the rules," he said. "So let me clarify them." He nodded once. Leon stepped forward and placed another folder on the table in front of me. Thicker this time. Inside were printed pages — photographs, addresses, names, dates. People I didn't recognise.

I flipped through them with numb fingers. Each page felt heavier than the last. Costa watched me read, not in a hurry.

"What's all of this?" I asked.

"Problems," he said. "Relationships. Activities. Events. Things that can be arranged into stories."

"I'm not a journalist."

"No," Costa agreed. "You're a writer. Journalists sell information to strangers. Writers sell meaning."

I stopped on a page and felt the air leave my lungs. A photograph of my house. Shot from across the street. Daylight. Clear enough to count the cracks in the driveway. Another photo — my late wife. Her car outside. Another — me leaving a café last week, looking down at my phone, unaware.

I looked up sharply. "You've been watching me."

Costa's expression didn't change. "Of course."

"For how long?"

He shrugged, a small movement. "Long enough. Pity about your wife, by the way. It didn't have to end that way."

"You did this to her!"

"Insurance, Mr Bagala."

"You fu —." Then I held my tongue. I tried to keep my voice rock steady. "What do you want? How many times do I have to repeat it?"

Costa leaned back and exhaled slowly, as if the question was tedious. "I want a book."

I blinked. "A book. That's it. A book. That's all you want from me?"

"Yes," he said. "A memoir, if you want to be precise."

The word tightened my stomach. The folder in the car. The sheet of rules. It was all funnelling into this like a drain. "You want me to write your life story?"

Costa smiled. "If you can call it a life."

I swallowed. "Why?"

Costa's gaze drifted to the half-drawn blinds, the grey city beyond. "Because there are men around me who believe they own the narrative. They believe they can control what's remembered. What's forgiven. What's been erased. I'm already dead to them. But before I go, I will leave my legacy for them to chew on." His eyes returned to mine. "And they're wrong about many things." He tapped the folder outlining his story.

I felt the urge to laugh again, but it didn't come. "So, you want to — expose them."

Costa's mouth twitched, amused. "Listen to you. Still moralising. Still looking for the clean motive."

I didn't like the way he could see through me. It made me feel paper thin.

"I'm not asking you to be righteous, Mr Bagala. I'm asking you to be exact."

Costa spread his hands and continued. "You exist in systems. Banks. Publishers. Tax offices. Phone companies. Airports. Most people think those systems serve them. They don't. They record them. I simply have access to everything about you."

The room seemed to tighten. The air felt thinner.

"I didn't steal anything," I said, weaker this time.

Costa nodded, conceding the point. "No. But you took what you were given. That's enough."

"What happens if I refuse?"

Costa's expression softened again in that pitying way that made my skin crawl. "You won't," he said.

My jaw locked. My stomach twisted. "You don't know that."

Costa looked at Leon. Leon reached into his jacket and placed a small USB drive on the table beside the folder. It was black, unmarked. Costa nodded at it. "That's the video of you scanning the ticket."

I stared. "That's —"

"Evidence, Mr Bagala. Not for the police. For me. In case you forget what you owe."

My mouth went dry. "That's blackmail."

Costa's eyes sharpened. "Extortion is such an ugly word. I prefer *structure*."

I forced myself to breathe. "You can't prove anything. The ticket was given freely."

Costa leaned forward slightly. "Do you know why we chose the lottery ticket?"

I didn't answer.

"Because it makes you complicit. It also makes you an accomplice. You can't keep the money without accepting the story that comes with it. And if you try to run — if you try to tell the police — you automatically become the thief in their eyes. The man who cashed a fraudulent ticket. A crime by itself that carries a very, *very* significant penalty."

"You engineered a winning lottery ticket?"

"We did. And your naivety is not at all surprising. Just look at the mess you've found yourself in."

I stared at him, horrified. "That's insane."

Costa's smile returned. "Is it?" He sat back. "You're the beneficiary. But also, a thief at the same time. That makes you controllable."

I felt something hot move through me — anger, shame, both tangled. "So what? I just write your book, and you let me go?"

Costa's eyes rested on me for a long time. The pause was deliberate. It was how he made people fill silence with their own fear. "Write well," he said finally. "Write truthfully. Write what I tell you, when I tell you, and do not improvise." He tapped the folder in front of me again. "And when it's done — we'll discuss what the word 'go' really means. But consider this also. Financial fraud is unforgivable. Not in the world we live in today."

My stomach tightened. There it was. The part Leon hadn't said in the car. There was no finish line. Only continuation. I looked down at the photos again — my house, my late wife's car, my life photographed like surveillance exhibits.

I sat very still. The city outside the tinted glass looked distant and harmless. Inside this room, everything had edges. "And if your associates find out?" I asked. "If the people you're talking about discover it?"

Costa smiled like I'd finally asked something intelligent. "Then we both die. If you refuse to give me what I want, two things are possible. We will kill you, or you get to rot in a prison cell. Don't choose the latter. I've heard it's worse than the quick death."

The simplicity of it was the real terror. No melodrama. No raised voice. Just a clean outcome. I stared at him. I was a word technologist. A paragraph engineer. But this time I had nothing to share.

Costa stood, smoothing his suit jacket as if the meeting was over. "You're going to start tonight," he said. "Then tomorrow, you'll receive instructions. You'll receive a location. You'll bring nothing except your hands and your memory." He looked at me one last time. "And Mr Bagala — don't treat this like a book you're writing to survive." He leaned closer, voice softer, intimate in the worst way. "Treat it like a book you're writing to *become*."

Then Mario Costa turned and walked out, leaving Leon by the door like a lock that had learned to speak. Leon opened the door for me and gestured down the corridor.

I didn't move at once. I stared at the folder, at the photos, at the USB drive sitting there like a black seed. Outside the tinted windows, the world continued. Ordinary life. Inside my chest, something had shifted. Because I understood now what all the money in the world really was. Not a gift. Not luck. A down payment. And the price was going to be me.

***

Leon didn't rush me. He stood by the door with his hands folded, posture neutral, more like a hotel concierge than a nightclub bouncer. I gathered the folder and the USB without being told. Leaving them behind felt dangerous in a way I couldn't articulate. As if refusing to touch them would count as refusal. And a bullet to the back of my head would not be an uncertainty.

The lift ride down was silent. Leon didn't look at me. I didn't look at him. The mirrored walls showed a man I didn't quite recognise — shoulders drawn in, eyes slightly too alert, like an animal that had learned the shape of a cage. The car ride back into the city blurred. When the Mercedes finally stopped, it was not outside my house, or even near it. It was on a side road off Lonsdale Street, quiet, half-forgotten. The kind of street people only used if they already knew where they were going.

Leon opened the door. "This is where you get out."

I stepped onto the pavement, folder under my arm. The car didn't wait for a thank you. It pulled away smoothly and vanished into traffic like it had never existed.

I stood there for a moment, breathing in the city like it might steady me. It didn't. The walk home felt longer than it should have. Every reflection in shop windows looked like someone following me. Every phone vibration made my heart jump. I kept expecting another message, another instruction, another tightening of the leash.

None came.

At my house, I locked the door, then checked it, then checked it again. I drew the blinds even though it was still light outside. I sat at the small kitchen table with the folder open in front of me and stared at the pages until my eyes hurt. There was no overt threat written down. No '*do this or else.*' Just information. Dense, clinical, meticulous. Dates, transactions, movements. Names that appeared more than once, always connected by money or absence. I realised something then that made my stomach turn.

Costa hadn't given me chaos. He'd given me order. He wanted to see if I could recognise it. If I could follow the logic. If I could understand the shape of what he was asking me to write. A memoir wasn't a confession. It was a map. I plugged the USB into my laptop.

For a second nothing happened. Then a folder appeared on the desktop. Inside were audio files. Dozens of them. Each labelled by date. Some going back years.

I clicked the first one. Costa's voice filled the room — calm, measured, faintly amused.

"Let's begin properly," he said. "I was born in Calabria in 1968 —" I shut the laptop. The silence afterward felt loud.

I stood and paced the kitchen, trying to massage stress from my shoulder, trying to dislodge the feeling that'd settled in my chest. It wasn't panic. Panic was sharp. This was slower. Heavier. Like something setting. I poured myself a drink even though it was barely afternoon. I needed the edge dulled. It didn't work. The alcohol just made the thoughts slide instead of stop.

By the time the sun went down, I understood something else. There was no version of this where I *didn't* listen to those recordings. Not because of fear — though there was plenty — but because curiosity had already taken hold. The same curiosity that cashed that lottery. The worst kind. The kind that masqueraded as professionalism. If I was going to die, either way, I wanted to know why. If I was going to survive but end my days in prison, I wanted that answered as well. I sat back down and opened the laptop again. This time, I listened.

Hours passed without shape. Costa spoke slowly, methodically. He didn't glamorise anything. He didn't apologise. He spoke like a man conducting an audit of his own life.

Names appeared. Disappeared. Sometimes with explanation. Sometimes not. I took notes without thinking about it. Dates. Connections. Patterns. My old habits kicked in, the ones I'd developed over years of writing fiction that tried to make sense of cause and effect. At some point, I realised my hands had stopped shaking. That frightened me more than anything else.

***

Near midnight, my phone vibrated.
A message.

TOMORROW. 9.00 p.m. BRING NOTHING.

No number. No signature.

I typed back before I could stop myself. *Where?*

The reply came a minute later.

SAME PLACE. DON'T BE LATE.

I slept badly. Not because of nightmares, but because of the absence of them. My mind didn't dream. It catalogued. I woke just before dawn with the sense that something had been rearranged inside me while I wasn't looking.

The day passed in fragments. I cancelled normal life duties. I ignored emails. I ate without tasting. Every normal obligation felt ridiculous, like paperwork after a funeral.

By 4.00 p.m. I needed to be outside for fresh air. I was choking on my own frustration, wondering where my life was heading. The answer in my head was sharp like a razor. *You're going to die. This is how it ends.* I couldn't imagine myself behind bars. So, I stepped outside.

Pounding the pavement, my footsteps matched my own heartbeat. Hard and furious. But as I walked, I heard from behind a set of footsteps approaching fast. I had an image in my head that maybe this was it. The end I thought about. I held my breath, hoping I wouldn't feel pain.

A woman appeared to my right. "Walk. Don't talk," she said in a thick British accent.

A man appeared to my left, absent of any words at all. I could see in my peripheral vision how this man walked with an awkward limp, something mechanical and not real. He was as tall as he was wide. A mountain of a man. I kept walking, just as instructed.

"Alfonso," the woman said. "In a moment we will about turn. Follow my instructions. Everything will be alright."

I didn't know why, the woman's voice was calming. I already felt my heart rate decline a little. But still not out of the danger zone. I asked who she was, bringing my voice down low. She didn't answer my question.

"All will be explained, Alfonso. Nothing to be alarmed about, I can assure you. Let's get to a place where we can chat, shall we?"

An about face later — the three of us turned in synchronicity. The unknown man and woman both closed ranks on my sides making me feel smaller than I truly felt.

Within five minutes, I was ushered into a café and found a small table toward the rear, out of earshot to anyone within the vicinity.

"Alfonso, I'm Maggie Gallagher, and this is Nathan Masters." She flashed an ID, but it was nothing I'd seen before. Not police or anything that resembled it. Maggie placed her ID away as quickly as she showed it. The only thing that made sense to me was the Australian Coat of Arms printed on a pale green background, at the bottom were the words *Australian Federal Government*.

Maggie sat first. Nathan didn't. He stood with his back to the wall, weight settled unevenly, eyes tracking reflections in the glass rather than the room itself. I understood instinctively that if anything happened, it wouldn't start where I was seated.

Maggie folded her hands on the table. Calm. Deliberate. The kind of posture people adopt when they're about to change the direction of your life without asking permission.

"You're not under arrest," she said.

I laughed once, sharply. "That's reassuring, isn't it?"

"It should be," she replied. "Because if you were, this conversation wouldn't be happening."

Nathan's gaze flicked to me for the first time. Not assessing. Confirming.

Maggie continued. "We know about your windfall. We know about Mario Costa. And we know about the manuscript you're working on under his scrutiny."

I opened my mouth, then closed it again. Denial felt childish. Confession felt dangerous.

I asked Maggie how she knew.

Maggie tilted her head slightly. "You live in a country that records things. Financial anomalies. Statistical outliers. People don't just receive sixty-one million dollars and disappear."

"I asked for privacy."

"And you got it," she said. "From the media."

Nathan shifted his weight. The sound of it — subtle, mechanical again — made my stomach tighten.

"Mario Costa didn't design the ticket to make you rich," Maggie said. "He designed it to make you visible to the *right* people. Both the good and the bad."

I felt something cold settle behind my eyes. "Then why haven't you stopped him?"

Maggie didn't answer immediately. She glanced at Nathan. He gave the faintest shake of his head.

Maggie continued. "Because stopping him isn't the same as neutralising him. And neutralising him requires patience."

"And me?" I asked. "What's my outlook in all this?"

Maggie's expression softened — not with sympathy, but with inevitability. "Not good I'm afraid. There're no doors open to you from his side. Costa has got you exactly where he requires you to be. You're his collateral. But you're also his leverage."

I pushed my chair back slightly, enough to signal distance without attempting escape. "If you're here to threaten me, save the time."

Nathan spoke then. His voice was quiet, even, Australian without decoration. "We're not here to threaten you," he said. "We're here to tell you the truth before Costa finishes the transaction."

I looked at him. Really looked. The limp wasn't weakness. It was his history. My head began to spin wildly.

Nathan continued. "Mario Costa doesn't intend to let you walk away," he said. "Not alive. Not imprisoned. Not silent. Not anything."

Maggie nodded. "The memoir isn't a legacy project. It's an insurance policy. Once it's complete, you become a liability."

I swallowed. "Then why not take the memoir off me now? I never wanted any of this."

"Because it's not finished," Maggie said plainly. "And because until it is, we don't have the information we need to move on him. We need the incriminating confessions. After that, he belongs to us. This goes much deeper than you can ever imagine, Alfonso."

Nathan leaned forward slightly, hands resting on the back of the empty chair beside me. "You're useful to us alive," he said. "And being unfinished will buy us the time to prepare."

The words landed hard. I stared at the table. At the faint ring left behind by someone else's coffee cup. "So, I know what Costa wants. What do you want from me?"

Maggie didn't hesitate. "For now, you keep writing. Don't rush it. Keep the strategy in play until we contact you again."

I looked up. "That's it?"

Maggie went on with instructions. "Don't be a fiction writer. Don't embellish. You don't editorialise. You don't summarise. You record. Precisely. That's what we need."

"And then what?"

Nathan answered. "Then we end Costa. Then we take down the entire syndicate." The bluntness took the air out of the room.

"And me? It seems I'm doomed every which way."

Nathan held my gaze. "That will depend on what you do with the memoir after you're done."

Maggie waved a hand and Nathan was silent. "Perhaps a plea bargain. And perhaps witness protection. We can't offer financial security. What we can offer is exclusive safety under our watch."

"A new identity and a new place to live," I laughed out loud. "Yeah, I've heard how that turns out."

"It's a much better option than a max security cell in solitary, Alfonso."

Maggie nodded. Silence settled between us, dense and final. Maggie passed me her card. "Someone will be in touch," she said. "Don't contact us unless you're told to." She paused, then added, "And Alfonso — right now, don't mistake our presence for protection. We hope you make the right choices."

They left the café the way they'd entered it. Without urgency. Without spectacle.

Nathan went last. As he passed me, he spoke just loud enough for me to hear. "Finish the memoir," he said. "Take things slow. Give us the time we need. Then decide *who* you want to be."

I sat there long after they were gone, staring at nothing. Costa thought he owned my future. He was wrong. But that didn't make me free.

***

At nine sharp, my phone vibrated.

GO OUTSIDE.

I stepped onto the street. A different car this time. Older. Unremarkable. Windows clear. A man sat in the driver's seat reading a paper. He folded it when he saw me. "Mr Bagala," he said. "Get in."

We drove north, then east, then south again, looping, sliding in and out of traffic in ways that made chasing impossible. Eventually we stopped outside an industrial building near the Yarra River — concrete, anonymous, half-lit.

Inside, the air smelled of dust, urine, and stale beer. Fluorescent lights hummed overhead. The room I was led into was smaller than I expected. A table. Two chairs. A recorder in the centre.

Mario Costa sat already waiting.

"No Leon tonight," he said pleasantly, wearing a forced smile. "I wanted this one personal."

I sat opposite him. My heart felt steady, which felt wrong.

"You listened," he said. "Good." He slid the recorder toward me. "Tonight, we start properly."

I hesitated. "You said not to bring anything."

"You brought yourself. That's all we need."

I took a deep breath and pressed record. And somewhere between his first answer and my second question, I realised the line I'd crossed wasn't behind me anymore. It was moving with me. And it wasn't done.

***

Costa spoke without flourish. No theatrical pauses. No false gravity. He didn't perform his life for me — he *delivered* it, piece by piece, like inventory. I learned quickly not to interrupt.

When I did ask questions, they weren't the ones I thought I'd ask. Not *how many*, or *who ordered it*, or *where the bodies were*. Those were distractions. Costa talked around them easily, the way men do when they've told themselves the story so many times it no longer had borders.

Instead, I asked about timing. About meetings that didn't happen. About deals that fell apart for reasons no one could explain. That's where the truth lived. He described his early years with a precision that felt surgical. Calabria. A father who believed work was punishment. A mother who understood silence as survival.

Immigration. Melbourne in the seventies, hot and ugly and unfinished. The Docklands. Construction. Laundering. Men who learned quickly that violence was easier than negotiation, but less profitable.

"I wasn't the strongest," Costa said once, almost conversationally. "That was never my advantage."

"What was?" I asked.

"Patience." He said it without pride. Like stating eye colour.

The recorder sat between us, its red light steady. It felt obscene that something so small could contain what he was giving me. Hours passed. At some point, coffee appeared. I didn't see who brought it in. I didn't ask.

Costa talked about money like it was weather. Something that moved in patterns if you knew how to read it. He talked about people the same way — pressure systems, fronts, predictable collapses. When he spoke about betrayal, it wasn't with anger. It was with irritation. Like a contractor complaining about shoddy workmanship.

"You don't punish betrayal," he said. "You replace it. Punishment is emotional. Replacement is structural."

I wrote. Not because he told me to, but because my hands needed to do something with the information. Notes in the margins. Arrows. Question marks. At some point, I realised I was no longer thinking about *if* this memoir would get me killed. I was thinking about whether it would be *worth* it. That frightened me. When the session at last ended, Costa stood and adjusted his jacket. "Good," he said. "You listen well. Now you go home and you write everything."

I was driven home the same way I'd arrived — without landmarks, without permission to orient myself. By the time I reached my home, my head felt full in a way that made sleep impossible.

I wrote instead. Not prose. Structure. Chronology. Mapping Costa's life the way he wanted it mapped. I told myself it was temporary. That once I understood the shape of it, I'd find a way out. That was the first lie I told myself.

Days passed. Then weeks. Sessions continued — sometimes in the boardroom, sometimes in anonymous rooms near the river, sometimes in places that felt deliberately unstable, like Costa wanted to see how distraction affected my listening.

More money hit my account. It wasn't frozen as I'd thought it might. I was torn. I had more money than I knew what to do with it. It made me feel filthy and used. But even so, my life was no longer starvation and mounting debt. My life stabilised. That was the second lie. Stability is just a quieter kind of danger.

I stopped telling people where I was going. Stopped answering calls. My world narrowed to Costa's voice and my own sentences. And the more I wrote, the clearer it became what he was really doing. A dead man's switch in literary form. A message from a dead body that will shake the foundation of his faction.

If anything happened to him, the memoir would surface — through channels I didn't know, through people I'd never meet. It would detonate reputations, dismantle alliances, drag men into the daylight who'd spent their lives underground. Costa wasn't writing to be remembered. He was writing to make sure no one survived him cleanly.

That night I understood with clarity. I couldn't sleep at all. I sat at my desk, staring at the latest chapter draft, and realised something else that made my stomach turn. I was no longer just recording his life. I was editing it. Choosing emphasis. Ordering events. Creating meaning.

I thought of Maggie. I thought of Nathan. I remembered their instruction. I took my time. I delayed as much as I could.

Costa rang me on occasion. "Where is that book?" he demanded. Time and time again. Delay after delay.

***

My phone buzzed.
A name this time.

MAGGIE GALLAGHER

After the phone rang, I answered.
"Alfonso, you've been hard to find."
My mouth went dry. "You know my number, just call me."
"That's not what I meant. Are you avoiding detection? Because you're almost good at it."
A pause. I could hear traffic on her end. Somewhere public. "How's the project with Costa? Coming along, is it?"
My heart kicked. "I think I almost have enough for a first draft. I'm writing what I'm told to write. Nothing more." I said carefully.

"Good. Keep it up," she replied. But something shifted in the way she spoke. "No more delays, Alfonso. Finish it."

Now I had both sides gripping my throat. The pressure was on. I closed my eyes. Costa's voice was still in my head, steady as a metronome. *You listen well.*

"And also, something else," I finally added. "My bank account hasn't been frozen."

Maggie responded after a pause. "Who said anything about freezing your account, Alfonso."

"I assumed it might be common practice under the circumstances."

"Not from us," Maggie said. "If you keep your end of the bargain, we'll do our best to keep ours. But that's not to say it won't happen. Chances are high that it might."

After I ended the call with Maggie, I sat there for a long time, listening to the quiet of my house. The place no longer felt like shelter. It felt like storage. I turned back to the manuscript. For the first time, I stopped thinking of it as Costa's story.

I began writing again — faster, with urgency, but with a new understanding of what every sentence was doing. I stopped worrying about elegance. Stopped worrying about fairness. Accuracy was now the objective.

The city went on pretending this was just another night. I was deciding how many people would survive it. I sat there in the dark, the glow of the screen reflecting off the window like a second life. I understood then that writing the memoir wasn't the point anymore. Surviving it was. And survival, I was learning, it always required payment up front.

By the time I'd finished, I sat at the desk and reread the last chapter, this time not as a writer, but as a witness. Costa's voice sat on the page with an authority that didn't belong to language. It didn't persuade. It instructed. Reading it back, I realised how little distance there was between transcription and endorsement. I was no longer neutral.

I closed the document without saving and leaned back, staring at the ceiling until the plaster cracks began to look like fault lines.

***

The next session with Costa took place two days later. Different location. A warehouse converted into offices near the port south of Melbourne. The smell of salt and diesel clung to the air, and every surface looked like it'd been chosen for how easily it could be wiped clean.

The warehouse office was colder than it needed to be. Not unfinished — *deliberately* restrained. Concrete floors polished to a dull sheen. Steel beams left exposed. Furniture sparse and heavy, like it'd been chosen to survive being thrown. There were no windows at eye level, only high panes near the ceiling that let in grey light without allowing you to see where it came from.

Costa sat already waiting. This time, there was no recorder on the table. That was the first warning. "You're late."

I checked my watch. I wasn't. "Traffic," I said.

Costa smiled as if indulging a child. "No," he replied. "Traffic is predictable. You were distracted."

I sat without being told. The chair opposite him scraped softly against the concrete. The sound seemed louder than it should've been. He studied me for a moment, then reached for a glass of water and took a sip. No alcohol. That was the second warning.

"Tell me," Costa said, setting the glass down carefully, "who else have you spoken to? Don't lie to me, Mr Bagala."

The question landed with aggression. This wasn't Mario Costa. This was someone else.

"No one," I said.

He nodded, as if I'd answered correctly. "That's the right answer. It's also the one most people give when they're lying."

I felt my spine stiffen. My mind needed to change the direction. Immediately. "You said not to improvise. I didn't."

Costa held his breathe and paused. "Very clever. But I'll indulge. I said not to improvise *the book*," he replied. "Conversation is different."

He leaned back slightly, interlocking his fingers behind his head. "You've changed," he continued. "Not in the way people usually do when they get frightened. You're quieter."

I said nothing.

Costa smiled faintly. "You've been measured. Measurement always leads to control. The question is by whom."

I forced myself to meet his gaze. "I'm writing what you asked for."

"Yes," he agreed. "But where is it, Mr Bagala. Surely after all this time, all this leniency you'd be finished by now."

That unsettled me more than criticism would have. He reached into a folder beside him and slid a single photo across the table. It wasn't part of the memoir. It wasn't even about him. It was about *me*. A photo of the meeting with Maggie Gallagher.

"You see," Costa said softly, "I don't mind outside interest. Outside interest is inevitable. What I do mind is divided loyalty."

"I don't have loyalty," I said. "I work for me."

Costa chuckled. "You're afraid. Fear is unreliable. Loyalty is worse. But alignment —?" He tapped the photo "Alignment is observable." He leaned forward now, close enough that I could smell soap and something faintly metallic. "If anyone offers you protection," he said, "they're lying. If anyone offers you a future, they're negotiating. What I offer you, Mr Bagala, is inevitability."

Silence stretched. Somewhere in the building, a pipe knocked once and went still.

"I want you to understand something," he went on. "The memoir is not insurance *against* me."

I waited.

"It's insurance *through* me. While I'm alive, it keeps people cautious. When I'm dead —?" He shrugged lightly. "It becomes something else entirely."

My throat tightened. "You talk like that doesn't concern you."

"It doesn't," he said. "I've already priced my ending."

That chilled me more than ever. He stood then, smoothing his jacket, circling the table slowly. "You're wondering if you'll make it out of here with your life."

I said nothing. My pulse thudded in my ears. Costa stopped behind my chair. I felt him there without seeing him. "If they're watching," he said quietly, "they're watching me. *Not* you." He leaned closer, voice dropping low. "And if they're clever, they'll wait until the memoir is finished."

I understood, with a clarity that hurt. Costa wasn't afraid of exposure. He was **curating the explosion.**

***

Maggie chose the place. That was how I knew we'd arrived at the end. Not a café this time. Not a moving conversation. A room with no windows and no personality, somewhere between government and nowhere. The kind of place designed to forget what happened inside it as soon as the door closed. She was already seated when I arrived. No Nathan.

That absence said more than his presence ever had. "You're finished," she said. It wasn't a question.

I placed the folder containing four hundred pages on the table between us. No flourish. No ceremony. The weight of it felt wrong in my hands — not heavy, not light. Neutral. Like a sealed verdict. "Yes it's here," I said.

She didn't reach for it immediately. She studied my face instead, as if confirming something she couldn't afford to get wrong.

"How many copies?" she asked.

"One physical," I said. "One encrypted digital. Stored separately."

Her eyes narrowed slightly. "Where?"

"You don't need to know."

She considered that, then nodded once. "That's acceptable."

I slid the folder forward. "This is the complete manuscript. Names. Dates. Transactions. The structure is intact."

"And omissions?" she asked.

"There're none. Only things you'll wish weren't there at all."

"I will also need all of the recordings from your meetings."

I passed Maggie the recorder I'd used completely intact. I also gave her the USB that Costa gave me.

That earned a faint smile. Not approval. Acknowledgement. She opened the folder and flipped through the first few pages, not reading — just verifying density. Evidence of weight. Of consequence. "You understand," she said, "from this point moving forward, things will happen very quickly."

"I know."

"And you understand, that when they do, Mario Costa will not survive the sequence."

I nodded again. "He knew that too. He was pricing his ending. He just didn't know who'd finalise the invoice."

Maggie closed the folder and pocketed the recorder with the USB, Silence paused time between us. Not awkward. Final.

"What happens to me?" I asked.

Maggie leaned back slightly. "That depends on what you do next."

I waited.

"You disappear," she said. "Or you stay exactly where you are. Quiet. Solvent. Uninteresting. And you get to choose which life."

"And witness protection?"

She shook her head. "You're not a witness. You're a custodian."

That word again. "I won't publish. And I won't pretend I don't know what's in the memoir."

"I wouldn't ask you to. But you will not interfere either. Clear?"

I nodded slowly.

She studied me one last time. "Do you regret it?"

I thought about the house. The silence. My wife. The money sitting in my account like a held breath. "No," I said. "But I don't forgive myself either."

"That's usually how it lands," she said.

She stood, took the folder, and tucked it under her arm like any other document. Nothing about her suggested she was carrying something that would ruin dozens of lives. At the door, she paused. "One more thing," she said. "Nathan wanted me to tell you something. He said you listened well. That doesn't happen often."

Then she left. The door closed without sound. I sat there for a moment longer, hands empty, feeling the absence settle in. Not relief. Not fear. Completion. The world around me continued unaware that a sequence had been set into motion that couldn't be recalled.

***

I didn't go straight home. That felt like a mistake waiting to happen. Instead, I walked. No direction. No destination. Just movement. The kind you use when you're trying to outrun the sound of your own thoughts. The city didn't notice. It never did.

I crossed streets on instinct, let crowds swallow me, drifted into quieter pockets where offices shut down early and cafés pretended to be closed while still watching people through the glass. I kept expecting my phone to vibrate. A message. A correction. Nothing came.

That should have reassured me. It didn't. By the time I reached the river at Southbank, dusk had flattened the sky into a dull metallic smear. The water moved slowly, carrying reflections it didn't care to keep. I leaned against the railing and stared down, thinking — not for the first time — about how easily people disappeared in cities like this. Not dramatically. Administratively.

"You shouldn't linger." The voice came from behind me. Calm. Close. Already inside my space. I didn't turn straight away. That felt important too.

"I thought you'd be busy," I said.

"Finished work early," Nathan Masters replied.

I turned then. He stood a few steps back, hands relaxed at his sides, jacket unbuttoned. The limp was there, just visible enough to remind me it wasn't a story. He didn't look like a man who'd just ended something enormous.

"Maggie has read the book," I said.

"Yes."

"And Costa?"

Nathan's eyes moved briefly to the water. Then back to me. "In progress."

I swallowed. "That's vague."

"On purpose."

Something settled between us. The kind that wasn't empty. The kind that waited.

"You told me," I said carefully, "that what would happen to me depended on what I did with the book after."

"Yes. I remember."

"I handed it over."

"You did," he agreed.

"So, we're done."

Nathan studied me for a moment. Not assessing. Not judging. Deciding. "Mario Costa believed stories don't end after they're told. He was wrong."

I felt something tighten. "What does that mean?"

"It means the book was never the danger. The *reader* is."

I didn't like that. "You're suggesting the memoir will never be open to scrutiny."

He didn't answer at first. Then he said something that was hard to believe. "Not publicly. But your hard work brought down an empire. Take solace in that."

I took a breath and thought about it.

"Maggie gave me the option to disappear."

"She was being kind."

"And you?" I asked.

Nathan took a step closer. Not threatening. Precise. "I think you're useful," he said. The words landed harder than Costa's ever had.

"Useful how?" I asked.

Nathan's gaze held mine. There was no warmth in it. No cruelty either. Just clarity. "You understand systems. You understand leverage. Silence. Timing."

I said nothing.

"You also understand that some truths can't be destroyed. They can only be *managed*."

The river moved below us, dark and patient.

"I'm not working for you," I said.

Nathan nodded once. "No. You're not. Not yet."

"What am I to you?"

He considered that longer than I liked. "An asset," he said finally. "One, we haven't decided how to classify."

I felt my pulse pick up. "So that's it? I just wait?"

"For now."

"And when you decide?"

Nathan's mouth twitched, not quite a smile. "Then you'll get a call. Same as before."

He stepped back, already disengaging. "One more thing," Nathan added. "You did well. Most people break, and much earlier."

Then he turned and walked away. But there was one question left. I needed an answer. "Wait," I said, "Your people still haven't frozen my bank account."

Nathan briefly looked over his shoulder and raised his hand. "You'll need it."

He kept walking and melted into the thinning crowd with the same efficiency as Maggie. I stayed where I was long after he was gone, staring at the river as the city lit itself up for the night.

The manuscript was no longer in my hands. That should have felt like freedom. Instead, I understood the truth at last. I hadn't escaped the story. I'd just been written into the sequel. And somewhere out there, Nathan Masters was deciding when — and if — it would begin.

BOOK FIVE

THE WINE CELLAR

I'd lived in this house long enough to know every noise it made. The hot water system clicked when the temperature dropped. The timber in the hallway groaned if you stepped on the third board from the linen cupboard. The garage roller door had a lazy shudder halfway down, like it couldn't be bothered finishing the job unless you held the button until it clunked into place. Normal noises. Safe noises. The kind you stopped noticing — until you were alone enough to hear them again.

That morning, the kettle boiled a fraction too loud in the quiet kitchen. I poured the water over a teabag, watched the colour bleed into the mug, and stared past the window at a row of fences and rooftops that all looked identical in the pale suburban Canberra light. Somewhere a dog barked. Somewhere a neighbour reversed out of a driveway, the tyres crunching over gravel, the engine coughing once before it settled into a steady idle.

Life continued. That was the dangerous part.

I'd left the news on the night before, the volume low, like background music for a man who didn't want to be alone with his thoughts. Ukraine again. Russia again. A map with arrows. A solemn-faced presenter using words that sounded clinical until you knew what they really meant. Escalation. Retaliation. Strategic. Tactical. American intervention.

A new phrase had been doing the rounds for weeks — early warning signs — spoken by people who didn't believe in them. Like superstition. Like reading tea leaves.

I believed in them because I'd watched my wife die of cancer and I'd learned what *'early warning'* really looked like. It wasn't dramatic. It was subtle, and it was ignored, and then it was too late.

I picked up my phone and scrolled the headlines. Same cycle. Same cadence. Talks failing. Sanctions. Threats. Another red line. Another *'unprecedented'*. I didn't need a PhD in geopolitics to recognise a pattern. I only needed a memory. But as I looked deeper, I noticed gold prices continuing to climb. Gold never rose ferociously. This time it seemed there was no plateau. I put the phone down and opened the pantry.

We had food. Enough for a normal week. Pasta, rice, cereal, a couple of tins — beans, tomatoes, one lonely can of peaches that must've been sitting there since the Howard government. Nothing wrong. Nothing dramatic. But I wasn't looking at what was there. I was seeing what wasn't. No depth. No redundancy. No margin for error.

You could live comfortably on an average income in an average suburb, with an average kitchen, and still be one delivery disruption away from hunger for the first time in your adult life. People thought the shelves were a permanent feature of the world. Like gravity. Like electricity. Like water before a drought. That belief was a luxury.

I closed the pantry and walked to the laundry. The tap dripped once, then stopped. I watched it like it might start speaking. When I was a kid, my father used to say the same thing whenever he watched the weather: *Storm's coming.* Back then it was something to complain about. A reason to bring the washing in. Now it felt like prophecy.

I heard the front door open — two quick clicks of the lock, and then the soft scrape of rubber soles on tile. I didn't move. I didn't need to. I knew the rhythm of her steps.

Charlotte.

"Morning," Charlotte called, like she was testing the temperature of my mood from the hallway.

"In here," I announced back.

She appeared in the kitchen doorway with her hair still damp, a gym bag slung over one shoulder. She was fit in the way people became when they were trying to keep life orderly — yoga, routines, little rituals to hold chaos at bay. She looked at the mug in my hand and then at the television, which was muted but still showing an analyst waving his hands at a graphic. "You're watching it again," she said.

"It's on."

"With you, it's always on, isn't it?"

I didn't like the edge in her voice. It wasn't anger. It was something worse — fatigue. The kind that made you start counting exits. I kept my tone even. "I like to know what's happening."

She stepped into the kitchen, unzipped her bag, rummaged for her water bottle like the conversation was a minor obstacle she could reach around. "What's happening is you're scaring yourself," she said.

I felt something tighten in my chest — not fear, not panic. A familiar frustration. The same feeling I'd had when doctors spoke in probabilities and my late wife smiled politely like optimism could beat statistics. "I'm not scared," I said. "I'm paying attention."

Charlotte took a drink. "Okay. Pay attention. But you're not sleeping. You're checking headlines at three in the morning. And now you've got lists that grow longer every day."

"Lists are useful."

"For what?" She gave me a look that tried to stay kind. "Michael. Come on. You live in Deakin. You're not in a bunker in Idaho."

I nearly laughed. It came out as a short exhale. "This is how it starts," I said, and regretted it the moment the words left my mouth. Her eyebrows lifted. "How what starts?"

The kettle clicked off again — re-boiled because I'd flicked it on out of habit without thinking. The sound was too sharp in the silence between us. I looked past her, through the window. The sky was clear. The fences still stood. The world still behaved. "That slow drift," I said. "The thing where everyone pretends nothing's changing until it's already changed."

Charlotte slammed her bottle down hard enough that it popped. "It's a war over there. It's always been a war somewhere. That doesn't mean it ends with us here."

"It might," I said.

She watched me for a beat, like she was searching my face for a crack she could patch. "This is about Andrea, isn't it?" There it was. The place people went when they didn't want to follow you into the room where your thinking lived. They blamed grief. They blamed trauma. They blamed anything that made your concern feel like a symptom instead of a calculation. I kept my voice low. "Don't do that."

"I'm not attacking you." She held up one hand, palm out, peace offering. "I'm just saying... you went through something horrible. You watched her fade away. You couldn't stop it. And now you're looking for the next thing you can't stop so you can—"

"So, I can what?" I snapped, sharper than I meant to. "Feel in control?"

Charlotte flinched. It was small, but I saw it. I hated that I caused it. I gulped. "Sorry."

She exhaled, eyes closing for a moment. "Michael… I love you. I do. But I can't live in a house where the apocalypse is playing an endless loop."

"It's not the apocalypse," I said. "It's the build-up to one."

She gave me a tired smile that didn't reach her eyes. "Are you hearing yourself, Michael?"

I did. That was the problem. I heard myself clearly, and what I heard wasn't madness. It was logic that nobody else wanted to carry.

Charlotte checked her watch. "I've got to go. I'm meeting Jess for coffee after class."

"Okay."

She hesitated by the kitchen counter. "Can you… maybe talk to someone?"

"I'm talking to you."

"Not like that." She softened again. "A professional."

I stared at the surface of the table; at the faint ring a mug had left from the day before. "I'm fine."

Charlotte's voice went quiet. "You're not fine. You're… braced. Like you're waiting for a car to hit the house."

I looked up. "What if a car *is* coming?"

She didn't answer straight away. She just shook her head, like she didn't know how to climb inside my reasoning without getting cut. "I'll call you later," she said, and left.

The front door clicked shut. Her car started. Reversed out the driveway. The sound of gravel. Then the sound of her car roared down the street.

I stood alone in the kitchen, cup cooling in my hand, and listened to the house breathe. My phone buzzed once — some update, some alert I'd set because I told myself it was '*being informed*' and not '*feeding obsession.*' I ignored it. Not because I didn't care, but because the conversation with Charlotte had left a sour taste of something hard sitting at the back of my palate.

I took my coffee into the garage. It smelt like dust and petrol and the ghosts of weekends I'd once spent fixing things for no reason other than the satisfaction of a job done. The shelves were stacked with old paint tins, Christmas decorations, a cricket bat I hadn't swung in ten years. The centre of the floor was open; concrete stained in a few spots where oil had spilled and soaked into the porous surface like a permanent confession. This space could become something else. It had volume. It had potential.

That's what my brain did now. It looked at normal things and saw alternate uses. It was the same part of me that used to read survival guides when I was a teenager, not because I wanted the world to end, but because I wanted to know I could endure it if it did.

I set the mug down on a workbench and stared at the wall. If I were going to do this, I needed to do it quietly. Carefully. In stages. Not because it was illegal to store food, but because people reacted badly to anyone who prepared for a world they didn't believe could change. They liked preparation only after disaster. Before that, it was '*paranoia.*' After that, it was '*wisdom.*' I knew which one I'd rather be.

I grabbed a tape measure, pulled it out with a metallic rasp, and walked the perimeter of the garage. Six metres by six, roughly. Enough to fit a car and still have workspace. The left side wall — brick, stable. The back wall — shared with the house, plasterboard over frame.

If I built against the left wall, I could conceal it behind shelving. If I claimed it was storage, or a wine cellar — Charlotte liked wine. Neighbours understood wine. Nobody panicked over wine.

I crouched and ran my fingers along the concrete. Cold. Solid. The kind of surface that didn't care about human fear.

I stood and opened the side door to the backyard. Air rushed in, smelling like cut grass and eucalyptus. The sound of the street was faint. Safe. I stared at that strip of ordinary suburbia — the fences, the clotheslines, the neat geometry of backyards — and I felt the strangest thing: grief, before the loss had even happened. Not for the world ending. That was too large. For the world being ignored. For people laughing at storm warnings while the sky thickened.

I went back inside and opened my laptop at the workbench. Not to doomscroll. To price things. To plan like a man who was tired of being surprised by inevitability. I started a spreadsheet. Water storage. Food rotation. Batteries. Medical supplies. Tools. Masks. Filters. A generator, maybe — if I could justify it without raising eyebrows. How much cash could I keep on hand without it feeling dramatic? What could I get delivered without someone asking questions?

As I typed, the quiet in the garage settled around me like insulation. In my head, I wasn't building a wine cellar. I was building time.

Time to think. Time to breathe. Time to be wrong and still live. And if I was right — time to survive long enough to decide whether survival was a gift or a sentence. The phone buzzed again. This time I picked it up.

A breaking news banner slid across the screen. Another statement. Another warning. Another promise that everything was under control. I stared at it until my eyes ached. Then I turned the phone face down on the bench, picked up the tape measure again, and started marking the driveway with a pencil. I kept the lines small. Neat. Precise.

***

I didn't tell anyone about my gold holdings. I kept it where I could feel its weight without seeing it. In the garage. In the back of my mind. It wasn't something you talked about casually. It was a decision you made quietly, the way you chose where to stand when you felt something coming. I knew if the worst came to worst, cash had no meaning. It would become useless. But gold? Gold speaks to everybody, and with it came power. Power to negotiate. Power to trade. In a world where supplies would mean life or death, gold would be the only answer to make things happen and to survive.

The build in the garage began with the cutting of concrete. I didn't rush it. I didn't act like a man running out of time — even though that was exactly what I was. Timber came in small loads. Concrete mix bought with other things to blur intent. Shelving rearranged so the changes looked accidental.

Day after day, I did little by little. Cutting concrete and removing rubble. Excavating dirt and removing it a barrow at a time. I finished with reinforcing the walls and installing self-contained shelving. A couple of bunks. A place for storing waste. Connection of power. Building a storage for a generator and finally an air vent.

After the wine cellar was complete, I stocked it with food and water, enough for a couple of weeks.

While I worked at getting things ready, did it in a way that I hoped the neighbours or Charlotte wouldn't notice. But Charlotte noticed anyway. She always did.

She stood in the doorway one evening, arms folded, watching me carrying things into a hole in the ground.

"Storage?" she asked.

"Wine cellar," I said automatically.

She didn't smile this time. "You don't even like wine, Michael."

"I like options," I said.

She stepped inside the garage, eyes scanning the space, the neatness that hadn't been there before. "Michael… what is this really?"

I put the two measures of water down and faced her. "This is me asking you to stay," I said.

She blinked. "What?"

My hands felt clumsy, like I'd waited too long to use them for anything honest. "I know what this looks like," I said. "I know how it sounds, but I'm not losing you because I didn't say it out loud."

She shook her head. "This isn't about us."

"It is," I said. "It's exactly about us."

She laughed, sharp and tired. "You're building a bunker in a Deakin garage."

"I'm building us time."

"That's not normal."

"Neither was watching Andrea die while everyone kept saying *'we'll see how it goes'*.

Her face changed at that. Not anger. Recognition. "I saw how that ended," I continued. "I saw what ignoring early signs costs. I'm not doing that again. Not with the world. Not with you."

She folded her arms tighter. "So, this is what? The end of everything?"

"I don't know," I said. And that was the truth. "But I know pretending nothing's changing won't stop it."

Charlotte looked away, toward the open garage door, the quiet street beyond. Kids' bikes lay on a lawn down the road. A neighbour's radio drifted faintly through the air. "People have always said the world's ending," she said.

"Not the world. Human race. Maybe a large amount of us will die. But the world will still be here."

She looked back at me. "And this time?"

"I think this time people are confusing normal with safe."

Silence stretched between us. "I don't need you to believe everything I believe," I said. "I just need you to believe that I'm not crazy. That I'm not doing this to feel important. I'm doing it because I don't want to be helpless again."

Her eyes softened. "I think you're scared, Michael."

It felt like tearing something loose to admit it. "Yeah."

Charlotte exhaled slowly. "Why didn't you say that earlier?"

"Because men like me get laughed at when we say things like that."

She stepped closer. "Okay, Michael. Say I believed you. Not because I want to. Only because I know *you* believe. And you know I love you, right?"

I nodded slowly, not wanting to scare her off. I had her attention, now I didn't want to lose it.

"Show me." Charlotte said it plainly like the words had no weight.

"What?"

"Show me what you've built. I want to see it."

I hesitated — then opened the concealed trap door in the middle of the concrete driveway. I heaved it open, feeling its full weight in my grip. The cellar light came on automatically, still connected to mains power. Solid. Calm. Real.

Charlotte stared. It wasn't dramatic. No blinking lights. No steel walls. Just depth. Shelter. Intent. "You planned this," she said quietly.

"Yeah." I nodded.

"For how long?"

"Long enough. But now I fear time is slipping away."

She walked down the roughly manufactured stairs and inside slowly, hand trailing along the wall, feeling the thickness of it, the effort. "This isn't madness," she said. "This is grief with a ruler."

I smiled. First in a while. "That might be the nicest thing anyone's said about it."

She turned to face me. "If you're wrong—"

"If I'm wrong, it's still a wine cellar. I'll live with that."

"And if you're right?"

I didn't answer. I could only imagine. My imaginings were chaotic and ugly both at the same time.

She looked around once more, then nodded. "Okay," she said. "Then we do it properly."

I frowned. "Do what?"

Charlotte rolled her shoulders like someone settling into a hard decision. "If we're preparing, we prepare together. No more secrets. No more pretending this is just a hobby."

Something loosened in my chest. "You'll stay with me on this?" I asked.

"For now," she said. "But if we're doing this, I need to understand everything. And I need to know where this ends."

I nodded. "So do I."

That night, we sat in the cellar with the door open, talking quietly while the radio murmured on low in the garage. We didn't argue. We didn't reassure each other. We planned. And when the first unscheduled emergency alert came through the following afternoon, Charlotte didn't look at me like I was crazy. She just reached for my hand and said, "Okay. Now I'm scared too."

I squeezed Charlotte's fingers. "Good," I said. "That means we're paying attention."

***

After much research, I finally located the Geiger counter in a place that smelled like dust and resignation. An old pawn shop located in a backstreet off Pirie Street, in Fyshwick CBD. It wasn't advertised in the window. No bright packaging. No urgency. Just a faded sticker near the register that said *Radiation & Survey Equipment —*

moving fast, like it was something people inquired about every day.

The shop sat off a service road I'd driven past a hundred times without noticing. One of those places that survived by not drawing attention to itself. Inside, shelves were stacked with oddments — measuring devices, meters, old military surplus with the paint rubbed thin from too many hands. Things built to last longer than the people who bought them. The man behind the counter didn't ask why. He just said it was becoming a pattern.

"Calibrated?" I asked.

"Last month," he said. "Battery's fresh."

He slid it across the counter. Heavier than it looked. Honest weight. When I picked it up, it gave a short, dry click — like it was clearing its throat.

Charlotte watched my face, not the device. "What does that mean?" she asked.

"Nothing," I said quietly, voice low. "Not yet. It will be useful when the time comes."

I attempted to pay by card. The man said, "No." Flat. Not making eye contact. Not like anything at all. I wanted to pull a few bills from my wallet, but then noticed the device had no price. "How much?" I asked.

"That depends on what you have," he said. "You can't buy something like this with cash, knowing what's going to happen. Cash is useless now."

"What?"

Charlotte stood back. "Michael? He knows."

I kept my voice low. "Probably more than we do. Let me play this."

I turned again to the shopkeeper. "Okay, if you don't want cash, what do you want?"

"Got any gold?"

I locked eyes with Charlotte. "He's a player. I have some gold but not here. It's back home."

Just then, someone else came into the shop. "Hey mate, I'm looking for something that reads radioactivity, got anything like that?"

The shopkeeper snatched the Geiger counter from my hand and offered it to the guy standing behind me. "It's yours if you have gold. Not cash. Not card. Gold."

"Aw shit," the guy said. "Sure, take my watch. It's eighteen carats."

"No, you bloody don't." Charlotte stepped in between them. "We were here first."

Charlotte grabbed her gold necklace and yanked it from her neck. "The chain is eighteen carats. The pendant is a nugget straight out of the ground. It's at least thirty grams of 99.99% pure gold. Will that do?"

"Charlotte, no," I said. She didn't hear me.

The shopkeeper took the chain from her and thrust it deep into his pocket, sliding the Geiger counter into my hands with one swift movement. The guy behind me said, "Oi!" but I ignored it and left the shop, Charlotte at my heels.

"Did you notice something strange?" I asked Charlotte.

"Nothing out of the ordinary for a pawn shop. Why?"

"There was no jewellery. Pawn shops sell jewellery, but he had none. Not a skerrick."

"What do you make of it?" Charlotte asked.

"The man is hoarding his jewellery. He's hedging. Why do you think that could be?"

Charlotte didn't answer but I could see the colour drain in her face.

"Here it is, Char. He's hedging because the day after tomorrow, jewellery becomes currency."

***

Back home, I turned the Geiger counter on in the garage. The clicks were faint at first. Almost apologetic. Background noise. The kind you could ignore if you wanted to.

Charlotte stood very still. "That's normal?" she asked.

"For now, it is. Background radiation. We live with it every day. What you're hearing is the breathing of the universe."

I walked the perimeter of the house slowly, holding the device out in front of me like a divining rod. The clicks stayed steady. Quiet. Manageable. But when I stepped toward the back fence, they changed. Not dramatically. Just enough.

Charlotte heard it too. I could tell by the way her shoulders tightened. "That's still okay?" she asked.

"It's not dangerous. Still within parameter."

In the wine cellar, I placed the Geiger counter within easy reach on a shelf, along with several packets of iodine tablets we managed to get hold of during the past few days. Each day I bought a few more to add to our growing collection. Just enough so people wouldn't ask questions. Just enough not to start a panic. Some were expensive, some weren't. But I knew in my heart that the value of money was something I stopped caring about. Now it was survival, and as long as I kept hold of my gold, I felt okay.

One of the items Charlotte brought down in the wine cellar was a small figurine of an eagle. Crystal and gold. Once she said it had meaning. Now she claimed it gave her hope. She sat it neatly on the edge of the shelf where I had placed the Geiger counter, as if the little eagle was there to keep watch over us. Maybe in a way it did just that. Hope was anything that kept us alive.

Charlotte and I didn't talk after that. We didn't need to. The next morning, the news stopped pretending. Not officially. Not with an announcement. It just… slipped. Broadcasters used phrases like *communication disruptions* and *unconfirmed reports*. Maps lost detail. Timelines blurred. Someone important stopped appearing on camera. Somehow, I knew the Geiger counter ticked steadily on a lone shelf in the wine cellar while Charlotte and I ate breakfast as normal at the kitchen bench.

Charlotte stared at me between sips of coffee. "Thank you for leaving it down there. I don't like that sound," she said.

"I know."

By midday, the power went out in half-hour bursts. Long enough to reset clocks. Short enough to convince people it was temporary. By evening, it didn't come back. The neighbourhood changed without realising it. People stood in their driveways talking too loudly. Someone started a barbecue they didn't finish. A car alarm went off and never stopped until the battery died, screaming into the dark like a creature that couldn't understand why no one came.

That night, I brought the Geiger counter to our bedroom and left it on the dresser. Charlotte protested at first but then relented after she heard the clicks growing stronger and louder. Not fast. Just insistent.

"Okay, we need to move," I said. "If nothing happens, then consider it a test run."

I didn't want to stress Charlotte more than I had to. But in the back of my mind, I knew time was retreating. I had everything in place. Everything needed in case of a devastating event. We moved through the dark silence and down into the wine cellar, hitting the start button on the generator I'd set up along the way.

Charlotte sat beside me in the cellar, knees drawn up, listening. "This is the last piece, isn't it?" she said.

"Yeah."

"What happens now?"

I didn't answer straight away. Because this was the part I hadn't rehearsed properly. Preparation had an end point. Survival didn't. And ugliness didn't arrive all at once — it crept in, slow and petty and human. "It gets smaller," I said finally.

She frowned. "What does?"

"The world," I said. "It starts shedding things. Rules. Courtesy. Truth. Then people.

We heard shouting somewhere in the distance. Not close. Not yet.

The Geiger counter clicked again. In a steady heartbeat.

I looked at Charlotte and saw the moment she understood that fear wasn't coming later. It was already here. And it wasn't loud. It was patient.

***

The cellar settled into a new rhythm after that. Not calm. Not safe. Just… contained. The generator hummed softly, a sound that had already become background, like breathing. The Geiger counter clicked on the shelf, steady now, insistent but not panicked. The world above us might have been tearing itself apart, but down here everything obeyed rules we both understood.

Charlotte sat cross-legged on a bunk, running her fingers along the edge of a crate, not really touching it. Thinking. I watched her without meaning to. She'd tied her hair back with an elastic she'd taken from her wrist. One of those small, practical gestures that said more than words ever did. She caught me looking and raised an eyebrow.

"What?" she asked.

"Nothing."

"That's never true with you."

I shifted closer, our shoulders brushing. The contact felt louder than it should have in the small space. "I was just thinking," I said, "that this probably isn't how you imagined things turning out."

She snorted softly. "I didn't imagine *any* of this."

"Me either."

She leaned her head against my shoulder. Not heavily. Just enough to say she was there. "I don't regret staying," she said. "This feels safe now."

I swallowed. "You don't have to say that."

"I know." She paused. "I want to."

Outside, something thudded in the distance. Not close enough to react to. Close enough to notice. Neither of us moved.

"Do you remember the night we met?" she asked.

I smiled despite myself. "You spilled red wine on my shoes."

"You were wearing those ridiculous leather ones."

"They were good shoes."

"They were pretending to be," she said. Then, quieter. "You didn't get angry at me. I expected you to, but you didn't."

"I was impressed by your aim."

She laughed — a small sound, quickly contained, like she didn't want to wake the end of the world.

I took her hand. Her fingers were cold. "You okay?" I asked.

"Yeah," she said. "I just keep thinking about how close we came to missing this."

"Missing what?"

She looked around the cellar — the shelves, the crates, the dim, honest light — then back at me.

"Each other," she said. "Really seeing each other."

I tightened my grip without thinking. "I'm sorry I waited so long to say it out loud," I said. "About being scared. About needing you."

She shook her head. "You said it when it mattered."

The Geiger counter clicked again.

Charlotte reached up and touched my face, her thumb brushing my cheekbone. It wasn't a romantic gesture. It was a check. A reassurance that I was still solid. "If this is the worst of it," she said, "then we're okay."

"And if it's not?"

She didn't answer straight away. She paused. Then said, "We'll be careful," she said finally. "With supplies. With decisions. With each other."

I leaned my forehead against hers. In that moment, love wasn't hope. It wasn't optimism or denial or bravery. It was choosing to stay present while everything else unravelled. We didn't kiss like people in movies do when the world is ending. No urgency. No desperation. Just a quiet, deliberate closeness, as if saying, *We're still here. We still recognise each other.*

When we separated, Charlotte rested her head back on my shoulder, eyes closed. "Wake me if it changes," she murmured.

"I will."

"And Michael?"

"Yeah?"

"Thank you for paying attention."

I watched her breathe, felt the weight of her against me, and understood something I hadn't before. Preparation had kept us alive. But love was the thing that made survival worth carrying forward. Above us, the world narrowed another inch. Down here, in the dark, we held the line.

***

We'd spent an entire night in the wine cellar. By morning, there was no change to the steady heartbeat of the Geiger counter. But that didn't mean nothing had changed.

After refilling the generator with diesel, Charlotte and I had breakfast in the usual way. It wasn't until after I switched on the television that we both noticed a massive shift in the world's demeanour.

Politicians were absent from speeches and arguments over global affairs. Now, it seemed there was no news at all. At first, I didn't notice, but Charlotte did.

"Don't you think there're more than enough commercials on TV right now?" she asked.

My eyes went to the TV. It was Monday morning, precisely 9.35a.m. There was no morning show. No weather report. No idiotic, meaningless live coverage of anything that usually made its way to the screen. Instead, we were watching vacuum cleaner demonstrations. *'Call now, but wait, there's more. Buy two for the one low price...'* Then miracle superglue. Then, ShamWow. Endless, one after the other.

"Where's the morning show?" Then it occurred to me. There were no politicians because they were all safely tucked away, sheltering from whatever was coming. There was no regular TV because no one had turned up for work. What we were seeing was a pre-recorded schedule that had run through the previous night. Except this time, nobody had bothered to switch it off.

Outside, I heard the first sounds of panic. Cars speeding away. People shouting at each other to get in the car. Doors slammed. A blood-curdling scream from the end of the street.

My eyes locked with Charlotte. "Wine cellar! Now!"

Leaving everything where it was, we didn't hesitate. We flew to the wine cellar, got ourselves in, battened the hatch and waited. We stayed for what seemed hours, held our breath, held hands and I pulled Charlotte tight into my chest not letting go.

***

The knock came just after midnight. Not loud. Not frantic. Three taps. Careful. Measured. Charlotte's eyes opened immediately. Mine were already open. We lay still, listening, the generator humming above us, the Geiger counter clicking softly on the shelf like a second clock.

Tap. Tap. Tap.

Someone knew how to knock without sounding desperate.

"That's not wind," Charlotte said.

"No. It sounds human."

I reached for the torch but didn't turn it on. Light was a decision now. So was silence.

Another knock. Slightly firmer this time.

"Michael," a voice said. Muffled. Male. Familiar enough to hurt. "I know you're down there."

Charlotte sat up slowly. "Do you know him?" I nodded. "Timothy. Two houses down."

The Geiger counter clicked.

Click.

Click-click.

Charlotte sucked in a breath. "How does he know?"

"Because people notice patterns," I said. "Even when they pretend not to."

Above us, floorboards creaked. Someone shifting weight in the house. After a while, the footsteps returned to the wine cellar.

"Michael," Timothy called again. "I'm not alone."

That was the line that changed things. I moved. Charlotte reached for my arm. Not to stop me. To anchor me. "What does he want?" she whispered.

I already knew. "He wants time," I said. "The same thing everyone wants now."

Another voice, this one thinner. A woman. Coughing. Wet. Close.

Charlotte closed her eyes for a moment. "Is she hurt?"

"Yes. I think so. It sounds like it."

"How bad, I wonder?"

I didn't answer. I didn't need to. We both understood what coughing meant now. It meant finding shelter at whatever cost. The knock came again. Louder.

"We don't need much," Timothy said. "Just somewhere to sit. Just for a bit. She's not doing well."

Charlotte looked at me. Really looked. The way she had the first time she stepped into the cellar. Measuring not the space, but the man and his companion.

"If we open that door," she said quietly, "we don't get to pretend this is private anymore."

"I know."

"If we don't—"

"I know that too."

The Geiger counter clicked again, steady as a heartbeat that didn't care about morality. I stood. Charlotte stood with me. We climbed the steps slowly, every sound magnified now that it mattered. At the top, I paused with my hand on the latch, feeling the vibration of the house, the presence of other people pressing in from the dark. I opened the door a fraction. Just a fraction.

Timothy stood on the driveway, eyes sunken, jacket pulled tight despite the mild night. His wife leaned against him, breathing shallow, her face grey under the light. Behind them, a teenage boy hovered, eyes darting, hands shaking.

"You were right," Timothy said. No accusation. No apology. Just fact. "We should've listened to you. To all your wild preachings."

Charlotte stepped up beside me. "How long has she been coughing?"

Timothy swallowed. "Since this afternoon."

Charlotte didn't look at me. She was calculating.

"They're putting it on for sympathy," I whispered to Charlotte. "He knows what we have but we can't Char. We just can't."

Silence pooled between us.

"We can't stay out here," Timothy said. "People are moving around. Someone smashed a window up the street." I looked past them. Shadows shifted at the edge of the road. Shapes where there hadn't been shapes before. Charlotte spoke before I could.

"We can't bring you inside," she said. "There's not enough supplies."

Timothy flinched like he'd been struck. "But—"

"We can give you water," she continued. "Food. Masks. Enough to get you somewhere safer than here."

After a pause. "There is nowhere safer," Timothy said.

Charlotte's voice didn't harden. It *settled*. "There is," she said. "But it's not here. And it's not shared."

The boy started crying. Quietly. Ashamed of it. I felt something tear loose in my chest.

"Michael," Timothy said. "Please. What will happen when the lights go out?"

I opened the trap door a little wider and handed Timothy the bag Charlotte had already prepared without me noticing. A bottle of water. Filters. Iodine tablets. Gloves. Two masks. Not enough. Never enough. "Don't go south," I said. "Head west. Stay off main roads. If the coughing gets worse—" I stopped. There was no end to that sentence that helped.

Timothy took the bag with shaking hands. "I thought you were mad," he said.

Charlotte met the woman's eyes and held them. No lies passed between them. Just recognition. "We're sorry," Charlotte said. And meant it.

They left quickly. Not thanking us again. Not looking back. They understood what they'd been given — and what they hadn't. I closed the door and slid the bolt. For a long moment, neither of us spoke. Then Charlotte leaned her forehead against the door and exhaled.

"That was the line," she said.

"Yeah."

"We don't get to be the people we were before."

"No, Char, we need to be much stronger from here."

She turned and looked at me. There was grief there. And resolve. And love that had survived contact with reality. "We'll carry this," she said. "But we won't carry everyone."

I nodded. On a lone shelf in the middle of the wine cellar, the Geiger counter clicked on. Steady. Patient. The world had asked. We had answered. And now the cost had a face.

***

It didn't arrive with sirens. That was the last thing I registered before the light. It came through the edges of the trap door above us. A white bloom that pressed itself through timbers, then through eyelids. It wasn't bright in the way fire was bright. It was total. A colour that didn't belong anywhere humans lived. Charlotte gasped. Not screamed. Gasped.

Within an instant, the Geiger counter screamed for her. The clicks collapsed into a single, frantic sound, like something alive trying to escape its casing. I moved without thinking. Hands on Charlotte. Down. Covering her head. The cellar seemed to shrink around us as the pressure arrived a half-second later. The house above groaned. Not a crash. Not an explosion. A deep, structural complaint, like timber discovering it was no longer part of a plan. Then the sound hit.

It wasn't loud. It was *dense*. A wall of noise that flattened my thought and turned the air solid. The generator coughed once, then steadied, then died. Lights went out. Dust shook loose from the ceiling and fell like snow on my skin.

Charlotte was saying my name, but I couldn't hear it properly. Sound lagged behind everything else, struggling to catch up. And then—Nothing.

The silence afterward wasn't peaceful. It was stunned. The Geiger counter continued to howl. I waited. Counted without numbers. One breath. Two. Three. Another flash followed, dimmer this time, as if whatever had done this was already moving on. Then the pressure again. Further away.

Instinctively, I reached for a kerosene lantern I'd left on a shelf for this exact moment and lit its fuse. The inside of the wine cellar exposed itself again. My other hand went for the iodine tablets and offered four of them to Charlotte before taking some for myself.

Charlotte's nails dug into my arm. Hard enough to hurt. I welcomed it. "Is it—" she started.

"Yes," I said. I didn't need to think about it. "That was it. It's over." Or so I thought. It wasn't just the explosion but everything else. Charlotte's breathing came fast, then shallow, then fast again. I pulled her into my shoulder and let her take in what had just happened.

"We're alive," she said.

"For now. From here, we need to keep things in check. We need to keep an eye on the radiation fallout and keep up the iodine."

The Geiger counter was unreadable. Numbers spiking, falling, spiking again like a heart that had forgotten how to beat properly. I killed the lantern to save fuel. Darkness felt safer. Smaller. Above us, the house continued to complain. Something shattered. Glass, maybe. Or crockery. Or both. Then came the heat.

Not flame. Not fire. A slow, creeping warmth that didn't belong underground. It seeped into the cellar through concrete and earth, the aftertaste of something unimaginably large.

Charlotte buried her face in my chest. "I can smell it," she said.

"So can I." Burnt plastic. Ozone. Something metallic. Something that reminded me of blood and electricity all at the same time. We stayed where we were. Minutes passed. Or seconds. Time had folded in on itself. The Geiger counter finally settled into a rhythm again — a fast, ugly rhythm that told me everything I needed to know without saying a word.

Above us, Canberra was no longer a city. I imagined it now as a gaping wound. I thought of the pawn shop. The empty shelves. The man who didn't want cash. The jewellery already gone. I thought of Timothy and his family walking west into a world that had just been erased.

Charlotte lifted her head and looked at me. Her face was grey. Calm. Focused. "What do we do now?" she asked.

This time, I answered honestly. "Now," I said, "we stay buried."

Another distant flash lit the cellar walls through layers of earth and the boards above. Then another. And another. The end of the world, it turned out, didn't arrive all at once. It passed overhead. And left us behind to count what was missing.

***

The dust came down long before we went up. It found every seam. Every breath. Every place we'd convinced ourselves was sealed. Fine, pale, almost pretty in the lantern light as it drifted down and settled on the shelves, the floor, our clothes. Fallout without drama. Fallout that didn't announce itself as dangerous. Charlotte wiped her face with the back of her hand, and I stared at the grey smear it left behind.

"Don't," I said.

She froze. Slowly lowered her hand.

I took a damp cloth from the crate and wiped her skin clean instead, carefully, like she was fragile glass.

"Everything's dirty now," she said.

"Not everything. But nothing's innocent. Not anymore."

The Geiger counter ticked like it had found its voice at last. Not frantic anymore. Confident. A steady, ugly cadence that made my teeth ache. This was the number I'd hoped never to see. We stayed underground for two days. Maybe three. Then I lost count. I stopped marking time when it stopped being useful. Sleep came in short, shallow bursts. Eating felt like theft. Drinking felt like negotiation. The heat faded. The smell didn't.

When the counter finally dipped low enough to make the word *possible* feel honest again, I didn't celebrate. I just nodded and started packing.

Charlotte watched me. We suited up in silence. Masks. Gloves. Hoods. Layers that made us clumsy and anonymous. The last thing I did before opening the trap door was turn the Geiger counter toward myself. It made its sound but now a warning. Still bad. Just not fatal.

I opened the door. The house was standing. That was the first surprise. The second was how wrong it felt. The walls had shifted almost a metre. Hairline cracks ran across the brick walls like veins. Every window facing east was gone, glass ground into the lawn and furniture flung outside by the pressure wave. The air was thick, stale, metallic. Charlotte stepped out behind me and stopped. "Oh," she said.

Outside, the street looked like it had been peeled back. Houses still stood, but they'd been stripped of softness. Roof tiles scattered like bones. Cars abandoned where they'd died, doors open, alarms long since exhausted. Ash lay over everything, dulling colour, blurring edges.

No birds. No engines. No voices. Just howling wind that dipped low then high, then low again.

We walked slowly. Deliberately. Every step chosen. At Timothy's house, the front door hung open. I didn't stop. I didn't look inside. Charlotte did. She didn't say anything. Just reached for my hand and squeezed once. Hard.

Further down the street, a body lay half-covered in ash. I recognised the shoes before I recognised the man. The bloke who used to argue about council rates over the fence. He'd made it as far as his driveway. Not far enough.

Charlotte turned away. "This is what you meant," she said quietly. "When you said it gets smaller."

"Yeah."

We didn't stay long. Exposure was a cost now, not a risk. Back inside, back underground, we scrubbed ourselves clean with water we couldn't afford to waste, stripping off layers like guilt.

That night, we heard voices again. Not knocking. Talking. People moving through the street. Careful. Searching. Charlotte and I sat in the dark, listening. "They'll come back," she said.

"Yes. They will. But when they come back, they'll only be part of themselves."

"More of them."

"Probably. We need to be ready."

She was quiet for a long time. Then: "If we hear them coughing—"

I didn't answer.

"If they're sick," she continued. "If they're dying."

"We can't offer help, Char. It's a different world now."

Her voice hardened, just a fraction. "What we did before. With Timothy. That was mercy."

"Yes."

"And the next time?"

The Geiger counter clicked. I thought of the bag we'd handed over. The water. The filters. The look in Timothy's eyes when he realised what we weren't giving him. I thought of the ash outside. The bodies. The way the world had rearranged itself around scarcity. "Next time," I said, "it's a decision."

Charlotte nodded. That was the moment I realised something had changed. Not the world. For us, love had brought us this far. It had softened the edges, given us reason to plan and wait and care. But love alone wouldn't survive what was coming next. What would survive was agreement. Boundaries. The ability to live with what we refused.

Charlotte reached for my hand again. "Michael, I'm going to have our baby…"

Above us, the city settled into its new shape — quieter, harsher, reduced to what it could no longer pretend to be. And beneath it, we learned the final lesson fallout had to teach: Survival doesn't just poison the land. It stains the people who remain.

THE WINE CELLAR: WHAT WE KEEP

The first time I went back up, I told myself it was only to check the air. That was the lie. It sounded practical, and practicality was something Michael understood without argument. I could've built a whole relationship on shared practicalities if I ignored what lived underneath them. We'd ignored plenty. Grief. Fear. The quiet violence of waiting for the next thing I couldn't stop.

Now we were living under the house like something ashamed to be alive. The wine cellar smelled different after *the blast* and blinding light. Before, it'd been concrete and diesel and packaged food — the neutral scent of preparation. After, it carried a thin metallic note that didn't belong underground. It lived in the back of my throat. It clung to fabric. It made everything taste like old coins. Even the water.

Michael was asleep in short bursts, his body refusing rest the way it had refused to stop working. Even in the dim lantern light, I could see the tension in his face, the slight twitch in his hands as if he were still measuring and cutting and calculating things in his dreams. He'd always been like that. A man who solved situations by building a plan around them.

I envied him for it. I hated him for it, too, in a way I didn't have time to unpack. The Geiger counter clicked on the shelf near the iodine tablets, steady but fast enough to keep my nerves raw. It'd become our second heartbeat. It told us when to stay buried. It told us when to move. It told us how generous the world was feeling. But what it didn't tell us was the kind of people we were becoming.

I sat on the edge of the bunk, placed my hand on my abdomen and pretended our child had grown enough for me to feel it move. I'd imagined the movement was new — small, not painful, but insistent. Like a reminder delivered without consent. You're not alone. You can't afford to be careless. You can't afford to be brave in the old ways. Michael knew. He'd known since the moment the words left my mouth. I'd watched something in him change when I told him — like a door locking from the inside. After that, he didn't talk about our pregnancy unless he had to. He treated it the same way he treated the cellar: not as a future father but as a problem to be managed.

I understood the instinct. I just didn't share the comfort. I reached for the notebook we kept near the lantern and wrote the date the way I'd always written it: day, month, perhaps in time there'd be a year. Then I stared at it until it felt like a joke. Dates belonged to a world that kept appointments. The world that promised tomorrow was shaped like today. But truth was different. Up top, everything was a world changed forever.

We hadn't earned that kind of certainty anymore. Michael stirred. His eyes opened immediately, alert, as if he'd never been asleep. "You're up," he said, voice low.

"I couldn't sleep."

He didn't ask why. There was no point. "The reading?" he asked instead, nodding toward the gadget that kept a check on radioactivity levels.

"Better," I said. "Not good. Just better."

He sat up, rubbed his face with both hands, and looked at me the way he did when he was trying to decide whether to argue. He was older than he should've been. Not in years — his face still held the shape it always had — but in the way his eyes had stopped expecting mercy from the world. "We should stay down another day," he said.

"We've already stayed long enough," I replied, but my calculations left me. "That's why we're alive."

I didn't deny it. I just stared at the hatch overhead, the trap door that separated us from what was left of the street.

Michael's mouth opened. "We can stay down here for as long as we have to. Radiation sickness isn't a joke."

He wasn't lying to me this time. I saw it in his eyes — he was thinking about our baby. I stood slowly, pulling my hoodie down over my stomach like it could hide the truth from physics. "I'm going up top," I said expecting the argument to form.

Michael pushed himself to his feet too fast, his knees cracking in the confined space. "No."

"Yes."

He looked at the gear I already stacked neatly in the corner — masks, gloves, plastic sheeting, duct tape, spare filters, iodine. The ridiculousness of it would've made me laugh in another lifetime. Now it was all we had. He thought hard about it. Gave it a moment or two.

"If you go up," he said, "you suit up properly."

"I know."

"And you don't go far."

"I know that too."

"And you don't touch anything."

"That as well."

"And you don't take your mask off."

"I know. I know."

He stepped closer and lowered his voice, as if the walls could overhear. "Char — you're pregnant."

"Yes, Michael, I know." I repeated it softer this time and watched his face flinch at my tone. He exhaled slowly, as if forcing calm to enter his lungs. "I'll go," he said. "Not you."

"No. You'll want to fix something. You'll see damage and start planning repairs as if repairs mean anything. You'll stay too long."

He held my gaze. He knew I was right. That was the problem with living with someone who loved you — eventually they learned how to hurt you efficiently. He nodded once, tight. "Then we go together."

I shook my head. "One of us stays. In case the hatch jams. In case — of anything."

Michael's eyes moved to the shelves, to the supplies, to the bunks. To the small world he'd built, and the way it'd become our only safe place. His expression changed. Then he said, "I'm not letting you go up alone. No argument."

I almost laughed. There was something in me that wanted to. The absurdity of it. The love wrapped around fear, trying to disguise itself as authority. I reached for his hand, squeezed it, and felt the tremor in his fingers. "I'm not asking permission," I said gently. "I'm telling you what I'm doing and it's final."

His eyes hardened, then softened. He stepped in and pressed his forehead to mine. It wasn't romantic. It was a check. A promise without words. "Five minutes," he said.

"Five," I agreed. "Promise."

He helped me suit up. Clumsy and slow, all of it designed for a world that still had instructions but no meaning. Mask tight. Hood up. Gloves sealed with tape. Spare filter in my pocket. Torch. Knife. Before I climbed, I swallowed iodine with water that tasted like steel and anticipation.

Michael watched me do it, silent, as if he could see the future in the way I grimaced.

At the top of the ladder, I paused with my hand on the latch. The trap door vibrated faintly. The world didn't stop when it broke. It just adjusted.

I cracked the hatch open a fraction. Light spilled in. Not the same as I remembered — warm and unfamiliar — but a pale, flat brightness filtered through ash and haze. It made the driveway look like a photograph left out too long. No sound came with it. That was what hit first. Silence. But what I didn't expect was the cold. It was winter in the middle of summer.

I widened the hatch and climbed out. The garage smelled like burnt plastic and damp plaster. The roller door had buckled inward as if it had tried to fold itself away from the blast. Glass from the small side window lay in glittering shards across the concrete floor, dulled by dust. A thin film of grey coated everything — tools, shelves, the workbench where Michael had once sat with his laptop like he was doing taxes instead of planning for the end of a world. And it was raining something black, like tar.

I moved carefully, torch in my left hand even though it was daylight. The beam cut a line through the haze, revealing particles drifting lazily in the forever-changed air. Even the dust was hostile.

I stepped to the open door and looked out into the backyard. The lawn was still there, somehow. I don't know how. It just was. But there was a thick carpeting of snow or ash everywhere, I didn't know which. The fence still stood. But everything was muted. The eucalyptus, leaves once green turned bronze, had dropped half its foliage onto an almost-winter land of grey. The branches stripped and brittle, like a thing that had survived at a cost.

I listened. No birds. No insects. Not even wind. The world felt held in suspension, like the moment after a scream while waiting to see who'd heard it.

I forced myself toward the front of the broken house. The hallway had cracked in places, plaster lines spidering along the corners. Our photos of a happier time lay face down on the floor, frames shattered. I recognised one — the beach, sunburnt smiles, a time when we'd been angry about small things. I didn't pick them up. Those versions of us were gone.

At the front door, I paused. Michael had reinforced it weeks ago, quietly. He'd said it was for security. I'd pretended to believe him. Now I ran my fingers along the deadbolt and felt the faint vibration of the house, the way it seemed to tremble under the weight of what'd happened and what might happen next.

I opened the door. The street looked like it'd been sandblasted back. Houses still stood, but they bore massive damage. Roof tiles scattered across lawns. Windows blown out on the east-facing sides. Curtains flapped slightly in empty frames. Cars abandoned at odd angles, one lifted onto its side. Doors ajar as if people had stepped out mid-thought and never returned to finish. Ash lay over everything, softened edges, faded colour. It made the world look gently ruined, like the aftermath of a quiet fire. That softness was the cruellest. It invited me to underestimate what it could do to me if I stayed out too long.

I stepped onto the porch, then down to the path. Five minutes, I reminded myself. Breathe through the filter. Don't touch my face. Don't touch anything.

Across the street, old Mr. Keating's house sat with its front door hanging open and loose on one hinge. He'd waved at us every morning for years. Always the same wave. Always the same smile. This vision in front of me now was extreme chaos. I didn't bother to look for him, knowing somehow the storm had taken him.

Two houses down, Timothy's place stood half intact. The fence was broken, a section leaning outward as if something had pushed through from the inside. The front window was gone, glass glittering in the ash. My stomach tightened against my unborn child. I told myself it meant nothing. People broke into houses. People looked for food. People looked for clean water. People looked for medicine. For anything that made them feel like they were still participating in a civilisation gone to ruin. But the part of me that'd been quietly learning under pressure — the part that would soon need to keep a child alive — didn't accept easy comfort.

I walked only as far as the letterbox. Even through the filter, the air smelled wrong. It had a sharpness to it, like dust-filled air after a tornado. I clenched my teeth.

I glanced down at the ash on the path and saw footprints. Crisp, recent impressions pressed into the grey. They led past our driveway, then back again. Someone had walked here. Looked. Returned. Maybe considered. I turned my head slightly and scanned the street.

No movement anywhere. But that didn't mean no one was watching. Even then it felt like eyes might be.

I stared at our driveway. At first, I didn't see it. My eyes slid over the familiar shape of concrete; the place

Michael had cut and reinforced and disguised so carefully. The hatch sat flush, hidden beneath a thin carpet rug and a dusting of ash, the seams almost invisible unless you knew what you were looking for.

I stepped closer, heart thumping. There, near the edge of the driveway, on the concrete beside the garden bed, someone had drawn a mark in pale chalk. A simple symbol — three short lines forming a rough triangle, like a child's version of a warning sign. It wasn't random. And I knew it wasn't graffiti. Placed too neatly, too deliberately. It sat just far enough from the hatch, right at the edge of the carpet rug. Just close enough to be a message for someone who understood what it meant. I stared at it until my eyes lost focus. My first thought was ridiculous: *Maybe it was there before.* But I knew our driveway. I knew every crack and stain and oil mark. I knew the way Michael would scrub at it clean on weekends when he was avoiding thinking about something else. That symbol wasn't there then. But now?

Someone came to our house. Someone had stood where I stood at this moment. Someone had looked at our driveway and thought about what might be underneath.

I backed away slowly, breath loud in my mask. I forced myself not to panic.

I turned and went back to our broken house, stepping over shattered glass, avoiding drifting dust. In the garage, I dropped to my knees beside the hatch. Lifting the carpet, my fingers working the latch with practiced speed. I lowered myself down into the cellar, pulling the trap door closed behind me with the same quiet precision we'd used when all this was still a secret.

Michael was waiting at the bottom of the ladder; eyes locked on mine. "Well?" he asked. "Was it worth the danger of getting not one, but two killed?"

I peeled off the outer gloves, hands shaking despite myself. "Someone's been here," I said.

Michael's expression tightened while handing me iodine. "How do you know?"

I swallowed hard before answering. "There's a mark on the driveway. Chalk. Right near the hatch. At the edge of the carpet."

Michael went still. It was worse than shock. It was like the confirmation of horror. He reached past me for the Geiger counter and checked it as if radiation could explain human intent. It clicked steadily, then screamed as he brought it close to me. "Char — get your clothes off and toss them outside. They're no good anymore."

The look on his face told me he wasn't amused. I did exactly as Michael instructed, but now I hadn't enough clothes to protect myself from the cold.

After a while we both calmed ourselves and tried to make some sense of what'd happened up top. He looked back at me. "What kind of mark? What did it look like?"

"Like a signal," I said. "Like they're telling someone else something. Like we've been marked."

Michael worked hard with words that refused to come. Then he came out with just a few. "This place isn't our secret anymore."

I nodded three times quickly. "Maybe they just suspect. But then maybe not. We must decide what to do next."

Michael took a slow breath and set the Geiger counter back on the shelf with more care than necessary. His hands hovered for a moment, as if he wanted to fix the air itself. Then he looked at me, and I saw the decision hardening, sitting behind his eyes. "We don't open it again," he said. "We reinforce it from inside."

I thought of the chalk mark. Of the footprints. Of the silence above. Of our baby inside me. "We're not staying here in this box forever, Michael."

In the dark, the lone oil lantern burned with a soft amber light casting long ghostly shadows inside an enclosed space, and I wondered how long it might last. I wondered what would happen if there were no more batteries or oil or even water. The cellar held its shape around us, pretending it was permanent. Above us, the hulk of a house that was once home began to learn we existed below it, and I thought it might think we were safe for a while but a little less than permanently.

***

We didn't speak for a while after I told him of the symbol. Michael did what he always did when fear arrived: he made it mechanical. He checked the hatch from below, ran his hand along the ladder rungs, inspected the latch, the bolts, the hinges — touching each piece as if certainty could be rubbed into the hatch through his skin. He was trying to turn an unknown into a list. Into a set of steps. Into something he could control. I watched him and realised something I hadn't admitted before. The cellar wasn't just shelter. It was his proof we were still alive. Proof that we hadn't been helpless. Proof that he'd been right. That he could keep us safe in a world that had stopped offering safety like it was a given,

Michael worked delicately at the reinforcements required to keep us safe from whoever was up there. He stood and looked around the cellar as if he were seeing it for the first time. The bunks. The shelves. The crates stacked with labels written in his neat, careful handwriting. The little systems inside the bigger system: food rotation, water limiting, battery stock, fuel measurements. He'd built a pocket universe and convinced himself it had rules the outside world would respect. "Did you touch it?" he asked.

"The mark? The symbol? No."

He nodded like it mattered. Maybe it did. Maybe in another world it would've. The air in the wine cellar still felt safer though. Cleaner. Smaller. Better than the ice-cold up top.

"How long was I up there?" I asked, though I roughly knew. A question I used to get Michael's mind back from where it'd gone.

"Four minutes exactly," he said. "Any more than that, I would've grabbed your arse and dragged you back in. You surprise me. You're not normally this reckless."

I let out a breath and a laugh. "Of course you timed it."

Michael didn't smile. He rubbed his face again, the skin around his eyes raw from exhaustion and worry. "We have to assume they're watching and calculating a raid on our supplies," he said. He glanced at me sharply. The look he gave me wasn't anger. It was that thing he did when I'd surprised him by being more ruthless than he expected. He was still getting used to the fact that the version of me who used to make dinner plans and complain about traffic had been peeled away by ash and silence.

Michael walked to the shelf where items were placed neatly and with precision. "Okay," he said finally. "We need to think about what's next."

I was about to explain the exact words. But decided to just let it go. I moved to the bunk and sat, letting my weight sink into the thin mattress. I imagined the baby shifting again, small as a whisper. I pressed a hand to my stomach under my tee-shirt, not to comfort myself, but to remind my body that I hadn't forgotten what it carried. Michael watched the gesture. His expression softened just a little for half a second. Then he hardened again, as if softness was so expensive. His eyes flicked away. He knew. But I could see the urge in him. The need to act. To do something. The worst part of fear wasn't that it scared you. It was that it made you crave movement even when movement was the most dangerous thing you could do.

"Michael. If we don't move, they'll break in anyway."

"We stop them."

"With what? A torch and a plastic kitchen knife?" I stared at him. "We need a plan. For our baby's sake."

He didn't answer at first. But then he said, "We don't have weapons. But we can prepare."

Michael had begun to calculate. He stood in the centre of the wine cellar, hands on his hips, eyes moving slowly from shelf to shelf. Not inventory this time. Not rations or batteries or water. This was a different kind of assessment. The look he wore was one I recognised from before everything broke — when he'd stared at a problem long enough that it stopped being abstract and started being solvable.

"We don't have weapons," he said again, quieter now. "But we do have mass. Heat. Leverage."

I frowned. "You're talking like you're about to build something."

"I am. I'm *MacGyvering* the situation."

I watched him move. He crouched beside the lowest rack, dragged out one of the old wooden wine crates we'd never bothered to unpack properly. Bottles clinked softly inside — most still sealed, some long gone. He ignored them, reached behind, fingers brushing dust and cobwebs, until he found what he wanted. A steel pipe. I remembered it. Leftover from when he'd rerouted the sump pump years ago. Too thick to bend easily. Too short to be useful for anything practical. I'd suggested throwing it out back then. He'd said, *might need it someday* and shoved it down here instead.

He set the pipe on a makeshift workbench. A reinforced table he'd built from scavenged timber and bolted into the concrete floor.

"What are you making?"

"A persuader," he said, after a beat. "Something that doesn't require bullets."

I folded my arms, suddenly colder. "You're talking about hurting someone."

"I'm talking about stopping them," he said. Then, after a pause: "Those are *not* the same thing anymore, Char. The sooner you realise it, the better."

He pulled open a drawer and laid the contents out with care. Not tools in the way people imagine tools. Not a neat workshop fantasy. Just what he'd accumulated over years of quiet preparation and half-forgotten projects.

"You brought all those meaningless items down here?"

"Do you see them as meaningless now?"

"Did you bring that bucket of electrical cords too?"

Michael looked at me with a half grin. "Yeah, all those cords you hated so much are all gone now. No need to worry."

He continued to place things out in a neat row. A heavy ball-peen hammer. A propane torch with one canister left. A pair of vice grips. Several steel brackets. A broken crowbar snapped clean near the curve. Rolls of duct tape. A box of roofing nails. He looked at the crowbar for a long moment, then picked it up and tested the weight in his hand. "This," he said, "used to be enough." He set it aside.

The torch hissed when he lit it, the sharp and aggressive sound in the enclosed space. The flame bloomed yellow then blue and white, reflecting off the concrete walls and making shadows jump like living things. He adjusted it with the precision of someone who'd done this before — not forging weapons, maybe, but solving problems with heat and force.

He clamped the steel pipe in the vice grips and braced it against the bench. When the torch touched it, the metal darkened, then slowly began to glow a dull, angry red.

I took a step back without meaning to. "Michael —"

"I need you to stay clear," he said gently. "The fumes aren't good for you."

Of course he'd thought of that.

The cellar filled with the smell of hot metal — sharp, acrid, unmistakable. Not like fire. Like something being forced to change its nature. The pipe began to sag slightly at one end, softening under the heat. He set the torch down and picked up the hammer. The first strike rang through the cellar like a bell. The second reshaped it. The third made it something else entirely.

Michael worked methodically, rotating the pipe, flattening one end into a brutal, leaf-shaped blade — sharp like a knife, heavy and tapered. The weapon was meant to crush, tear and to slice clean. No wasted motion. No anger in it. I realised then that this wasn't panic. This was adaptation.

When the metal cooled slightly, he reheated it, then bent the shaft at a shallow angle so the head sat forward heavy. He reinforced the bend with one of the steel brackets, bolted and wired tight, then wrapped the grip with layered tape and cloth torn from an old shirt — thick enough to absorb shock, rough enough not to slip. Finally, he weighed it in his hands. It wasn't elegant. It wasn't subtle. It was undeniable.

"If someone comes through that hatch?"

He met my eyes then. At my stomach. At the future we were trying to keep breathing. "Then they don't come through twice."

Michael leaned the weapon against the wall beside the ladder, close enough to reach without thinking. Close enough to be part of the cellar now. Part of the system. For the first time since I'd come back down from the surface, the Geiger counter wasn't the loudest thing in the room. It was the quiet understanding between us. Michael looked at his weapon as if it was a finished project to be proud of. "That's mine," he said. He passed the ball-peen hammer to me. "That's yours."

***

In the silence, the cellar held the conversation the way it held everything — trapping it until it became heavier. I felt my stomach tighten. Something was wrong. I knew it. I'd been circling the thought for days. Avoiding it by focusing on supplies, filters, iodine, lists, or anything that felt clean.

The first pain wasn't pain. It was pressure. A tightening low in my abdomen, dull and insistent, like my body clearing its throat before saying something it didn't want to say out loud. I froze on the edge of the bunk, breath held, waiting for it to pass. Everything passed eventually. That had become the rule. This time it didn't.

Michael was across the cellar, adjusting something on the hatch, his back to me, shoulders tense with purpose. I didn't call his name. I didn't want to interrupt the version of him that still believed preparation could outrun consequences.

Another tightening came. Sharper this time. Enough that I had to brace my hand against the mattress.

No —

Not now —

Not here —

Oh, God —

I'd been careful. Careful with iodine. Careful with time above ground. Careful with food and water and rest. I'd done everything right in a world that no longer rewarded it. A warmth spread between my legs that didn't belong there. My heart pounded, fast then shallow, as if it were trying to outrun the rest of me. I stood too quickly and felt dizzy, the cellar tilting slightly, the lantern light smearing at the edges. I pressed a hand hard against my stomach, not to protect the baby — because deep in my body, I already knew — I needed to feel something solid under my palm. I took one step, then another, toward the far corner where we'd stacked spare clothes and medical supplies. The tightening came again, unmistakable now. Rhythmic. Purposeful. My body had made a decision without consulting me. I reached the crate and fumbled it open, hands clumsy, breath coming in short, sharp pulls. Gauze. Bandages. Antiseptic wipes. Things meant for cuts and burns and the kind of injuries that made sense. Nothing in there for this. Of course there wasn't. The old world hadn't prepared us for endings that happened quietly underground.

When I looked down, there was blood on my thighs. Between my legs. Darker than I expected. Heavier.

I sat back on the concrete floor. My legs wouldn't hold me anymore. "Oh," I said aloud, the word slipping out before I could stop it. It wasn't a cry. It wasn't even grief. Just a perception coming up to the surface.

Michael turned at the sound. He crossed the cellar in three strides. "Char?" Then he saw my face. Then he saw my hands. The blood. Everything in him stopped except his eyes.

"No," he said immediately, like it was a command. Like the word itself could still function as a barrier. He dropped to his knees in front of me, hands hovering, unsure where to touch. "No, no — maybe it's just — sometimes there's bleeding. I've read —"

"It's not that," I said. My voice somehow steadier than I felt. It scared me. "It's already happening."

He shook his head once, sharply. Just once. Just enough to tell me he was unsure. "You don't know that."

"I do, Michael."

Another cramp tore through me, stronger than the others. I gasped despite myself, fingers digging into the concrete below my body. Michael grabbed my shoulders then, firm, grounding, like he was trying to hold me in place.

"I'm sorry," I said. The words came automatically, reflexive, like they'd been waiting their turn. "I'm so sorry, Michael."

His face twisted, something breaking through a controlled surface. "Don't," he said. "Don't you dare apologise. This isn't —"

"I know," I said. "I know what you're going to say."

But knowing didn't stop it.

The pain came in waves, each one stealing something from me that I couldn't see but could feel leaving. I bit down on my lip to keep from making noise. Noise felt dangerous. Noise felt like it might summon something else to the cellar.

At some point Michael wrapped a blanket around my shoulders. At some point he pressed gauze between my legs, his hands shaking despite how carefully he tried to hide it. At some point he started whispering things — facts, plans, reassurance stripped of belief.

I stopped listening.

I stared at the lantern instead. At the way the flame wavered slightly, burning the oil down into nothing, converting substance into light and heat and then absence. That felt familiar. That felt like us.

When it was over, it wasn't dramatic.

There was no single moment. No clear line.

Just exhaustion. A hollowing out. A silence inside me that hadn't been there before. And tears. I cried. For hours into the small space. All the while, Michael held me close. Held me tight, like he was anchoring me to my own reality.

Michael sat back on his heels, his hands still red with dried blood, his face grey. He looked smaller somehow. Less engineered. "I couldn't fix it," he said, barely audible. "Couldn't save it."

I leaned my head against the concrete wall and closed my eyes. "It wasn't something you could fix, Michael. It's just what happens."

"But I should've —" His voice broke then, finally, completely. "I built all this. I planned everything. I was ready for strangers. Radiation. Hunger. I wasn't —"

"For this," I finished off for him.

He nodded once, violently, like the motion hurt.

I rested my hand on my stomach again. It felt different. Quieter. Like a room after the furniture's been taken away. "I think," I said slowly, choosing the words with care, "that our bodies knew before we did. About the world. About what kind of place it is now."

Michael bowed his head and pressed his forehead to the floor, crying uncontrollably. I let him cry. He needed it.

Michael didn't touch me at first. He sat beside the bunk, close enough that I could feel the warmth of him through the thin blanket, but careful, like he was afraid his weight might collapse something fragile. The lantern burned low, its flame steady now, disciplined. The cellar had returned to pretending it was just a tiny room. I stared at the concrete wall and counted my breaths.

Michael reached for the basin and rinsed his hands slowly, methodically, even though they were already clean. He dried them on his shirt instead of the towel, like he didn't trust softness. Then he came back and sat again. "Can I?" he asked.

I nodded.

He slid one arm behind my shoulders, not pulling me in, just resting there — an offer, not a demand. I leaned into him a moment later. He adjusted immediately, shifting so my weight rested more comfortably, his hand flattening against my upper arm, warm and steady. We stayed like that for a long time. "I'm here," he said finally.

"I know you are —"

"I mean —" He stopped, swallowed. "I'm not going anywhere. Not into my head. Not into plans. Not into the next thing. I'm here. With you."

Something in my chest loosened at that. I hadn't realised how much I'd been bracing for him to disappear into systems and measurements and future dangers. Into anything that wasn't this moment. He shifted again and reached for my hand. His thumb brushed over my knuckles, like he was mapping something he didn't want to forget. "I keep thinking," he said quietly, "that if I hold you right, maybe your body will forgive itself."

I closed my eyes. "That's not how it works."

"I know," he said. "But I still want to try."

He pressed his forehead gently against the side of my head. Not a kiss. Something steadier than that. A contact point. A way of staying connected without asking anything in return. "I loved our baby," he said, voice rough but controlled. "I never said it out loud. I didn't let myself. I thought if I treated it like a problem, I could keep the baby safe." He paused. "Turns out I was wrong."

I turned my head just enough to look at him. His eyes were red, rimmed with exhaustion and something softer underneath it. He didn't look away. "You didn't fail," I told him.

"I know. But I still hurt."

I nodded. "Me too."

Michael tightened his arm around me — not enough to hold me too tightly — just enough to remind me I was being held in his embrace. His other hand slid down to my back, resting there, firm and warm. Protective, but not possessive. "I can't fix this," he said. "But I can do this." He shifted again so I was more fully against his chest. "I can hold you. I can make sure you eat. I can sit with you when it hurts. I can stay."

The words landed so genuinely. How could I not love this man?

"I don't need you to be strong," I said quietly.

His breath hitched once. "Good. Because I don't feel strong."

We stayed there, breathing together, his heartbeat slow and solid against my ear. The cellar creaked softly around us. Michael did the bravest thing he knew how to do. He stayed in our pain that we both shared together.

***

I'd stopped counting the days only because the days somehow blurred and time itself smeared itself into confusion. The names of each day didn't matter anymore. I had no idea what they were. Michael routinely dowsed the lantern to save fuel. We'd lit it only in cases where we needed light for the bare necessities. To do the things we needed to survive. The rest of time was spent in totality.

"Michael. Please. We need to think about going," I said. "Just look at us. Our water is running out. We have no batteries left. And food? I don't think we've eaten anything for —."

After I'd said those words, the Geiger counter quit as if the damn thing was listening in. Michael went to the shelf in the total darkness and after a short rustle, he found it. I heard him shake it, then again violently. He swore words at the top of his voice, ignorant to anything or anyone who might be above us. "Fuck this shit." Then slammed the device hard down.

"I agree with you, Char. It's time to move."

That was when we both heard it. A sharp tap on the trap door above us.

We both froze at the sound.

The knock came again. Not loud. Not urgent. Just deliberate. Three short taps on the trap door, spaced enough to say whoever was up there knew exactly what they were doing.

Michael moved beside the ladder. In the dark, I could hear the shift in his breathing before I saw him move. His hand went instinctively to the weapon leaning against the wall. Mine went to his arm.

"Wait," I whispered.

The knock came a third time. Softer now. "Please," a voice said from above. Hoarse. Familiar in shape, wrong in tone. "Michael. It's me. Timothy."

Michael lit the lantern; my eyes hurt for a second then adjusted.

"Timothy?" Michael said.

He looked at me. There was no question in his face, only estimation tempered by something much older — neighbourhood, memory, obligation.

I nodded once. Slowly.

Michael climbed the ladder and cracked the hatch just enough to speak. Cold air spilled down, carrying with it a smell that made me feel immediately ill. It wasn't the smoke or ash. Sickness.

"Step back," Michael said quietly. "Both of you."

There was a pause, then the scrape of shoes on concrete. When Michael lifted the hatch he fully climbed out, I followed up the ladder far enough to see.

In the freezing temperature, Timothy stood at the edge of the driveway, barely recognisable. He'd lost weight — too much, too fast. His clothes hung from him like they'd belonged to someone else. His skin had taken on a waxy, yellow-grey pallor, stretched tight across his cheekbones that jutted sharply. Open lesions wept ugly streaks on his skin. His lips were cracked and bleeding. Dark bruising mottled his neck and jaw. One eye was swollen and half shut. The other fixed on us with something like relief, edged with desperation.

Timothy's hair had begun to come out in uneven clumps. Beside him stood his son. Thin. Quiet. The son's hand was clenched tightly, knuckles white. His face streaked with dirt, eyes too large for it, taking everything in without blinking.

"Jesus," Michael said under his breath.

Timothy gave a humourless half-smile that ended in a raspy cough. He bent forward slightly, hand braced on his knee, fighting it down. When he straightened, there was blood on his teeth. "She's gone," he said. "My wife." No preamble. No easing into it. "Anna didn't make it. Two days ago, now."

I felt the words hit like I'd dropped something precious. "I'm so sorry, Timothy," I said. It sounded inadequate even as the words left me.

Timothy nodded once, like the phrase meant something only because it was expected. "She went fast at the end," he said. "Didn't even know where she was." His voice shook, then steadied again by force. "I stayed. For him." He rested his hand briefly on his son's shoulder.

Michael reached for iodine and offered it. "Take as much as you need."

Timothy barked a dry laugh that turned into another cough. "We're all sick," he said. "Just at different speeds. The iodine won't help us now." He wiped his mouth with the back of his hand. "You said to go west. It's worse there. Plenty of the dead. You get sick not with the radiation, but with the disease from the bodies. But our group's heading east. A dozen now, maybe more of us along the way. People are saying Molonglo River past Fyshwick is clean. Or cleaner. That there's a refuge set up near the water. Filters. Tents. Doctors — what's left of them."

"You sure that's not just rumour?" Michael said.

"Everything is rumour," Timothy replied. "But people who went ahead sent word back. Water's drinkable. Not perfect, but it won't kill you straight away. Might do if you drink too much of it. But at least you get some time."

The son looked at Michael then. Didn't say anything. Just watched him with a kind of careful hope that made my throat tighten a notch more.

Michael looked back at the house. At the driveway. At the hatch that had kept us alive and sealed us away from the world at the same time. "It'll take days to get there," he spoke.

Timothy nodded and coughed hard. Raspy hard. He took a moment or two just to clear it. When he spoke again, his voice had changed. "It'll take a day or two to push past the city. They said roads aren't there anymore. Just — ruin. They said it's blocking the clean path out."

I knew then, before Michael spoke again, before he looked at me again. Staying wasn't living anymore. Michael came back to the ladder and stepped down. He met my eyes in the dim light of the cellar. "Pack," he said simply. "Take only what we can carry."

I didn't argue.

We moved quickly. Water first. Filters. Iodine. Food stripped down to calories and weight. The notebook. One blanket. Michael hesitated at the shelf, then took the dead Geiger counter. Next was his weapon made from once useless junk. He grabbed it and slung it across his back without any ceremony.

I took one last thing. The eagle figurine I valued so much. I packed it neatly in my pack. When we climbed out for the last time, the cellar yawned below us — dark, stocked, useless. A monument of preparation that had reached its limit.

Timothy watched us seal the hatch. His son stood close, shoulders hunched against the cold, eyes never leaving our hands.

"We go now. It's early in the day," Timothy said. "Less exposure."

Michael nodded. "We'll keep pace with the group."

I looked east. The sky was a pale, sickly grey, the sun reduced to a dull smear behind ash and cloud. Before stepping out for good, Michael took the blanket from our bunk, the only one we had and wrapped it around my shoulders, pulling it snug.

Somewhere east beyond the horizon was water. Or the idea of it. Sometimes that was enough. As we started moving, the son walked close to Timothy's side. Timothy stumbled, caught himself, and kept going anyway.

I fell into step beside Michael. Behind Timothy and his son and a group of people numbering roughly twenty, walking slowly and with measured steps, some limping, all of them coughing. Michael reached for my hand without looking. He held it tight. Behind us, the house disappeared into the haze. Ahead of us, the road stretched east — uncertain, dangerous, alive with rumour but cluttered with ruin exactly as Timothy described.

Light was a generous word for what filtered down through the grey clouds. The sun was there somewhere — reduced to a pale disc behind a ceiling of grey that never seemed to thin. It gave no warmth. It didn't rise so much as *appear,* like a tired thing dragged into the sky out of obligation. Shadows were soft and directionless, as if even they had given up on certainty.

As we walked we passed shadows of people forever etched into the scenery by instant vaporisation. The road east was still recognisable, but only just. Bitumen had blistered and cracked in long, jagged seams, like dried mud at the bottom of a dead river. In places it'd buckled upward, lifted by heat and shock into warped ridges that forced us to slow, to pick our footing carefully. White lane markings had faded to ghosts beneath a film of ash, the idea of direction lingering after its usefulness had long passed.

We stopped without being told to. Michael took my arm. Hard. His fingers dug in like he needed something solid to remind himself the ground still existed.

"Char," he said. I followed his gaze west. Where Parliament House had once sat — low and deliberate, pressed into the hill like it belonged — there was now a crater.

Not rubble. Not ruins. An open gaping wound.

The hill had been scooped out as if by a giant hand, the earth torn open and cauterised at the edges. The crater was wide and deep, its inner walls fused into blackened glass and twisted stone. Whatever hit hadn't merely destroyed the building. It'd erased the idea of it. No columns. No recognisable structure. Just a bowl of slag and ash filled with stagnant water that reflected nothing but a quick death.

Someone whispered, "They hit it directly." No one corrected him.

We hooked right and continued.

Buildings thinned quickly. The suburbs gave way to open ground stripped raw of ordinary housing.

I grabbed Michaels elbow, "Where is everything?"

He said one word. "Vapourised."

"We were expecting a ruin not just empty."

"Technically it's still a ruin. But just disappeared."

We thought we were at least halfway to the river. Paddocks that once rolled green now lay flat and colourless, covered in a powdery grey crust that puffed up around our boots with every step. Fences leaned or lay collapsed entirely, posts burned black at the base, wire slack and tangled like something that had tried to crawl away and failed. Here and there, machinery sat abandoned — tractors, irrigation rigs, a burned-out ute half sunk into the earth — metal warped and rusting already, as if time itself had accelerated out of control.

Nothing moved.

No birds cut the sky. No insects rose from the grass. Even the wind felt reluctant, stirring only enough to lift ash into slow spirals that drifted across our path and settled again without urgency.

The smell was constant. Burnt vegetation. Old smoke. Something chemical underneath it all that made the back of my throat tighten and my tongue taste faintly of rust. We walked with our scarves pulled high, breathing shallow, learning quickly not to open our mouths unless we had to.

We passed a group of dogs where they'd fallen. Some lay close to fences, bunched together as if they'd tried to escape something invisible. Others were scattered alone in the open, bloated and stiff, eyes clouded white. The ash clung to their hides, muting their appearance, making even death look smaller. No scavengers touched them. Nothing came to clean up what the world had discarded.

Timothy stumbled often. His son never left his side. They moved as one unit — Timothy dragging his weight forward through sheer will, Timothy's son adjusting his pace instinctively, leaning back just enough to steady him without pulling him down. Timothy's son never complained. Never asked how much further. His silence was heavier than any crying would've been.

Further along, we passed a convoy of vehicles that'd never made it. A line of cars sat jammed across the road, some nose-to-tail, others skewed at odd angles as if abandoned mid-panic. Doors hung open. Windows shattered outward. Luggage spilled onto the road — suitcases burst, clothes half-buried in ash, a child's backpack lying on its side with cartoon animals faded and unrecognisable, already scavenged for its contents by someone else.

Michael didn't look inside the cars.

Neither did I.

The group walked around them instead, eyes forward, as if the road itself demanded respect for what it had witnessed. The land rose gradually, the terrain changing as we moved east. Gum trees presented themselves, then became skeletal. Eucalyptus trunks stood stripped and blackened, their bark hanging in long ribbons that stirred faintly when the air moved. Leaves crunched underfoot — not the dry crunch of autumn, but a brittle, dead sound, like stepping on paper that would never soften again.

By mid-afternoon, if that was accurate, uncontrolled coughing spread through the group. It started quietly — one person, then another — until it became a constant background sound. Some spat blood. Others wiped their mouths and kept going without comment, as if acknowledging it would somehow bring some relief.

The sky *never* changed.

Afternoon came only because our bodies said it must have. We rested briefly in the shadow of a low rise that offered little protection. No one sat for long. Rest felt dangerous. Like if you stopped moving, the land might decide you belonged to it. When we started again, the road dipped and the horizon opened. Somewhere far ahead — too far to see clearly, too far to trust — I imagined water.

A river cutting through the land. I didn't know if it was real or just my mind trying to keep my legs moving.

Michael squeezed my hand once, just to prove we were still together.

We walked on, eastward, through a country that no longer recognised us, carrying what we could and leaving the rest behind — houses, plans, names, and the shape of the lives we thought we'd been living.

Molonglo River waited somewhere ahead. Or it didn't. Either way, stopping was no longer an option.

***

By the last stretch, we stopped counting the distance. Energy dwindled. Energy had become something we rationed as carefully as water. Steps replaced kilometres. Breaths replaced time.

No one said how many we'd lost. The gaps in the line told the story well enough. Packs abandoned by the roadside. A scarf tied to a fence post. A shoe left where someone had sat down and never stood again.

The first death had stopped us. A woman near the back had collapsed without warning. One moment she was walking, shoulders hunched, eyes down. The next she was on her knees, palms pressed into the ash as if praying to the ground. She didn't scream. She didn't cry out. She just folded.

Someone knelt beside her. Someone else called her name. She never answered. We stood there longer than we should have, the group uncertain, afraid that moving on would make it real. Michael checked her pulse. Once.

Then again, slower, as if he could coax it back through patience. "She's gone," he said finally.

No one argued.

We didn't bury her. The soil was too hard, too shallow, too contaminated. Digging would've cost hours we didn't have, strength we couldn't spare. In the end, we did nothing that resembled dignity. We moved her off the road, wrapped her in a blanket someone surrendered without comment, and placed a stone on her chest so the wind wouldn't uncover her face.

Then we walked on.

After that, it happened faster.

An older man who sat down to rest and never stood again. A teenager who started coughing blood in the morning and was silent by midday. One of the group simply fell behind and was gone by the time we noticed — no sound, no signal, just absence.

Each time, the pause grew shorter.

Grief was replaced by design.

Can we afford to stop?

Can we carry them?

Will this kill us too?

The answers were always the same.

No.

No.

Yes.

Timothy was getting worse. His skin had gone translucent, veins visible beneath it like bruises trying to escape. His cough was constant — deep, wet, tearing at him from the inside. Sometimes he stopped walking entirely, doubled over, one hand on his chest, the other gripping his son's shoulder like it was the only solid thing left in the world.

"Dad," his son would say. Just once. Always quietly.

Timothy would nod and straighten and keep going. At some point, one of the men offered to carry Timothy's son's pack. Timothy refused with a sharp shake of his head. Pride wasn't the right word for it. It was something thinner. More fragile. As if letting go of anything else would finish him.

The land changed again as we drew closer to the river. Burned bush gave way to flattened empty spaces. Large numbers of bodies appeared, those who had attempted and failed getting to water. Some lay where they'd fallen. Others were piled together under tarps or plastic sheeting; the work of people who'd still believed there would be time to come back for them. There hadn't been.

We stepped around them without comment. By then, even the children who were with us had learned not to ask.

My legs shook constantly from depletion. Every muscle felt hollowed out, as if the strength had been scraped away and replaced with grey static. Michael stayed close, adjusting his pace to mine without speaking, his hand firm at my elbow when the ground dipped or my foot dragged.

We didn't talk about the baby. There were no words left for that.

Late in the day — when the sky should've been changing but didn't — we lost another. A man near the front simply lay down on the verge and closed his eyes. "I'm done," he said calmly. "You go on."

Someone tried to argue. Someone else cried.

Michael looked at me. I looked back.

We kept walking.

Behind us, the man's voice faded into the ash.

By the time the land sloped downward, and the air began to smell faintly — *faintly* — less dead, there were barely a dozen of us left. The group moved like ghosts, spaced out, silent, each person locked inside the narrow tunnel of effort required to keep one foot moving in front of the other. Then, through the haze, we saw it. The river. Water.

Molonglo River ahead, dull and grey under the poisoned sky, its surface barely moving, as if it too were holding its breath. Around it, shapes resolved slowly Not salvation. But something like pause.

Someone near the front laughed — a short, broken sound that turned into sobbing. Another dropped to their knees, hands pressed to the ground, overcome not with joy but with the sheer relief of stopping.

Timothy made it three more steps. Then he collapsed.

Michael and I were there immediately. Timothy's chest hitched once, twice. His eyes found his son's face. "You stay," he whispered. "You hear me? You stay."

His son nodded furiously, tears cutting clean tracks through the ash on his cheeks.

Timothy's hand loosened. That time, we didn't move him. We couldn't.

Michael closed Timothy's eyes. His son didn't shed tears. He just sat beside his father, silent, until someone gently helped him to his feet and urged him toward the water.

As we reached the edge of the river, I looked back once. The road behind us was littered with what the journey had taken — people, things, pieces of ourselves we hadn't noticed falling away. The land didn't mark them.

Didn't remember. We did. And then, finally, we stopped walking.

THE WINE CELLAR: THE COST OF WATER

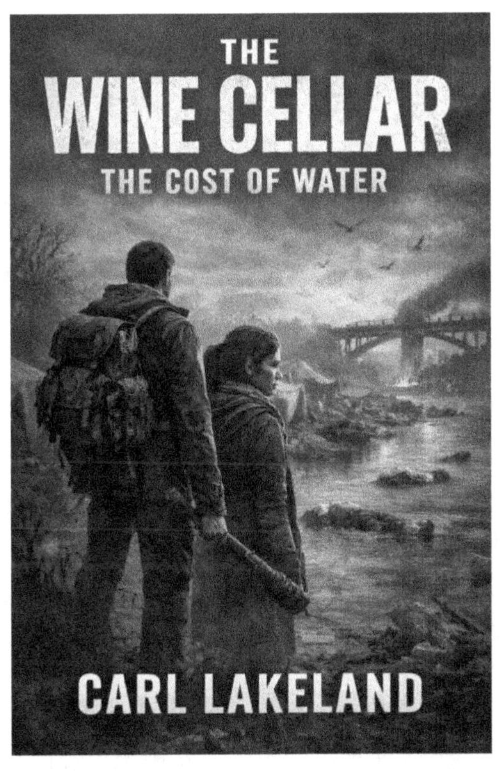

Every street we'd crossed on the way out of Deakin had rewritten the rules a little more. Noise drew eyes. Eyes drew questions. Questions drew hunger, and hunger drew people who stopped asking permission.

By the time the Molonglo came into view, we were moving like a thing with one shared nervous system — heads down, shoulders tight, every footstep placed with care as if the ground could punish us for being careless.

The air changed first. It wasn't the pleasant dampness you'd expected near water. It wasn't cool. It wasn't fresh. The air carried a taste — thin, and wrong — like licking an old piece of metal. Under that was something worse, something human and sour, a smell the body recognised even when the mind refused to give it a name.

I stopped at the edge of a stand of half-dead shrubs and held up my hand. The group of sixteen souls compressed behind me. They were a bunch of ragged beings who'd learned that stopping was sometimes the only way to stay alive.

I stared through the branches at the riverbank. Dirty white tents with red crosses rose from the waterside. They were set up in rows the way someone once expected order to matter. The sides sagged. A few had collapsed entirely, poles snapped, fabric draped like dead skin over ribs. Tarps flapped and slapped lazily against stakes that still held, stubborn like old habits. There were plastic water containers — bright yellows and some red colours that didn't belong in the landscape — tipped on their sides like toys left out by a child who'd gone inside and never come back.

It looked like a refuge, but it felt more like a lie.

Charlotte stepped beside me, close enough that I could feel her warmth through the layers of dirty fabric. Her face was streaked with soot and exhaustion. The last few days had scraped the softness from her expression. She didn't ask questions the way she used to. She studied the scene. She assessed. She made decisions with her eyes. "You see anyone?" she whispered.

I shook my head slowly. "No movement at all."

"That isn't good, isn't it?"

"No," I said. "That's never any good."

Behind us, someone shifted their pack, a buckle clicking softly. The sound carried in the still air. "Quiet," I murmured without turning. The buckle stopped moving. The group held itself still.

The river ran beyond the tents, a grey ribbon under a sky that couldn't decide whether it was still allowed to be blue or even green. Ash covered everything. It settled into corners and seams like the world was trying to cover itself over. I watched the water for a long time, waiting for the kind of evidence that told my feelings I was wrong. A ripple. A fish. A bird dropping in to drink. Anything. But nothing came. Just an echo of something. I didn't know what. An echo of ghosts that once was.

The boy — Timothy's son, Liam, a kid of about sixteen years — stood a few paces behind our group, his eyes fixed on the river like it was calling him. He didn't blink or show emotion much anymore. When he did, it was slow, like he was under water.

I tightened my grip on the strap of my pack. The weight dug into my shoulder. It should've been comforting, having supplies. It wasn't. It just reminded me that everything we had left that belonged to us was carried on our backs almost with guilt. After a moment, the group started gravitating toward the river. I wondered about what we might find.

On arrival at the riverside and tents, the ground was uneven, churned and pocked. Footprints hardened into the ash like fossils. There'd been a crowd here once — dozens, maybe more — moving in and out of the camp, doing the things people did when they still believed in systems. Fetching. Sharing. Arguing over rations. Living in the thin optimism that someone was coming. Now the footprints went everywhere and nowhere, overlapping until the direction was meaningless.

The first tent I reached had its flap open. The fabric was stiff with dust. A cheap camp chair lay on its side, one leg snapped, as if someone had stood up too fast and didn't care what they broke in the process. Inside was a sleeping bag, half-unrolled, with a dark stain near the bottom. I didn't step in. I didn't have to. My brain filled in the rest.

Charlotte hovered behind me. "Any supplies?"

"Maybe," I said. "Maybe not worth taking even if there were."

That was the new calculation: not what you could use, but what it might do to you. I moved along the row. There were empty MRE bags littering the dirt. Plastic bottles crumpled up like fake fists. A child's shoe. One lone sneaker, small, bright blue, sitting in ash like a punctuation mark. I felt sick looking at everything laying around randomly. I crouched and touched the edge of the sneaker with the tip of a finger. Damp underneath, even though everything else felt dry. I stood again without looking longer than I had to.

"Michael," Charlotte said softly.

Her eyes were on the river. I followed her gaze. Bodies floated there, but the brain tried to reject them at first. My eyes told me they were just logs. They told me they were just random debris. They told me it was just the way the water twisted around shadows. Then a pale human arm rolled slightly in the slow current, fingers open like a weak wave. I shuddered and stopped breathing.

The river was littered with them. Scattered like something had washed them in and then changed its mind about letting them go. Bodies were snagged on branches. Some were half-submerged in the mud. Some lay face down, backs rising like little islands under wet clothing. Simply too many to count.

I took a step back without meaning to. Then the smell of the dead hit harder. It rose from the water in a sickly wave. Sweet, rotten, putrid. It crawled into my nose and sat there not leaving.

Someone behind us made a sound — half gag, half chuck. The group's tension spiked. I could feel it — the way panic travelled through people like electricity. Charlotte's hand found my forearm. It wasn't to restrain me, but to anchor me. "We should leave," she whispered, urgently.

I stared at the water, at the bodies, at the camp that had once meant hope. "We can't," I said. "Not yet."

"Michael —"

"We can't," I repeated, and forced my voice lower. "We came here for water. We don't leave without knowing for sure. Maybe we can boil and purify the life out of it."

Charlotte looked at me the way she used to when I'd been building the cellar — part disbelief, part hatred for my logic, part relief that someone had logic at all. She nodded once, reluctantly. The truth was, she didn't have another plan either. I moved closer to the river. Just close enough to see what the water looked like where it touched skin.

The surface wasn't normal. It had a film — thin, iridescent in places where light hit it. Oil-slick rainbow on grey water. That could've been fuel. It could've been contamination from the city. It could've been blood. It could've been any number of things. But it also meant everything ended the same way: drink it unpurified and die.

I pulled my scarf up over my nose. The cloth did nothing against the ugly smell. I scanned the camp again. Empty. No voices. No fires. No human movement. No scavengers. That was wrong too. A camp full of bodies and abandoned tents should've been crawling with desperate people stripping it bare, unless the people who got here learned something fast and lethal and spread the lesson without words.

My eyes tracked along the line of tents. A cluster near the water that looked more intact than the rest. One tent had a tarp slung over it like extra protection. The tarp's edges were weighed down by rocks. Something was kept out — or something was kept in. I walked toward it, carefully. My boots crunched lightly in the ash. Each step felt loud. Charlotte stayed close. Behind us, the group stood still, but I could feel their puzzled gaze burning into my back.

I reached the tarp-covered tent and used a finger to lift one corner. Inside, there were supplies. A half-crate of bottled water — plastic bottles with labels still intact. A box of medical gloves. A packet of bandages. A small stack of iodine blister packs in a zip lock bag, water-damaged but still recognisable and good enough to add to our existing supply. Someone had been rationing carefully. Someone had been organised enough to keep everything moisture free.

Then I saw the sleeping mat in the back. It wasn't occupied. It was just… arranged. Like someone had lain on it and then been lifted off. There were marks in the dust where a body was dragged. I dropped the tarp corner and backed away.

Charlotte's voice was barely audible. "They left in a hurry."

"Or they didn't leave at all."

Her eyes flicked to the river. She didn't argue.

I turned back toward the group and suggested they stay put while I investigated further. After a while. After scanning the area and trying to make sense, I walked back up the slope to the group, trying to keep my pace calm. My heart didn't cooperate. "We're not staying here," I said. "Nobody goes to the water. Nobody touches anything that's been in it, or near it."

A woman in the group scratched her head. Maybe confused. Her lips were cracked, eyes hollow. "But… the bottles…"

"I saw bottled water. We'll take what we can carry. But we'll treat it like it's contaminated until we can prove it's not."

"How do you do that?" someone else asked.

I didn't answer right away. The truth was I didn't know for sure. Not without the one thing I'd been carrying for this reason. The Geiger counter sat in my pack like a silent complaint. Dead. Soundless. No power to drive it.

I looked at Liam. He'd drifted closer to the riverbank without anyone noticing, eyes locked on the water. His face still had that thin, faraway look of grief. He'd been holding it in for too long — holding the death of his father inside him like a stone.

"Liam," I said.

He didn't respond.

"Liam," I repeated, sharper.

His eyes flicked to me for a second. I feared something inside him had cracked.

"Liam, stay back from the river," I told him. "It's not safe."

He stared at me, expression unreadable. Then he looked past me again, back to the water.

Charlotte stepped forward, her voice softer than mine. "Liam. Please, stay away from there."

After a look of confusion with a couple of groans, Liam headed over and rejoined the group. The group shifted uneasily. People didn't like what their eyes were telling them.

My attention turned away from Liam and I made myself focus. One problem at a time. Water. Radiation. Toxicity. All those things, I needed to know. I suggested to the group that we needed to gather supplies — anything dry, nothing else.

A man named Joel — broad shoulders, a face that always looked like he was in the middle of saying no — nodded once. "And the water?"

"Leave the water for now. I'll work it out."

I stepped away from the group and unshouldered my pack. The straps slid off with a rasp. I lowered it carefully onto the ground, like it contained something fragile. In a way, it did. The Geiger counter. I stared at the pack for a moment longer than necessary. There were things inside that felt more like talismans than useful devices. Items you carried not because they were magic, but because they represented a line between guessing and knowing.

I unzipped the pack. My hands moved through the contents in a sequence I knew by touch — spare socks, plastic sheeting, tape, a small pouch of tools, the last of our sealed food. I reached the hard plastic shape and wrapped my fingers around it. I pulled it out. The Geiger counter looked older than it had back in the cellar. Everything looked older, aged by necessity.

Charlotte watched me. "Any battery left?"

"That's what I'm hoping. There might be just enough left to give a small indication."

Hope was a dangerous word. It always had been. Now, hope was practically a weapon. I glanced back at the river again. Bodies. Ash. Silence. And the tents like a stage after the actors had long fled.

I turned the Geiger counter over in my hands. The power switch was stiff with dust. I thumbed it once without flipping it, feeling the resistance like a warning. If it came alive and read high, we'd lost the river, and everything after became instantly harder. If it didn't come to life at all... we're blind.

Behind me, someone whispered my name, and I heard fear in it. I didn't turn. I just held the Geiger counter a little tighter and stared at the water like it owed me an answer. Then I flicked the switch. And waited to see whether the world was going to tell the truth or stay quiet.

***

Nothing happened. For a second I thought the switch was jammed. The Geiger counter sat in my hands with the same dead weight as an ordinary brick, the kind of object that only mattered because of what it might promise. I thumbed the toggle switch again, harder this time, as if pressure by itself could create an electric charge. Still nothing. No click. No tick. No faint static heartbeat. Just quiet. I stared at the blank faceplate until my eyes started trying to invent movement in it. A survival trick. See a pattern — see a way out. The truth was simpler. Dead battery. I let out a slow breath and felt the air drag that metallic taste across my tongue once again.

Around me, the camp stayed empty. The river stayed full. Charlotte watched my face like she'd learned to read it in a new language. "It's gone," she said softly.

"It's not gone," I replied, though I didn't believe it yet. "It's just… empty."

Behind Charlotte, the group had started to move — careful, tentative steps between tents. People were scanning the ground for anything useful, but they were doing it the way you searched a burnt building: fast, quiet, terrified of touching the wrong thing. I could feel their restraint. They were listening to me even as they scavenged. That wasn't trust. That was dependency. It didn't matter what you called it. The result was the same: if I made the wrong call, I carried the blame and all the outcomes.

I lowered the Geiger counter to my lap and opened the battery compartment with a fingernail and persuasion. Dust fell out. The smell of old electronics, dry and faint, like a memory of safety. The battery inside sat there like a joke. No bulge, no leak. Just spent. I rocked it in its cradle, and nothing changed. I turned it over, checked the contacts. Clean. No corrosion. The device was simply out of motivation.

Charlotte crouched beside me. Her knees popped, a sound that used to be normal. "Can we replace it?"

"With what?" I asked, sharper than I intended. I reined it in. "We don't exactly have a shop nearby, Char."

Charlotte glanced toward the river and then back to the tents. "There might be batteries in the tents."

"Maybe," I said. "But the battery has to match the device."

She gave me a tight smile and a huff. "You really are fun at parties, Michael."

I almost smiled back. Almost. Then the smell from the river shifted and reminded me there were no parties anymore. Nor would there ever be again.

I stood, keeping the Geiger counter in my hand like it was still relevant, and scanned the camp one last time.

"Michael," Joel called softly from a few tents away.

I looked up. He was standing beside an open tent with his head half inside, rummaging carefully. He held up a small tin like he'd found treasure. "Baked beans," he said with pride.

"Take it," I said. "But keep it separate. Everything found here stays separate until we *know* what we have."

Joel nodded and tucked it out of the way for collection later.

I shifted my attention to Liam. Again, he'd cut away from the group. Separated himself like a lone sheep. He wasn't scavenging like the rest. He wasn't even standing still. He was walking with a quiet purpose down the slope toward the water's edge, eyes fixed on it like it was home.

"Liam," I called.

He didn't stop, didn't respond.

The sound of my voice pulled everyone's attention. Heads turned. Bodies held, like a herd hearing a twig snap.

"Liam!" I snapped, louder.

He slowed half a step, almost irritated, then kept moving forward again.

Charlotte started after him instinctively. I caught her arm. "Don't," I hissed. "I don't want you anywhere near it."

"I'm not letting him —"

"I know," I said. "But you don't go near that water. Not ever. It's a death trap of disease."

She stared at me and clenched her teeth in frustration. She hated this part — the part where the love for another got turned into rules. Then she nodded once, hard, and stayed back.

I moved. I didn't run. I took long strides down the slope, boots slipping slightly in the ash. The smell got stronger with every step. The water's surface held that strange film like a skin.

Liam reached the edge and stopped. He stood there, toes almost touching the mud, staring down into the grey. I could see his reflection in it, broken by the slow current and drifting debris. It was like the river was trying to take him apart before it even touched him.

"Get back," I said. "Now."

He looked over his shoulder at me with eyes that were too calm. "It's water," he said. "I'm thirsty."

"Liam. Don't be stupid. We need to boil it before anyone drinks."

He turned back to it. "I – I need a drink."

I took another step forward and stopped a safe distance from the water's edge. The mud looked wet in a way that didn't feel natural. The air above the river seemed heavier, as if the river carried more than just water and bodies.

Liam's shoulders rose with a sharp inhale. His hands clenched, then relaxed. He stared at the bodies as they drifted by, caught and released in slow loops. And then he stepped forward into the river as if pulled.

I moved faster. I grabbed the back of his jacket and yanked him away from the edge. He spun, furious, and shoved at my chest. "Don't touch me!"

I held him at arm's length, not in anger. In containment. "Listen to me," I said. "If that water is hot — radiation, chemical, disease, whatever — it doesn't just kill *you*. It also kills anyone who tries to save you. ***Do you understand me***?"

His eyes flicked past me to Charlotte, to the group. Then back to me. He didn't answer.

I saw it land in him. I released him slowly. "Go back to the group. It's not worth the trouble," I said, almost pleading. "Help us find a battery. Keep your mind active."

Liam backed up a few steps, gaze still pinned to the water like he couldn't let it go. Then he turned and walked up the slope, stiff and noiseless.

I watched him go until he reached the group. Charlotte moved toward him cautiously like she might spook him.

I turned back to the river, then to the Geiger counter still in my hand, and felt a blunt, ugly truth settle. I wasn't just blind. We all were. And being blind on a riverbank full of bodies was not a problem you solved with optimism. I climbed back up to the tents. Joel met me halfway.

"I need a battery, Joel. Find one."

Joel glanced around like the group might be listening. But then came a new promise that might solve my issue. "There's a guy, Darren —" Joel jerked his chin toward a man I didn't much like on principle. Skinny, quick-eyed, always watching like a watcher watches a watcher. "— he carries a trannie radio," Joel told me "What'd ya think?"

"You shitting me?"

I followed Joel's nod and saw Darren kneeling by a pile of tinned baked beans that he'd found. I approached. I didn't introduce myself. I had no time for the pleasantries. "Darren, is it?"

He looked up. "Yeah?"

"Gimme your radio."

He reached into his pack and produced a small 1980s Radio Shack. A radio, the kind you'd buy from a servo on a road trip and forget it was in the glove box.

"This thing's cactus anyway," he said. "No signal anywhere. Useless."

"I don't need it for a signal." I crouched beside him. "Open the battery compartment."

He looked at me like I'd asked him to hand over his last meal. Then, with visible reluctance, he popped the battery cover off. A single battery, size C. I needed a D. Not the size I needed. Of course.

Darren's voice was thin. "It still works. Power's power."

"No," I said. "It's wrong for what I need."

I looked down at the battery again. Wrong size meant it wouldn't seat correctly. It wouldn't make contact. It might sit loose enough to rattle, break connection, kill the reading. But then I had an idea, something I watched on YouTube.

I strode with urgency back to the group, cutting across pock-marked dirt and patchy brown dead grass. I got there out of breath, sweat breaking out on my skin despite the cold. "Anyone here smoke?"

The group eyed me strangely as though the words settled out of character. Someone in the group held up a hand. "I have them, but I don't have a light." From his breast pocket, he produced the packet of Horizon Blue, flipped it open and offered me one. I snatched the entire packet from his hand. It offended him. "Hey, mate. That's all I have."

"It's not for the smokes," I said, tipping it up and emptying the cigarettes back into his hand. I reefed out the foil and handed the empty packet back.

I stepped away, voices of puzzlement behind me. I got myself back to the riverside as fast as I could go, meeting up with Joel halfway there.

The idea was simple, stupid, obvious. Which meant it might work. I opened the Geiger counter's battery compartment again. The cradle made for a specific length had no concern. The contacts sat in fixed positions. If I could shift the battery just enough — bridge the gap — make contact — then I didn't need a perfect match after all. I just needed an unbroken circuit.

Joel watched me with suspicion. "What're you doing?"

"I'm *MacGuyvering* a new battery," I said. "But it might be just a mindless hack that doesn't work."

He laughed without humour. "With cigarette foil?"

I didn't answer. I didn't have the time for details. I tore a strip of foil, then folded it, once, twice, compressing it into a tight little pad. The foil crinkled softly in my hand; my hands went to work.

Charlotte leaned closer. "Is it safe to do that?"

"Nothing's safe," I murmured. "But it might be accurate enough."

I placed the wrong-size battery into the Geiger counter's compartment. It sat loose, leaving a gap at the contact. I slid the folded foil into the space between battery and terminal, careful not to tear it. I pressed it down until it wedged in tight. Then I held the device up and shook it lightly. No rattle. No movement. It stayed seated. Exactly what I wanted.

Joel watched me with birdlike eyes, his mouth slightly open. "That's… actually a thing."

I nodded. "It's a thing," I said flatly. "Here's hoping it'll work."

My hands were steady, but I felt my pulse kicking in my fingertips. It wasn't from excitement. It was from the weight of what this reading would decide. I closed the compartment, turned the Geiger counter in my hands, and thumbed the switch again.

For half a second nothing happened, and my gut dropped a centimetre or two. Then the counter clicked once. A dry, sharp click — like a tiny metronome clearing its throat. Then it clicked again. And again. The sound built fast, accelerating, not into a steady rhythm.

The counter's little speaker began to squeal under the load. The clicks were too fast to count. Too fast to be background. Now, as I stood there, it began to scream out a single unbroken tone.

Charlotte's hand clamped around my forearm. Hard. "Michael —"

Oh no, I kept telling myself. No, this is not good.

I didn't look at Charlotte. I stared at the display. The numbers jumped. Spiked. Didn't settle. It was like the device hit panic. Devices didn't panic, they reported. Which meant this wasn't borderline. This wasn't a 'maybe'. This wasn't a 'be careful'. This was certain death waiting to take your life and throw it back at you.

My mouth went dry. For a moment the whole camp seemed to fall away and all I could hear was the Geiger counter shrieking, crying out loud in my hands, telling me in the only language that mattered, that the river was not water. It was pure, constant, poison.

Joel stepped closer, eyes wide. "Bad?"

I swallowed. "Worse than bad, mate. We all need to move back. Now."

My eyes went up and hit the group standing bunched together high up on the embankment. I gestured to everyone with a single hand. They all understood. The group's fear rose like steam.

Joel took a step back from me as if my voice itself was contagious. "Turn the bloody thing off," he whispered.

"No," I said. "I need to keep testing to get the real picture."

Charlotte's grip tightened on my arm. "Michael, no! It's enough!"

I shot her a look. "You're still here? Char, I need you to clear off!"

Charlotte did exactly that. One step back. Two. She spun and stepped away. I knew her. She'd never create panic amongst the group. The steps she chose were measured. Precise. Exact.

I looked back toward the group, to their faces. Liam watched everything. His eyes locked to what I was doing like it was a verdict. The counter kept screaming. I stepped away from Joel and walked closer toward the river — holding the Geiger counter out in front of me. With each step closer to the river, the chorus didn't ease, just climbed in pitch. The squeal sharpened. The display kept bouncing upward like it was trying to escape the limits of its own scale. I stopped five metres from the water's edge. The distance felt like approaching a cliff. The Geiger counter screamed higher, screaming its horror.

I lowered my eyes to the mud near the bank. Dark, wet, smeared with ash. A slow lick of water crept over it and retreated again, touching and withdrawing like the river was breathing.

The counter went insane. The counter didn't just stay high. The needle slammed to the right.

It wasn't just the bodies. It wasn't just a few pockets of contamination. The river itself was hot. It was no longer a resource. It was a boundary. I stepped back quickly, but with the urgency of a man retreating from a fire where death was waiting in a taxi. When I reached the group, only then did I switch the Geiger counter off.

Peace fell so abruptly it felt like the world had been muted for a moment or two. Nobody spoke to themselves or to anyone. The only sound heard was the tarp flapping somewhere in the background and the sluggish whisper of water moving past dead things. I immediately reached into my pack and grabbed iodine knowing I had a limited time before contamination hit my thyroid. I popped out two, no three tablets and shoved them in my mouth.

"Anyone here get close to that poison?"

A hand went up, then two, then three.

"Take these," I said and shared them around. I gave four tablets to Charlotte. Three for a dose. One extra for safety.

Joel broke the hush first. "I'm assuming we can't stay here."

"Not unless you'd want to fry then glow green," I said.

A woman in the group spoke out. "But the refuge — why would they set up here if —"

"Because they didn't know," I said. "Or they knew too late."

Someone behind her whispered, "Jesus Christ."

Charlotte looked at me with a kind of controlled horror. "How long does it take before it's too late?" she asked me quietly.

"Depends how you get exposed," I said. "Drink it — fast. Bathe in it — faster. Touch it, then touch your mouth, your eyes..." I trailed off shaking my head. There was no benefit in painting the full picture. She'd already imagining it.

Liam stepped forward suddenly, pushing past Charlotte like he couldn't contain himself anymore. "It's just water, isn't it?" but this time his voice was frayed. Defiant. Desperate. "It has to be just water. I can't do this anymore." He stared at me, studied my face for an answer. I had nothing.

For a split second in time, I saw the boy he was, before his father died. Before the street went still. Before ash turned everything into the same colour of greys and blacks. I opened my mouth. And before I could say anything, Liam turned and ran toward the river.

"Liam!" Charlotte screamed.

The group surged instinctively — people moved to grab him, to tackle him, to save him in the only way humans knew.

"Stop!" I roared to the group. The word cracked like a whip.

They all froze in their tracks.

I sprinted after Liam hoping to get there in time. I went for his jacket, reaching out, fingers hooking in hard. He twisted away with the prowess of a rugby league professional — wild, sudden strength — and I missed.

Liam hit the water with a splash that sounded too normal. Too ordinary. Like a kid diving into a lake on a hot summers day. The river accepted him without complaint. No argument. For half a second he was submerged, and the human part of me — every instinct, every piece of old wiring — screamed to go in after him.

Charlotte, I noticed, took a couple of strides forward, both hands outstretched. I couldn't decide if it was for Liam, or for me.

Joel moved too.

"NO!" I yelled, and the sound came from somewhere deeper than my throat. "Stay back!"

They both stopped, torn between rescue and survival, between reflex and reality. Liam broke the surface. He stood waist-deep for a moment, hair plastered to his head, eyes wide as if he'd expected the river to do something else. Then he began to wade toward the bank, clumsy, slow, his arms moving strangely.

I backed away from the edge, hands raised, palms out. "Liam, come out," I ordered, voice low but urgent. "Get out and don't touch anyone or anything. Do-you-understand?"

He stumbled up onto the mud, coughing, noxious toxicity pouring off him. His clothes clung to him like a second skin. His body looked wrong, and the sheer speed of change turned my blood to ice.

His face had gone pale grey, as if the colour was drained out of him. His lips trembled uncontrollably. He blinked fast, then slower, like his eyes were struggling to keep working. He raised his hands, covered in open lesions, cracked and bleeding, and he stared at them with confusion, as if he didn't recognise who they belonged to.

Charlotte covered her mouth with both hands and made a sound that was half sob, half scream, and somehow held it in.

Liam took two steps forward.

I stepped into his path instantly, blocking his movement. "Stop," I said. "Stay right there, Liam."

He stared, trying to understand my cruelty. Behind me, I felt the group's fear convert into something else — horror with nowhere to go. The Geiger counter in my hand felt suddenly obscene, like I'd used it to summon Liam to his own demise. I didn't move toward him. I didn't comfort him. I didn't put a hand on his shoulder. He swayed on his feet. His breathing became shallow and fast. His eyes rolled slightly, as if the world was tilting too hard.

He whispered words but they didn't register. Whatever came out were rattling, gargling sounds that spelled nothing understandable, not a language I recognised.

Charlotte's voice came out broken. "Liam! Oh my God!"

Liam tried to step forward again. His knees buckled. He fell onto the ash-covered mud with a wet slap, and his body began to shiver, convulsing, violently. Within a few moments, he was soundless.

I turned to the group, forcing my composure. "Nobody touches him."

Charlotte took one step toward Liam and stopped, tears cutting lines through the grime on her cheeks. She looked at me like I did something monstrous.

I moved to the edge of the group and spoke instructions clearly. "Gather dry supplies. Quickly. Anything sealed. Anything not touched by river. Then we leave."

***

The Molonglo River was lethal — worse than that. The refuge was a graveyard. And Liam died because the old world didn't care about consequences or grief. I looked back toward the tents, to the scattered supplies, to the ash-covered ground. And that's when I realised something else. Darren, the transistor radio guy, was gone. The skinny man with the quick eyes. He wasn't scavenging. He wasn't standing with the group. He wasn't anywhere. I scanned the camp rapidly — between tents, behind tarps, toward the tree line. Nothing. He'd vanished while all our attention was on Liam and the river.

Charlotte noticed my shift and followed my gaze. "What?"

"Darren's gone. Wonder if anyone's seen him."

Joel turned quickly, eyes moving across faces. His expression hardened. Joel's question sat in the air; unspoken like a second mortality we didn't need.

"We don't look for him. We leave," I said.

Joel nodded, stepped away at once, and joined back with the group.

I glanced back at the empty tents, the river, the bodies. Darren made his choice. If we stayed longer, who knows the consequences even with iodine protecting our front line of defence.

Charlotte's voice was quiet when she spoke to me. "Where do we go? If not here, then there's nowhere."

I looked north along the riverbank, where it disappeared behind trees and a broken city that once was home. The bridge over Lake Burley Griffin was the only answer. Once crossed, we'd head east out of the city and connect with the Federal Highway. Somewhere far east was Lake George — if it was still water and not poison like the Molonglo.

"It'll cost us days, maybe a week." I spoke. "We should make it. We have enough supplies to get us there but if anyone lags we can't afford the delay."

Nobody argued with that. Everyone knew the price. I shouldered my pack again, the strap biting into the same sore place it always did. The Geiger counter went back inside, useless now but still vital as proof. The iodine tablets felt suddenly precious in a way that made my gut twist.

I gave the group one last instruction without looking back at Liam's body. "No one drinks. No one touches the river. If you feel sick, you tell me immediately. If you hide it, you'll die and take someone else with you. Don't let it be you."

They nodded. Silent. Grim.

Charlotte moved close to me again, her hand finding my sleeve. She didn't speak. She didn't need to. Her touch was light — just contact enough to say *I'm here* without asking anything of me.

We started walking north, following the dead river toward the bridge we hoped was still intact and could be crossed. Behind us, the tents flapped in the ash wind like they were trying to wave us goodbye. And the river carried its bodies downstream like it had all the time in the world.

***

We walked north with the river on our right and the city broken apart on our left. No one spoke for a long time. The sound of our boots on ash and broken ground filled the silence, dull and rhythmic, like a clock counting down something nobody wanted to name. The river followed us faithfully. It bent and narrowed, slipped between dead reeds and half-submerged debris, but it never left us. Sometimes it ran close enough that I could hear it moving — slow, thick, like it was dragging weight with it. Other times it dipped away behind trees or concrete embankments, only to return again a few hundred metres later, patient and unavoidable. I didn't look at it unless I had to.

Behind me, the group had fallen into a loose column. I'd spent most of the journey staying central. Walking somewhere in the middle of the pack with Charlotte keeping pace at my side. Something had changed. I didn't know what. Now, the group gravitated to my rear and I led the way. As I talked, I had all ears. As they spoke questions, I answered them. And each and every one of them was silent without words unless it was important.

"Haven't you noticed?" Charlotte said softly with a smile I hadn't seen in a while.

"I've noticed something. What it is, I have no idea."

"Michael, they all look up to you. You've become leader to them. People need a leader. That's you."

I didn't respond. I wasn't sure yet how that made me feel. I never liked responsibility especially if it was thrust upon me by unforeseen circumstances.

Charlotte eyed me sideways. Her smile widened as she took my gloved hand. "You're protector now. *Michael the Protector.*"

With the words coming from Charlotte, I instinctively checked for my *persuader* slung on my back. The weapon I'd made from scraps and junk back at the cellar was now elevated in status. It wasn't just there for the protection of me and Charlotte. It was now there for the protection of everyone. With that thought, I wondered the cost if I had to wield it. Would it be enough to protect us? Perhaps one day, I'd live long enough to find out. And if indeed it was an effective answer to our survival at whatever was out there.

As we walked I looked west — to where Parliament House had once sat, pressed into the hill like it was authority made permanent. Now there was only a crater. A direct hit. Fused stone. Twisted metal. A wound in the land that still bled poison downhill into the water below. Power hadn't protected itself. Instead, power had drawn the strike, costing countless lives and what was left over will resonate for years and decades to come.

Joel walked a few paces back, scanning constantly, the way men did when they'd accepted that danger no longer revealed itself without jumping you from behind. The group kept close to him, as though trying to conserve heat even though the air was bitterly cold.

Darren was still missing. I'd expected to see him ahead of us by now — ducking out from behind a tree, grinning like he'd found a shortcut or a stash. That kind of person didn't disappear quietly. They wanted to be seen. Wanted credit. But the riverbank stayed empty. Which meant he'd gone somewhere else. Or something had happened fast enough to claim him. Neither situation made me feel better.

We reached a stretch where the bank rose sharply, forcing us up onto cracked concrete that once supported a pedestrian path. Graffiti peeled away from walls in long strips, words half-erased by heat and compression. A child's bike lay on its side near a bent railing, tyres flat, the chain rusted solid. I stopped and raised my hand.

The group halted and compressed automatically. I supposed they were learning my signals the way soldiers did, even if none of us wanted to name it. I scanned ahead. The path curved around a stand of trees where the river dipped out of sight. Beyond that, the river opened up to Lake Burley Griffin. The land opened into once manicured lawns and gardens. All gone now. Instead, burnt ground, broken infrastructures — culverts, stormwater drains, the skeletal remains of picnic shelters. A bridge over Lake Burley Griffin was just beyond that.

Charlotte leaned in slightly. "There," she pointed.

I nodded. "The bridge looks untouched. Good." I took a breath and felt the weight of what I hadn't said yet settle deeper into my chest. Every step north was a step away from certainty. And heading east might be just as poisonous. Every which way I thought about it, I realised, staying put was way worse than that, possibly unsurvivable.

"We stop here and rest for five minutes," I said to the group. "Then we move again."

I pulled my pack off and knelt, unzipping it just enough to check the iodine tablets. Inventory checks became a reflex, something to do with my hands when my head wanted to spiral. We had fewer than I'd liked. I snapped the pack closed and stared into the distance as if I could find an answer somewhere out there.

Charlotte watched me. "How many do we have?"

"Enough," I said. "A thousand tablets, maybe more."

Joel approached, voice low. "We need to talk about Darren."

I met his eyes. "We will when we set up for the night."

"Now," he insisted quietly. "Before someone else disappears."

I nodded once. He was right. Fear liked quietness too much. I turned to the group. "Circle up."

After I had all ears; "I don't know the whereabouts of Darren. I don't know why he left or where he went. If anyone saw something, say it now."

A man in the group spoke up. "He was watching you. When you fixed the Geiger counter. He looked interested. Too interested if you want my opinion."

Another one added. "I never trusted him. We shouldn't have brought him with us."

Then another. "That man knows about the iodine. He was about to pinch it for himself."

I scoffed. "What?"

"It's true," Another one said. "While your back was turned. I bloody stopped him. Sneaky little bastard."

That was all I needed to know. But I still owed it to everyone to at least put it to a vote.

"Those in favour of searching for Darren, raise your hand."

No one did. We left it at that.

"But what if he gets with another group?" someone else said. "That becomes dangerous for us."

"It will," I agreed. "I guess we'll just have to deal with it should the case arise."

I felt the group's attention narrow, waiting for me to close the loop. To make sense of it. To make it smaller. "It doesn't matter," I said, "the short is this; he's not with us anymore. Which means two things."

I held up a finger. "First: we assume he's alive and acting in his own interest."

Another finger. "Second: we assume anyone else he meets up with might compromise our existence."

Charlotte swallowed. "Because of the Geiger counter?"

"Because of the counter," I confirmed. "And because of the tablets."

Joel's mouth tightened. "So, we're marked."

"Maybe," I said. "Or maybe just visible." Neither option was good. I let my hand drop. "From here on, nobody leaves the group alone. Nobody scouts ahead without me knowing. If you need to take a piss, you take a buddy and you stay within sight."

The group looked briefly at each other, nodded, murmured among themselves and became unified.

"Alright," I said. "Pack up. We move."

As we started walking again, Charlotte fell into step beside me, close enough that our shoulders brushed occasionally. The contact grounded me more than I wanted to admit.

"You have your gold with you?" she asked quietly.

"Yeah. I brought the entire stash I had back home. But I don't know if it would matter now. We'll see what happens."

She absorbed that without comment. After a moment, she said, "You knew this would happen didn't you?"

I didn't deny it. "I knew *something* would. Why did you think building the wine cellar was so urgent."

We walked on. The river reappeared again, narrower here, flowing faster through a choke point between concrete banks. The water looked darker, heavier. I kept my eyes off it and focused on the far bank, on the scrub beyond, on anything that wasn't moving wrong. A shadow flickered ahead. I raised my hand instantly. The group compressed behind me. I scanned the tree line. Nothing obvious. But the feeling stayed — the sense of being watched and measured.

Joel whispered, "You see something?"

"Maybe," I said. "Or maybe I'm finally paying attention." I stepped forward slowly, every sense stretched tight. The shadow resolved into a figure stepping out from behind a broken signpost just short of the bridge. Then another. Then two more. They didn't rush us. Didn't shout. Two of them had high powered weapons. They stood there facing us, spread across the path in a way that said they'd done it before.

My hand slid down to the weight at my side without thinking. Charlotte inhaled sharply. I felt it more than I heard it. The nearest man lifted his hands slightly, palms out — not surrender, just signal.

"Easy," he said. His voice was calm, almost conversational. "We're not here to hurt anyone. We don't want any trouble."

I stopped walking. "So, what are you here for?" I asked.

He smiled faintly. "Supplies. Same as you. Same as everyone."

Behind me, I felt the group tighten. I kept my voice steady. "We don't have anything you'd be interested in."

The man's smile widened just a fraction. "You've got iodine. This guy, Darren. He told us all about it. One of your mob I suppose. Said you also have a Geiger counter tucked away in that pack of yours."

The words dropped into the space between us like a stone. Darren. Now I know where he'd gone.

"Darren. Where is he?"

The guy shrugged. "Probably dead. He didn't have anything to trade for toll. So, we didn't let him cross the bridge. The idiot decided to swim for it. Not sure if he made it all the way."

Charlotte's fingers brushed my sleeve. Not gripping. Asking. This was the moment the road narrowed. And whatever I said next decided if we'd cross the bridge over Lake Burley Griffin.

***

They stood like they belonged there. Not posturing. Not fidgeting. Not rushing to close the distance. Four of them spread across the cracked path, with another two half-visible fifty metres beyond, placed where they could watch without being obvious. It was the kind of spacing you only learned by doing this more than once.

The man in front — mid-forties, lean, beard trimmed short — kept his hands visible but relaxed. A knife sat openly on his belt. A statement without bravado. Silence was a tool. People who talked too quickly were usually trying to fill it because they were scared of what might happen if they didn't.

"And I suppose you want the Geiger counter," I said.

His eyes flicked, just once, to my pack. He didn't bother denying it. "That, yeah. Hard thing to miss. People don't carry those unless they know something. And the iodine as well. That'll get you across."

Charlotte leaned in, voice tight. "What if we say no?"

The man smiled at her, not unkindly. "Straight to it. I like that. I'll take everything you have. All the tablets, and the counter."

Behind me, Joel swore softly under his breath.

"That's not happening," I said.

The man didn't react. No flare of anger. No threat. "Then we don't let you across. Like your Darren. But you can get across eventually by tracking around," he pointed west. "But by the time that happens you might end up skintight and crispy."

I glanced past him, down the path. The bridge east was just there. The river underneath littered with floating bodies more than at Molonglo.

"Like I said before. Your Darren didn't make it. He couldn't deal. But you've got something interesting enough to buy yourselves a toll."

Charlotte's breath hitched. "You can't control a bridge if people need to cross?"

He avoided Charlotte and just pointed west again. "Toll or keep walking. You decide."

I studied him more carefully. His clothes were layered but clean. His boots were intact. The others wore similar gear — scavenged but maintained. These weren't panicked survivors. They were organised.

"How many are you?" I asked.

He smiled again. "Enough."

That answer told me more than a number. I shifted my weight slightly, letting the hush stretch again. The group behind me was tense but quiet as though they'd learned when to let me speak. "You know what iodine does," I said.

He nodded. "Buys time."

"Not forever."

"Nothing's forever."

"It's the difference between sickness and death," I said. "Between walking and collapsing."

He shrugged lightly. "That's true. That's why you'll hand it over."

"And you want all of it."

"Yeah. Everything you got."

I let that hang for a moment, unslung my Persuader, then said, "You won't get it."

The man's eyes sharpened, just a fraction. "You're willing to get your people killed over pills?"

I didn't raise my voice. "I'm willing to not kill them by not handing over the one thing that keeps them alive."

A murmur erupted between the man and his followers. Not dissent. Interest. He considered me more carefully. "You're the one who decides, then."

"Yeah."

"And they follow."

"They're still alive," I said. "So far."

He chuckled softly. "Fair comment."

Charlotte's hand brushed my back. A warning. A question. I knew what she was thinking:

If not the tablets, then what?

I answered it out loud.

"I can trade, but you can't have the iodine. That's not negotiable. The counter stays with me. That's not negotiable."

The man's smile faded slightly. "Keep walking toward Capital Hill. Or Capital Crater these days. That's your choice." He turned and headed back to the bridge.

"Wait." I got his attention and he turned around.

"You haven't told me your name. If you're going to walk away and leave us to our fate, the least you can do is give everyone here something to remember you by."

The man thought about saying nothing. I saw it in his eyes. But there was also something sitting there just behind his conscience. He paused breathing heavily at first, then he shrugged. "It's Brian. My name's Brian. Before the world went to shit, I had family just like anyone. All of them gone now."

"Brian. You've made your decision," I said, "but I want you to remember something first."

"Go on," he said nonchalantly in a tone that was flat and unbothered.

"Have a look at all their faces," I pointed back to the group. "These are people just like you. They're exhausted. They're tired. Some of them are just surviving by balancing on a strand. What you see around you, everything here. Everything that's happened. This was out of a decision not made by us. It was a decision made by the hand of one person. That person wasn't even here in this country. That person wasn't even human enough to see what pressing a button would take away from the entire planet. The result of one man's stupidity? You're living in the same horror that we all are right now. We're all the same end outcome of a world gone mad. And now, every single one of us, left over and living, have the responsibility forced upon us to make the right decisions and to keep going. To keep surviving. I get where you are. We're the same. I'm just asking for a fair chance. A crack at continuing, finding a balance, and to find a place to live out the years we have left."

I reached into my pack slowly, keeping my movements visible. I pulled out a small cloth pouch, worn soft from handling. I loosened the tie and tipped it just enough that the contents caught the light. Gold. Not coins. Not jewellery. Small bars and rough pieces, shiny. Bright. Unmistakable. The man's breath changed.

Behind him, one of the others leaned forward without meaning to.

"This," I said, "is currency that doesn't expire. Doesn't dissolve in water. Doesn't need explaining."

The man held my gaze, calculating. "You're offering that for toll."

"Our group needs to cross safely. No ambush. No trailing us. No warnings sent ahead."

He laughed quietly. "That's a big ask."

"It's a clean one," I replied. "You get something that holds value everywhere. We keep the tablets and counter that keeps us alive and walking."

He rubbed his beard, thinking. "Gold doesn't stop radiation."

"No," I said. "But it stops people."

That earned me a look. Respect, maybe. Or recognition.

"And when you're past the bridge?" he asked. "What stops us from taking the tablets and counter anyway?"

I met his eyes without blinking. "You won't try. Because we believe in fair trade. And because you're outnumbered."

He studied me for a long moment. The wind shifted, carrying the smell of ash and river rot between us. Finally, he nodded. "You've done this before."

"Not like this," I said. "But I know how deals work when the rules don't."

He turned and spoke quietly to one of his people. They conferred in low voices, eyes flicking toward us, toward the pouch in my hand.

Charlotte leaned in, whispering, "Will it work?"

"It will. This is exactly the reason I had the gold with us in the first place; Char. Greed never changes. And because the alternative is Capital Hill. It'd be more toxic than the river."

The man turned back. "We'll take payment up front. Then you can cross."

"No," I said. "You let us cross and I'll leave it on the road at the other side."

He frowned. "What if I don't trust you?"

"That cuts both ways," I replied.

Another pause. Longer this time. "I'll instruct the others to stay here. I'll escort you across alone. You can give me the gold after you cross."

I nodded once. "Done."

Then he spun and went back to his men. I saw them talking. One reacted badly. Yelling broke out. They talked each other down and the words between them settled. Brian came back, two others followed.

I placed my hand down on the Persuader. Something changed. Maybe negotiations had failed. I prepared for a fight. I locked eyes with Joel. "Be ready," I whispered.

Joel instantly drew his blade. I saw others in the group prepare. Charlotte took her ball peen hammer from her belt.

Brian returned, reaching us, the two men behind him shouldered their weapons. Two others in his group did the same.

"I cleared it with the others," Brian said. "Today's a toll-free day for you lot. Keep the gold. Keep everything."

I looked back over my should to the group and shook my head. They knew the sign and stood down. Joel resheathed his knife. Charlotte stood, back straight and amazed, breathing with a sense of relief."

"This isn't a sick trick?" I asked.

"Not a trick. What you said made sense. Perhaps we're all the same as each other after all. Take your group and go before I change my mind."

"Much obliged." All the words I could come up with.

I looked back to the group. "Shoulder packs, we're moving."

In a single file, the group advanced past Brian and his men. I stayed until the last of the group crossed to the other side. I watched them closely making sure a trap wasn't tripped.

Before leaving, I asked Brian what he did before everything happened. Before the world changed.

"I was a policeman," he said. But it doesn't matter anymore, does it?"

I let the silence settle there for a while.

"Then, why not join us?" I asked. "We could use your experience."

"Where ya headed?"

"To water. Lake George."

"Waters there might be worse than here."

"Maybe. But what if it's not?" What if there's a settlement or a refuge there. It has to be better than surviving here, Brian."

He thought about it. "We have supplies and weapons, but we don't have what you have."

I looked at him. "In my opinion, the more people we have as a group, the better the odds we have to survive. We do this together."

He looked at me with a half-smile. "Okay, I'll get my things.

***

We didn't stop again until the light began to fail. By then, the river was finally behind us — not out of sight, but out of reach. It ran lower now, cut away from the road by scrub and broken land, like something ashamed of itself. I kept checking the wind, the slope, and the distance. Old habits. I didn't trust water anymore, not even when it behaved.

With the death of Liam, and the missing Darren, we became fourteen. That all changed with Brian and his men adding to the group, bringing us to twenty-two.

We made camp on high ground, far enough from anything that moved or reflected light. No fires. No talking louder than breathing. Packs down in a loose circle. People sat where they landed, backs to the trees, heads bowed, conserving whatever they had left.

I took inventory without writing it down. Writing things down felt like tempting fate. Charlotte sat beside me, knees drawn up, arms wrapped tight around her. Her face was pale under the grime. Shock had a way of settling late, once it knew you were safe enough to feel it.

"We crossed," she said quietly.

"Yeah."

She nodded. "How much trust do we give them, Michael."

"Like everything now. Only time will tell. But regardless, we'll know soon enough."

"And you're willing to risk it?"

"I only know this, Char. The more numbers we have, the stronger we become. Along with everything that we have. Supplies, tools, whatever. It's safety in numbers for the group's survival. And we still have a long way to go."

I watched the horizon as the sun collapsed into smoke-stained cloud. The sky went that deep bruised blue that only comes after something irreversible. Somewhere behind us, Canberra was still dying. It would keep dying for years. Maybe centuries. The river would carry it all downhill, patient and thorough.

Someone near the edge of the group began to cry — soft, embarrassed sounds, quickly swallowed. No one moved to stop it. No one told them to be quiet. Grief didn't make noise anymore. It leaked.

I reached into my pack and took out the Geiger counter. The thing looked ridiculous now. Plastic. Lightweight. Silent. All that power, reduced to a warning it could no longer give. I turned it over in my hands and thought about how much faith I'd placed in a few clicks and a needle. How much blood it had cost to listen to it anyway.

I set it down on a rock between Charlotte and me. "I'm not carrying it tomorrow," I said.

She looked at me. "Why?"

"Because it already did its job." I tapped it once. "It told us what the world is now. I don't need reminding."

She didn't argue. She rarely did anymore. Instead, she reached into her pocket and took out one of the iodine tablets.

She held it between her fingers like something fragile. "This saved us," she said.

"It bought us time."

She studied the tablet, then closed her hand around it. "Time costs things too."

I looked out at the dark. At the land that no longer cared what we needed. "Yeah," I said.

A few people slept. Most didn't. They watched me when they thought I wasn't looking. I felt it settle on my shoulders — not pride, not power — responsibility. The quiet understanding that if I was wrong again, there would be no forgiveness left to spend.

Charlotte leaned her head against my arm. "Do you think Lake George is clean?" she asked.

I thought of the Molonglo. Of the bodies drifting like punctuation marks. Of how water remembered everything. "I think we'll find out," I said.

She smiled faintly. Tired. Real. "And if it isn't?"

I didn't answer straight away. Because the truth was, I already knew. "We'll keep moving," I said. "That's the only thing that still works."

The night closed in properly then. No stars. Just cloud and ash and the low murmur of people trying to convince themselves they were still here. Before I slept, I buried the Geiger counter beneath the rock where we'd rested. Not deep. Just enough. A marker of where certainty ended. I didn't say a word when I did it. Some things don't need ceremony.

We walked at first light. And we didn't look back at the water.

ABOUT THE AUTHOR

Carl Lakeland is an Australian author of suspense and spy thrillers, known for his lean, fast-moving narratives and grounded realism. Drawing on personal experience and a deep interest in intelligence operations, military history, and human resilience, his stories explore loyalty, sacrifice, and the unseen costs of conflict.

His work blends action-driven storytelling with emotional depth, focusing on characters shaped by hard choices and irreversible consequences. Carl lives in Australia, where he continues to write fiction that favours authenticity over spectacle and tension over excess.

9 781764 476058